D1330326

A NOTE ON THE AUTHOR

CARLOS ACOSTA was born in Havana in 1973 and trained at the National Ballet School of Cuba. He has been a principal at the English National Ballet, the Houston Ballet, the American Ballet Theatre and the Royal Ballet, and has danced as a guest artist all over the world, winning numerous international awards. He is the author of the autobiography *No Way Home: A Cuban Dancer's Story* and made his film debut in *New York, I Love You*.

www.carlosacosta.com

A NOTE ON THE TRANSLATOR

FRANK WYNNE has won four major prizes for his translations, including the 2002 IMPAC for *Atomised* by Michel Houellebecq, the 2005 Independent Foreign Fiction Prize and the 2008 Scott Moncrieff Prize. He is also the translator of Tomás Eloy Martínez's *Purgatory* and won the 2012 Premio Valle Inclán prize for his translation of Marcelo Figueras's *Kamchatka*.

www.frankwynne.com

PIG'S FOOT

Carlos Acosta

Translated from the Spanish by Frank Wynne

B L O O M S B U R Y
LONDON · NEW DELHI · NEW YORK · SYDNEY

First published in Great Britain 2013
This paperback edition published 2014

Bloomsbury Publishing Plc
50 Bedford Square
London WC1B 3DP

www.bloomsbury.com

Bloomsbury Publishing, London, New Delhi, New York and Sydney

Bloomsbury is a trademark of Bloomsbury Publishing Plc

A CIP catalogue record for this book is available from the British Library

ISBN 978 1 4088 3372 8

10 9 8 7 6 5 4 3 2 1

Typeset by Hewer Text UK Ltd, Edinburgh
Printed and bound in Great Britain by CPI Group (UK) Ltd, Croydon CR0 4YY

Para Berta y tía Lucía,
ambas victimas de la misma enfermedad.
Y para Charlotte y Aila

To the roots goes the honest man. A radical is simply this:
a man who goes to the roots
José Martí

There is beauty in the breakdown
Frou Frou

Author's Note

Pig's Foot is set in a fantastical alternate version of Cuba inspired by the landscapes, the different cultures, the rough magic and the turbulent history of my country. Inevitably it is peopled by historical figures – politicians, dictators, boxers, architects and philanthropists – whom I have taken the liberty of treating as fictional characters. Just as I have Melecio create the Bacardí Building in Havana (actually designed by architects Rafael Fernández Ruenes, Esteban Rodríguez Castells and José Menéndez), so too I have him spontaneously declaiming verses, among them 'Deseos' by Salvador Díaz Mirón. I am indebted to him, to all the authors I have read and to all those who have inspired me.

Carlos Acosta

Part One

The Village

A Few Important Details About Me

Bueno . . . OK . . . the first thing you need to know about me is I never knew my mother or my father, in fact I only found out their names a couple of months ago. My memories begin on the day I came home from primary school dragging a dead cat by the scruff of the neck. I must have been about seven at the time, and I remember the cat had eaten my lunch. My grandma grounded me – obviously – and I wasn't allowed out to play for a week. She told me it was no reason to go round strangling things. I tossed the remains of the cat on the ground, then punched the front door so hard I fractured my wrist. All this stuff I remember as clear as day. But before that is like an empty space inside my head. Sorry, maybe I'm not making much sense; what I mean is I don't have any memories of what happened before. I was a pretty normal kid, just like the other *chiquillos* in Barrio Lawton as far as I remember, though my grandparents always insisted I was different. They told me I had been born in a place called Pig's Foot – *Pata de Puerco* – in the deep south of Cuba on the far side of El Cobre. According to them, I slid down my mother's legs into the mud like a slug.

Can you imagine? Like a slug. And that as soon as my mother plucked me up out of the muck, I started howling like I'd been stuck with a fistful of needles. Pig's Foot sounds to me like one of the weird recipes Grandma used to concoct, but from what I was told both my grandparents and the parents I never knew were born there and one day I would have to go back.

'Mark my words,' my grandpa used to tell me all the time, 'no man knows who he is until he knows his past, his history, the history of his country.' 'The old guy's losing his marbles,' I thought, 'the first sign of old age!' But then one day I suddenly found myself utterly alone. It's impossible to imagine the man you will become when you find yourself alone. I don't know if you understand what I'm saying. Take me, for example: years ago it would never have occurred to me to set foot in Santiago, let alone to hang on every word I ever heard my grandpa say, as though somehow his words might be the cure for my affliction. That's how I came to build a world around a tiny village called Pata de Puerco, a place I've never been but one I inhabited through the memories of that poor old man, the memories Commissioner Clemente wheedled out of me in the course of a long and painful interrogation, the memories I'm happy to relate to you now, no hard feelings.

Before we get started, I should point out that Clemente, the short, bald prick with the big 'tache who calls himself a doctor, is actually Grand Wizard of the Cuban branch of the Ku Klux Klan. I suppose you think I'm making this stuff up, but I swear to you that even in 1995 there are evil people in Cuba. And Commissioner Clemente, with his gang of

4

whiteshirts, is one of them – whenever I see him it's like I have a rock in my stomach. That's why when he asked, instead of telling him my real name – it's Oscar Mandinga, in case you're wondering – I said: .ان تصرفكَ هذا يليقُ ببهلون تبا! دعني وشأني أيها الأرعن/. I answered the son of a bitch in Arabic. After that, what happened, happened; Commissioner Clemente brought the darkness, hammering me with questions until he literally split my skull in two.

So like I said, my name's Oscar Mandinga – pleased to meet you – now, back to the hazy past that was my childhood. The only thing I knew about my grandparents was that years earlier they'd moved from Santiago de Cuba to a *barrio* called Lawton in the city of Havana and opened a laundry business that brought in just enough to put food on the table. I have no problems remembering '*El Buen Vivir*' – The Good Life laundromat – since I worked there as a kid, but even back then, I never heard any stories about my grandparents, never saw any photos of them when they were young. As far as I knew my grandparents had been born old, because the day I opened my eyes the first thing I saw was a tall, black, toothless old man – my grandpa – and a little grey-haired old woman with shy, sandy eyes – my grandma. They were sweet, affectionate old things for the most part and I've got to say they brought me up well. At The Good Life they taught me the meaning of hard work and thanks to them when I was little I learned to cook, to clean, to take out the trash, in short to be methodical and reliable. But that's no use to me now because that bald bastard Commissioner Clemente won't give me any work. Though what with the 'special economic period' in force these days in Cuba, no one's got any work.

For all I know you're one of those ignorant morons who thinks books are for timewasters. If so, let me tell you straight up that I don't give a rat's ass what you think because I love reading the classics – though to be honest, I'll read pretty much anything from *Sputnik* magazine to the cartoons in *La revista pionero*. Art is my life, and it's such a pity that in Cuba it's gone to the dogs in the '90s. Round here, people say that when you've made enough good art you've earned the right to turn out bad art. Bullshit! You used to be able to go to the theatre in Havana, but these days there's bound to be a power cut right in the middle of the ballet or the operetta. Everyone's permanently worried and constantly complaining – everyone, that is, except my grandparents, who still insist the Revolution – power cuts, rationing, shortages and all – is the best thing that ever happened to this country. When I say it, I sound like a fruit loop.

Anyway, back to the important stuff, to Pata de Puerco and its origins. This is the story of my ancestors exactly as I told it to Commissioner chrome-dome Clemente before his band of whiteshirts turned up and took the sun away for ever.

Oscar and José

In the 1800s, Pata de Puerco was just one small corner of a sweeping plain with a few scattered shacks between the Sierra Maestra mountains of Santiago de Cuba and the copper mines of El Cobre. My grandpa used to say a passing stranger would have thought the tocororos in the trees had just learned to sing. The Accursed Forest and the surrounding swampland teemed with crocodiles that roamed around like tame dogs, having not yet decided that mud was their favourite place to wallow. It was a lush, green place surrounded by picturesque bowers of twisted trees and jungle creepers, which created grottoes where it was possible to walk for miles without seeing a ray of sunlight. The earth was so red people said it was not soil, but the spilled blood of Indians dried by the sun. Deer and hutias scuttered through the grasslands and wild dogs had learned to live in harmony with man, whose numbers were so scant in this far-flung corner of Cuba it seemed like the last place God made.

The Santisteban family arrived here in 1850. They were looking for a place to live, an idyllic, out-of-the-way place far from the metropolis. As everyone knows, the Santistebans were a powerful slave-trading family who, with the Aldamas and the Terrys, controlled the sugar trade the length and breadth of the island. They owned a workforce of more than fifteen thousand slaves, in addition to the railroads, the stores and the credit houses they possessed.

It was here in Pata de Puerco that Don Manuel Santisteban decided to live out the rest of his days. There are many stories about how he came to build his house, but the way my grandpa told it to me, one day Don Manuel stopped by the ruins of the oldest sugar plantation on the island, a ruined mansion that had once belonged to the conquistador Hernán Cortés back when Santiago de Cuba was the capital of the colony. 'Here shall I die,' announced the powerful slave trader and, without wasting a minute, ordered a new plantation house be built over the crumbling ruins. No crocodile was ever seen in the area again after Doña Isabel Santisteban ordered that all the lush vegetation be hacked down. Cuba, she insisted, was a country of sunshine and not a single ray could pierce the shade of the towering trees. And so the parrots, the hummingbirds and the tocororos also vanished for ever from this beautiful place.

A number of small squat, rustic houses were planted like sombreros around a vast estate measuring some twenty *caballerías*. Between these houses rose the majestic residence of Don Manuel, his señora and their two children, a mansion with tall windows and labyrinthine corridors. The slave quarters, situated 200 metres from the main house, were built of brick and tiles and had a single door and a lone, barred window on one side which allowed in scarcely enough air to breathe. A watchtower, used to keep a lookout for runaways and to keep an eye on the workers, was erected between the slave quarters and the sugar mill and from the top you could see all the way to the stables and the canebrakes.

Among the seven thousand slaves living on the plantation itself was Oscar Kortico, who came from a long line of Korticos: Negroes barely four feet tall who were shipped to Cuba in small numbers and in time vanished from the face of the earth leaving no sign that they had ever existed. A pygmy race from East Africa, from a land as cracked and barren as the surface of the planet Mars, the Korticos were expert hunters and knew the secret ways of plants. Too late did Don Manuel realise just how strong these people were, for when he tried to order a new consignment of Korticos, he was told there were none to be found on or off the island – the earth had opened up and swallowed them. He had been planning to replace the Mandingas – the tallest Negroes and those most suited to forced labour – with Korticos whose appearance belied not only their strength, but the laws of physics. Despite their height, they were as strong and sturdy as the Mandingas and much cheaper to keep, since they ate half as much as other Negroes. But after the shipment that brought Oscar, his mother and his father to Pata de Puerco, no Kortico ever came to Cuba again.

To his dying day, my namesake Oscar Kortico had the same diminutive body, the same thin, slightly elongated childlike face, the same round, black eyes, the same prominent cheekbones that looked like runnels for those tears he never shed. This is how my grandpa described him to me, adding that although Oscar Kortico was a bitter man (something many people confirm) he had known happiness (something many more deny) if only as a child; this inexplicable, elusive feeling was embodied by his mother, the creature he most adored and who returned his great, his boundless love.

Her name was Macuta Dos and she worked on the plantation feeding the animals, cleaning the grounds and drawing water from the well. Since she was a strong, muscular Negress, they set her to cutting cane with the menfolk and gave her so many backbreaking chores that often she worked twenty-two hours a day. The two hours she had to herself, she devoted to her son Oscar who had learned never to complain, though already in his heart he sensed that something was amiss with the world. Those two hours were enough for Oscar: shrugging off her tiredness, his mother would play with him and sometimes tell him stories and fables, like the legend of Yusi the Warrior, a God of the Kortico pantheon, a creature gifted with exceptional powers who, it was said, could lift a cow with just one hand.

After much insistence from Oscar – an insistence that involved howls and wails but never tears – Macuta Dos explained to him that his grandparents had died of old age; that one of his uncles had been shot as a runaway slave and the other carried off by a terrible disease – some curse, some horrifying thing that had caused first his ears and then his testicles to swell. She told him that his father had escaped into the mountains at dawn one morning only to be dragged back that same afternoon dead, the skin flayed from his body, his face unrecognisable. Her only legacy, she told him, was an ancient amulet, a leather necklet strung with a shrivelled pig's foot. Oscar and this amulet were her only fortune.

Oscar Kortico immediately rushed to tell this story to his best friend José Mandinga, who clapped his hand to his mouth in horror. José tried to cheer him, saying that what had happened was destined to happen and that surely now his luck would change for the better. But one night the overseer came to the slave quarters to take Oscar's mother to a small dark room where she was to be bred with one of the tall, brawny Negro bucks because, by Don Manuel's reckoning, such a pairing would produce a good litter of whelps. The boy clung to his mother like a tick to a dog. Macuta Dos pressed the pig's-foot amulet into his hand and told him she would never forget him. Oscar begged to know why she was being taken from him.

'Because such is the lot of a slave.'

'What is a slave?'

'An animal, *hijo*, an animal.'

With a vicious tug, two men wrenched the pair apart and took Macuta Dos from Oscar's side for ever.

In this moment was the wellspring of Oscar Kortico's bitterness. For a whole month, he murmured the story of Yusi the Warrior to himself and refused to play with his friend José. He looked for his mother only in the darkness, expecting that she would suddenly appear through a wall or that at least the men might come and take him to be with her in that small dark cell. Every day he pressed the amulet to his chest, trying to lose himself in the scent of pig's foot that reminded him of his mother. He could not imagine he would never see her again. Six months later, he was sold to an Italian merchant named Giacomo Benvenuto, who lived some ten miles from El Cobre. There, Oscar was given the surname

Benvenuto and set to work as a houseboy in the kitchen and doing chores around the residence.

Though they dressed him in finery, still the other children called him 'the black flea' because of his diminutive stature and treated him like a circus freak. It was here that Oscar truly learned what it meant to be a slave. Little by little there blossomed within him a hatred of the world and most especially of children; a hatred he would carry with him to his grave. He felt as though there was no one he could trust; that he had been forsaken by love, by friendship, by peace. By everything, in fact, but the bitterness that burned like an eternal flame in his chest, reminding him of his miserable existence. He brooded about the meaning of the word slave. 'You are an animal.' This was how he felt, like a brute beast, something confirmed one day when, while he was fixing some kitchen shelves that had been eaten away by termites, he found himself surrounded by a gang of children led by the plantation owner's son. Striking the pose of a lion tamer, the Italian boy informed his entourage that Oscar was living proof of simian intelligence.

'As you can see,' said Giacomo, 'a monkey can fix shelves. He doesn't feel anything inside because he's an animal, but he can talk, he can even read if you teach him. And see – he's proved he knows how to use a hammer. Let's give this magnificent creature a round of applause.'

'Oscar, Oscar, Oscar the orang-utan,' chanted the other children.

Suddenly, Oscar saw black. His teeth drew blood from the Italian boy. Not enough blood to warrant the death sentence, but enough to have him put in the stocks and given several lashes, then locked up in a dark cell for a week.

On his release, he was relieved of his domestic chores and set to work in the fields; it was here that he spent his adolescence and grew to become a man. In all that time he never met a woman who made him happy. He believed that no woman would ever be able to love his diminutive stature, or the bleak pessimism that had become his distinguishing trait. And so he had no choice but to lose his virginity to a sow. It happened one day when Benvenuto's overseer ordered Oscar to work in the barnyard. After the sow came a boss-eyed nanny goat that wouldn't stop bleating. Before long, Oscar Kortico's fame had spread to nanny goats, sows and mares for miles around.

Then came the war of independence which, as I'm sure you know, began in 1868 (10 October, if I'm not mistaken . . .). By now, Oscar had turned eighteen. Giacomo Benvenuto and his family had fled back to the country they'd come from. It was Oscar who brandished the torch that set the sugar mill ablaze. The following day, he set off for the Santisteban plantation in search of his mother. He found only a heap of ashes and charred bricks. It was then that he joined forces with the Mambí Liberation Army under the command of General Maceo at their camp east of Baracoa.

Meanwhile, José Mandinga, Oscar's best friend, was skulking through the streets and the taverns of El Cobre.

Unlike Oscar, who never had much luck with women, and seemed to have inherited from his mother the curse of enduring a life without love, José was always lucky with the opposite sex. At thirteen, he had lost his virginity to Mamaíta, a Negress who worked in the infirmary and could easily have been his grandmother. In secret, he learned from Mamaíta the mysteries of how women should be kissed and caressed in what she called 'touchy-touchy lessons' held every Sunday when the other slaves went out, some to have fun in the local taverns, others to go swimming in the river. On the pretext of curing his cold or scolding him for some misdeed, Mamaíta would take José to the infirmary. He would arrive back in the slave quarters late at night, tired and sore. 'A pig fell on me,' was his invariable excuse. His mother peered at him with her eagle eyes, secretly thinking that the more pigs fell on her son, the better equipped he would be for life.

José was a Mandinga like his father Evaristo and his mother Rosario, who worked in the sugar mill, turning the wheel, sowing, cutting and harvesting cane. Sometimes Evaristo would send José to have a horse shod or Rosario would give him chores around the infirmary, where the slaves used as wet nurses were housed. By the time he turned eighteen, José was a six-foot, broad-shouldered, muscular Negro. He had had sex with almost all the unmarried female slaves on the plantation. His blood brothers admired him, and longed to be like him since José had a charm that led others to treat him with affection and respect.

José often asked his parents what had become of Oscar and when finally they told him his friend had been sold, the boy spent a long time fretting about their answer. For months afterwards, he kept a close watch on the white overseer; he would peer through a chink in the door of the slave quarters at night before he went to sleep and every time he saw the overseer he would run and hide, terrified the man was coming to take him and sell him. But neither he nor his brothers nor his parents were ever sold. His was a different fate.

Some months before war broke out, the slaves led an uprising that would go down in history as the Slaughter of the Santistebans. Beginning with the dogs and ending with the family, not a soul on the property was left alive. The bodies of Don Manuel and Isabel Santisteban and their children were strung up from the watchtower. After the slaves had burned everything, they went their separate ways, fleeing for the caves or the hills. José, his parents and his brothers hid out in the Accursed Forest where they quickly contracted yellow fever. Within a week all but José had died. This is how the young Mandinga boy, like so many who had lost everything, came to be roaming the streets of Santiago.

When word finally reached Oscar that José, whom he thought of as his only surviving family, was now a vagrant and set out in search of him, scouring the streets, the taverns and the dive bars. Finally, among the ruins of the sugar plantation where both boys had been born, he stumbled upon a bundle of foul-smelling rags.

Oscar asked what had happened and José told him about the Slaughter of the Santistebans. Most of the slaves, he told Oscar, had been caught and hanged. He told his friend how his own family had died of a strange sickness that had turned their bodies into human furnaces. The Kortico shook his friend by the shoulder and said: 'You should join the *mambí* army. Killing those bastards is the only way we will ever be free.' José spat on the red earth and turned back to sleep.

'Damn it, José, these white men are the ones who brought the sickness to Cuba.'

Hearing this, José suddenly sat up and stared hard into Oscar's eyes. His friend explained that many times he had seen the Spanish spreading disease through the swamplands, that this was why runaway slaves were always found stiff-legged long before they reached the refuge of the caves.

'I'm telling you, they are the ones who brought the sickness,' Oscar said. 'Now is the time to avenge your family for all the pain they suffered.'

The Mandinga spat on the ground again, but this time to let the Kortico know that he was prepared to fight. José extricated himself from the pile of putrid rags and climbed up behind Oscar on his horse and together they rode back to the *mambí* camp.

During the ambush on the Palma Sopriano convoy in Victoria, José slew fifteen Spaniards with a machete and returned to camp with two horses and eight rifles. In the Battle of Juan Mulato, Oscar and José killed forty-two Spaniards. When, during the fighting at Tibisí, Oscar and José each slew thirty enemy soldiers, the *mambí* soldiers christened them 'The Duo of Death', and General Maceo personally decided to take them with him to the rally at Mangos de Baraguá in March 1878. Lounging in their hammocks after the battle, Oscar confessed to his friend that he loved war, because 'you get to go to so many different places, places you've never been'.

'I know,' said José, looking at him askance, 'but right now, just get some rest, and don't go dozing off. You might dream I'm a Spaniard and hack me to pieces with that machete.'

Betina and Malena

The day following the Battle of Tibisí, José strolled through the morning mist down towards the river to wash the blood and filth off himself. In the distance, he heard a deep, rasping sound and realised he was not alone. He could make out the figure of a woman scrubbing clothes against the stones by the riverbank and carefully crept towards her. Seeing how beautiful she was, he stood, transfixed.

Betina and her younger sister Malena lived alone in a little shack on the outskirts of Manzanillo. Her father had been the sort of man who, in a cheerful mood, would hit her and call her a stupid, ugly whore; in a black mood or in drink, he would lock her in the chicken coop and beat her until she howled in terror. Only then would he release her, telling her she was as dumb as her mother. He died in 1877, a year after General Martinez Campos marched into Havana. Betina's mother was to die many years later in Weyler concentration camp.

It was Betina's dream to find a kind and decent man, someone who would give her a family. Now twenty-five and no longer a virgin, her chances were slight. She had had lovers who beat her, stole the pittance she earned washing laundry at the creek, and then abandoned her. Whenever this happened, she would hole up for days, sometimes weeks, crying an ocean of tears and vowing to take her own life by eating raw earth like the Indians.

Time passed and she put her dreams behind her and became a tough, hard-headed, sometimes foul-mouthed woman who believed only in working to survive. She no longer washed her hair or shaved her armpits. Years of scrubbing laundry had made her delicate fingers as calloused as a farmhand's. But though she neglected her appearance, her beauty was so startling that wherever she went, men threw themselves at her feet and women glared at her with passionate jealousy. Many a woman dreamed of possessing those lustrous locks, those brooding almond eyes, that body as curvaceous as a Greek amphora.

When he saw Betina kneeling, her hips swaying as she slapped the laundry against the rocks, something stirred in José and he felt his breeches swell. Lust coursed through him like a rutting animal. He wasted no time with words, but immediately proposed sex, showing her his bulging flies.

'I don't know what you're thinking. I may be black and ignorant, but let me tell you now that I am a decent woman.'

'Of course, señorita, that's why I am attracted to you.'

'Because I'm decent?'

'No, because you're ignorant.'

Betina angrily snatched up the laundry basket and was about to leave but José blocked her path. She was ignorant, he explained, just as he and all the Negroes he knew were ignorant; this was why he liked her.

'I saw you kneeling there, swaying your hips, and I thought of my mother.'

'How could you think about your mother with your breeches fit to burst?'

José replied that he loved his mother more than anything in the world and did not know whether this boundless love was the cause, but whenever his mother came back to the slave quarters after work, José felt a thrill run through him that paralysed his body and his breeches would begin to swell. It had first happened when he was fourteen. As he spoke, he stared down at his crotch with the mischievous, feline smile of a naughty child. Betina told José that she had not been born yesterday and asked him to be so good as to leave her in peace because she had too much laundry to do to waste time talking to him. Just then, José grabbed her roughly and clapped his hand over her mouth.

'Shhh.'

He froze, staring up at the overgrown hill looking for some sign to confirm his suspicions. He picked up Betina's laundry basket and, holding her firmly by the arm, dragged her into a dense thicket off the path then pointed to two Spanish soldiers riding towards the river. He signalled to Betina that he would be right back and, like a streak of lightning, vanished into the trees.

Betina felt a cramp in her shoulders and in her belly. She watched as one of the Spaniards dismounted and tethered his horse to a tree. Then, glancing warily around, he walked towards the river. Confident there was no one nearby, he walked back towards his horse. Betina stumbled, the trees around her rustled and the soldier glanced back in her direction. He walked towards Betina, cocking his rifle and signalling to the soldier he had left behind.

'Don't expect your friend to answer. He won't be talking any more.'

Startled, the Spanish soldier spun round and found himself face to face with José who was holding a blood-smeared machete.

'This whole area is surrounded by *mambís*. If I were you, I'd go back the way I came. Unless of course you want to die.'

The soldier froze, his rifle aimed at José's chest, gauging the courage in those coal-black eyes and weighing it against his own. He hesitated, the rifle trembled in his hands.

'So. Do you want to die?' roared José.

The soldier fled. Racing back to his horse, he stumbled on a large boulder and, looking down, discovered it was the head of his friend, his hat still in place. In a flash, he leaped into the saddle and vanished.

'Now that you've seen that I'm not all bad, I think I deserve to know your name . . . Mine is José.'

'My name is Betina, but my opinion of you hasn't changed.'

Betina covered her legs as best she could as she settled herself behind José on the horse. The Mandinga gave her a smile that was all his own, and a sly, passionate gaze. Betina's lips parted to reveal teeth that looked as if they had been sculpted by an artist. It was the first time José saw her smile and he felt sure it would not be the last.

Having left her outside her shack, José headed back to the *mambí* camp. He told Oscar what had happened, adding that

Betina had a beautiful sister who, to judge from her height, was a Kortico like him.

'I've told you before,' Oscar said, 'I want nothing to do with women. They all want babies and I will never be able to rid myself of my loathing for children.'

José insisted that Oscar needed to root out the bitterness from his heart, that a good woman might do just that. But Oscar wanted to go on killing Spaniards.

'You have already killed so many. If you carry on like this, you'll turn into the orang-utan you despise so much.'

The Kortico sprang to his feet and drew his machete.

'What are you saying?'

'What I'm saying is I am not an animal and neither are you. We are both entitled to forget war and blood, fire and disease, to forget the dark past and begin again.'

Oscar simply frowned, staring into his friend's eyes. Then he sheathed his machete and sat down again, muttering that he was not about to change his mind.

'You do what you like. I'm going with General Maceo to the rally at Mangos de Baraguá.'

But the following day, José managed to drag his friend to the house where Betina and Malena lived. Just as he predicted, Oscar and Malena fell in love the moment they set eyes on each other and, with time and much effort on his part, Betina was persuaded to change her mind about José. The two couples were married beneath an avocado tree, settled in Pata de Puerco and lived happily in the little village as time slowly impelled them towards the inevitable: towards the dark, despised abyss, towards oblivion.

★ ★ ★

While the war against Spain raged on, Pata de Puerco huddled in its isolation and its misery, drawing slowly farther and farther away from the rest of the island. The villagers experienced the war from afar like a wound that throbs when one is asleep. For many, years of fighting and of hunger had killed off any hope that the war might be a temporary ache that would soon pass. And though the battle had not troubled to visit their tiny village, in the distance they heard the roar of cannons and the screams of the dying. The *patapuercanos* never truly understood the meaning of war, of so many dead; they went on living, forgetting and dying. Fried chicken wings and *churros* with chocolate. I don't know why that suddenly popped into my head – maybe because I've been talking about war and famine, and the only war I know is the one being waged in my belly.

Now, I know it's not like anyone is ever going to ask, but if they ever do, I want you to make it clear that my namesake, Oscar Kortico, with José, Malena and Betina were the true founders of the village of Pata de Puerco. At the time, many people believed that the area was still cursed after the Slaughter of the Santistebans. It was José and Oscar who cut the paths through the forest and dug the well with their bare hands. It was Betina and Malena who planted the red flame tree that marked the northern boundary, next to the cemetery for men and animals. It was they who encouraged the peasants from all around to move here. Slowly, from the four corners of the island, the hopeless began to trickle in, those searching for the end of the world, for some place where they could shut out the memory of war and begin again.

José and Oscar helped the Santacruz family build a shack

next to the cabin of Ester the midwife. Shortly afterwards, Silvio and Rachel Aquelarre and their baby daughter arrived from Baracoa and built a simple house in a clearing behind that of Oscar and Malena. The pale-skinned Jabaos, a family of eleven, settled near the ruins of the old Santisteban sugar mill. They always roamed the plains and the uplands in groups of five at least. Gradually, Pata de Puerco filled with life, with youth. From nothing, it grew to become a hamlet of a dozen crude shacks connected by pathways like red veins. *El Callejón de la Rosa* – Rose Alley – was the dirt road that connected the hamlet to El Cobre, the nearest town, where there was a church and where respectable families lived.

It goes without saying that the inhabitants of Pata de Puerco were illiterate Negroes who lived off the land. Not one of them had money enough to buy livestock. My grandpa used to say that people moved slowly in those days, and still more slowly in that part of the world. Days seemed to last thirty-five hours rather than twenty-four. But there was no need to hurry since there was nowhere to go, nothing to buy and no money with which to buy it. The only shop for miles around was Chinaman Li's store a mile and a half along the road to El Cobre.

It was in 1896 that José and Betina had their first child, a beautiful little girl who had a reddish-black complexion, bushy eyebrows like her mother and the same mischievous eyes as her father. They named her Gertrudis. Her first birthday was another day of backbreaking labour for Oscar and José. Out in the fields digging yuca and picking beans, they got to talking about Yusi the Warrior. It all started when José

23

stabbed his machete into the ground, killing a huge scorpion. Oscar chided him, saying that scorpion venom could be used to cure all manner of illness; that was how Yusi had healed his own wounds. José ventured the opinion that Yusi the Warrior had never existed, a comment that enraged his friend.

'Besides, why do we need scorpions when we have someone in the village who can cure anything?' José pointed his curved blade towards the path as Ester the midwife appeared. Ester was a fat, reclusive Negro woman with large breasts who almost always wore a smock smeared with coal dust and a brightly coloured scarf wrapped around her head. For her services as a midwife, she accepted whatever patients could afford to give – a chicken or a pair of rope sandals. Little was known about her, where she came from, or whether she had ever had a family. People said she was the lover of El Mozambique, the most hated man in all of Pata de Puerco whom she often visited.

José told Oscar that Ester's tits could cure any illness, and not just the bellyache everyone suffered from. Ester's breasts and buttocks might even have cured the fever that had killed his family in the Accursed Forest. Oscar paid no heed and went on filling his sack with cassava.

'You know what I like best about babies?' José went on. 'The way they pee on you. It's like a benediction. Geru used to pee on me all the time, but now she's growing up she doesn't do it any more. I can't wait for our next child to be born so it can start all over.'

Hunched over his work, Oscar said nothing. José patted him on the shoulder and told him not to worry, that some day it would happen to him.

'It's already happened to me and I don't want it to ever happen again.'

José looked at his friend for a moment, bewildered. Finally, he said, 'I know it's impossible to ever know anyone completely, but I'm sure that . . .'

'They used to tie me to a post with ropes, José.'

'Who?'

'The children on the plantation. And do you know what they did?'

José shrugged.

'One after another they pissed on my face. And I can tell you now it's no benediction.'

The two men stood, staring at each other. The bitterness in Oscar's eyes was so blatant that José felt his heart fill with an infinite sadness.

'Six weeks, José,' Ester the midwife called from the dirt road.

'Six weeks to what?'

'Betina is six weeks gone.'

'Pregnant?'

'Congratulations!'

Ester picked up her basket and hurried off. José hugged Oscar, lifting him off the ground, then gathered up his sacks of cassava and ran back to his house.

'Come on, Oscar, and bring Malena, this calls for a celebration!' he shouted.

Head in his hands, Oscar stared after his friend but did not say anything. He picked up his sacks and trudged home.

The house of José Mandinga and Betina de Flores, crafted from wood and royal palm, had three bedrooms, two for the children they dreamed they would have. That's how my grandparents always described it, and though I never saw it, I feel I know the place by heart. The front door was flanked on either side by windows that were always wide open, letting air and light flood into a narrow rectangular living room that was simple and unadorned. A passageway led to the bedrooms which opened on to the corridor, so there was no privacy. At the end of the corridor was another door that led outside to the privy and the open fire on which they cooked.

Malena rushed in excitedly. The polar opposite of her sister Betina, who never conceded defeat in difficult situations, Malena preferred to let others make her decisions for her; she never offered an opinion, she was meek, quiet and withdrawn. Her dream was to have a son she would name Benicio. Like her sister, as a girl she had had no luck with men, but unlike her, Malena had waited in silence for her man to come, never complaining, but never giving up that faint, flickering hope. She was not pretty like Betina, but she had the look of a faithful wife about her that women have when they long to tend to a house, a husband or a child, and this gave her an alluring, mysterious air. An air that could fascinate men. But there were no men. War had done its work, carrying off the men, most of them to their deaths.

Malena hugged her sister and then hugged little Gertrudis. Oscar stood stiffly in the doorway staring at Gertrudis with owlish eyes.

'I'm so happy for you, sister,' said Malena. 'Now I know I will never catch you up.'

Betina said that actually having babies was easy, they simply needed to try harder. At this, she shot a conspiratorial glance at Oscar, who was standing like a fence-post in the doorway. José told him not to look so glum.

'Look, Geru, look who's here ... Uncle Oscar ... remember Uncle Oscar? Go give him a big kiss,' he said to little Gertrudis who tottered over to Oscar and grasped his thumb. José's friend was sweating merely at the sight of the small child tugging at him. Betina asked when Malena and Oscar were planning to have a child, sarcastically insinuating that perhaps the long wait was because Oscar could not get it up. Malena tried to change the subject, asking her sister if she was having morning sickness yet, but Betina insisted that it was high time Malena had a baby, that it was foolish of her to hide the fact that she desperately wanted a child. Oscar set Geru down on the ground, walked over to Betina and said, 'Maybe some day we might get a dog, but right now we don't want anything that eats, shits and farts.'

'Your selfishness will be your undoing, Oscar,' said Betina.

Oscar drew his machete but José put a restraining hand on his friend's chest and told him to hold his temper, not to forget that he was in his house talking to his wife. His stocky frame towered head and shoulders above Oscar.

'She may be your wife, but she would be wise to hold her tongue if she wants to keep it. And she should stop meddling in our life.'

José told Betina to go and lay the table and told his wife and his friend that it was time to stop eating shit. 'Let's eat food instead,' he said. Betina and Malena immediately withdrew to the kitchen.

While the women were cooking, the men sat at the table. José said that he would have to find work to earn some money because the land they farmed yielded barely enough for them to survive. According to Abel Santacruz, there was work to be had in the cane fields around El Cobre, and he planned to go there and try his luck. Oscar, intently observing every detail of what little Gertrudis did, was not listening. At one point, the little girl tottered over and stood in front of him, staring down at his bare feet, then she clutched her stomach and from her mouth spewed a thick liquid that befouled Oscar's right foot. The Kortico immediately rushed to get a bucket of water and went out into the back yard. He tipped the water on to the ground and, having created a pool of mud, plunged his vomitous foot into the sludge. Malena asked what was going on. José watched, smiling to see Oscar rubbing his feet like a wild colt.

What was going on was this: the Korticos – a tribe in which the men, despite being only four feet tall, had penises that were abnormally long and thick – believed in African gods, as did all the slaves brought from Africa. Among the most important of these was Olofi, God of Creation, lord and master of all living things, who granted man the power to create other living beings, but only with His blessing. Olofi would mark those privileged to bear children with the vomit of a child. Once this had happened, the couple were obliged to conceive within a year. Men who were not marked out were required to tie their foreskin with string in order to avoid pregnancy. According to Kortico tradition, Olofi's will could be negated only by a ritual performed on a riverbank that involved sacrificing an animal to the god and twenty lashes with a whip made of goat hide.

'Come on, Oscar, sometimes life doesn't turn out the way we plan. There's nothing you can do.'

'No,' said Oscar, 'There is another way.'

He explained to everyone how, according to tradition, the will of Olofi might be revoked. José and Betina looked into Malena's sad eyes. It was not the best solution, but at least it offered a release from the spell, a way of circumventing the will of the African gods.

Heads bowed, Oscar and Malena returned to their shack which was green inside and out. It had a timber floor of royal palm through which grew weeds and wild mushrooms. The cabin had a living room and one bedroom and windows that were riddled with termites. Because of the damp, the walls inside were covered in moss, turning the shack into a green and fragrant forest.

'Don't you understand, Malena, I would do anything for you, but I could never be a good father to this child. What if he were to grow up to be more miserable than me?' Malena stroked Oscar's head as she gazed into his eyes: his happiness mattered more to her than anything in the world and so, if having a child would be a problem, it was better not to have one. Oscar was mollified. He smiled like a baby, kissed his wife tenderly and made love to her as never before knowing that, as long as Malena was by his side, he would never be lonely.

The following day, José went to talk to Abel Santacruz, Silvio Aquelarre and the father of the Jabao family and persuaded them to join him and Oscar working on the sugar plantations east of El Cobre. Each man chipped in two pesos for a horse and cart to make the journey there every day. They would get up at four in the morning and work eight hours a day for one peso a month. Though the pay was miserable, everyone – except Oscar – gave thanks to God that they had money to provide for their families. With one daughter growing up and another child on the way, José could ill afford the luxury of starting a revolution – something Oscar frequently suggested. Three weeks after they started working on the plantation, the five men set off as usual for the cane fields. When they got there, Oscar organised a meeting of thirty *macheteros*.

'These white men are exploiting us, and I don't want to go on being a slave. I have two solutions: either they give us better working conditions, or we cut the bastards' heads off. I would be happy with either.' José gave his friend a sidelong glance and spat on the ground, waiting for the reactions of the other workers. The first to speak was Señor Jabao, who said Oscar was right, that the *macheteros* at La Villas were paid three pesos a month while those they worked for were exploiters. Someone named Matías said that he was tired of revolution, that he had spent his whole life fighting war after war and now that he had his own house he simply wanted a little peace.

'Your house doesn't belong to you any more than mine belongs to me, or have you forgotten who owns the land? The war is still raging, but when it's over, you'll see, they'll throw you off this land. Oscar here says that if we had a little more money in our pockets, we'd be better off. Why don't we just make our protest and see what happens?'

José's words were met with utter silence. One of the *macheteros* moved into the centre of the circle. A tall, black, broad-shouldered giant of a man with powerful arms, who looked as though he had been lifting weights since the day he was born. He was shirtless, and the muscles of his chest and abdomen were unusually chiselled. He wore the same sackcloth trousers worn by all the *macheteros*. Grandpa looked into his eyes and said they were unfocused, as though he was not actually seeing, but rather hearing voices no one else could hear.

'Bravo, bravo,' said the man, clapping his hands slowly as he stepped into the middle of the group, 'Fine work from brothers Oscar and José. I can imagine what their wives will say when they come home empty-handed. With no job, no money, but their honour intact – because I think that's what all these fine speeches are about. Now, I don't know about the rest of you, but a man cannot feed his family with honour. And how many men here have children to feed?' A forest of hands shot up. 'Raise your hand, José, too; go on, Gertrudis is still a child. And we know your friend the dwarf here has no kids. He might have a wife, but the way he's going he won't have her long, nor will the rest of you if you listen to the shit that . . .'

He did not have time to finish his sentence. Oscar hurled his machete and, had the other man not ducked, it would have hit him square in the forehead. Instead the machete sailed past, wounding the *machetero* standing behind him. Before José could react, Oscar hurled himself on the man, grabbing his throat. The man was a giant and Oscar looked like a small boy climbing a coconut tree. 'I'll kill you, you bastard,' screamed the Kortico. José and four of the other workers waded in to separate them. After a long struggle they finally managed to pull Oscar off.

'You see what I mean? This man is an animal. That's what

you'll all be if you carry on the way you're going,' said the big man, rubbing his neck. José told him to leave before the situation turned ugly. Then he walked back to the crowd of *macheteros* and told them to forget everything that had been said. Let each man go his own way. In the tense atmosphere, slowly, one by one, the workers headed off to the canebrakes to begin their eight hours of backbreaking labour.

'Where did he come from?' asked José on the road back to Pata de Puerco. The infamous Mozambique was the most hated man for miles around. He too lived in Pata de Puerco, on the outskirts of the village, though no one ever saw him. He never came out of his house, not even for a breath of fresh air. 'One day we'll pay that son of a bitch a visit, hey, Oscar,' said José, whipping the mare to get her to move faster. Oscar simply stared out at the horizon. Señor Jabao told José to forget the idea because El Mozambique had seven vicious dogs that would not let anyone come near the house.

'He really had it in for you! Are you sure you don't know him?' asked Aquelarre. Still Oscar stared into the middle distance. Then Abel Santacruz interjected to remark that while he hadn't wanted to say anything, a bird in the hand was better than two in the bush. He apologised to Oscar, insisting that though he intended no criticism, but these were hard times and they should give thanks to God that at least they had work enough and money enough to put bread on the table. Oscar turned to glare at him and José immediately sensed what was coming next.

'Gentlemen, let's just forget what happened. Hey, Oscar, you know today is your goddaughter Gertrudis's birthday? Don't tell me you forgot.'

'What do you mean, we should give thanks to God, Abel?' said Oscar. 'You're talking as though God provides for us. Get it through your thick skull: we're slaves, each and every one of us, and we'll die slaves if we go on thinking like sheep. It doesn't matter that people say slavery has been abolished, it doesn't matter how much times have changed, the Negro is still a Negro, and he'll live his whole life in mud and filth.'

At these words, silence closed in. All that could be heard was the creak of the cartwheels across the flatland. José went on talking about Gertrudis, about how much she'd grown, how she talked like a parrot, how she scampered around. Oscar interrupted him.

'I'm not going back. So I want my *reales*.'

'What *reales*?' asked the others.

'The two pesos I put in to buy this mare and cart.'

José said that if he wanted his two pesos he would have to wait until the end of the month when they were paid, because none of them had a *centavo* between them. Then he went back to prattling on about Gertrudis until Jabao tapped him on the shoulder to let him know that Oscar had jumped off the cart and was hurrying towards the overgrown hill. 'Don't worry. He'll soon calm down,' said José and spurred the cart on towards Pata de Puerco.

At three o'clock in the morning, José was woken by a hammering on his door. Half-asleep, he opened it to find Santacruz, Aquelarre and Jabao standing there with horrified looks on their faces. 'You have to see this, José.'

The four men ran to the place where the cart had been tethered. The mare lay sprawled on the ground, her tongue sticking out. One of her hind legs had been hacked off with a machete. Having examined the body of the animal, the four men concluded that this carnage was motivated by old bitterness, the grudge of an unhappy man, it was an act of vengeance. José spat on the ground and said, 'This is something I'll never forgive him for.'

He patted each man on the back, telling them to say nothing of what had happened but to leave the matter in his hands. Santacruz, Aquelarre and Jabao went back to their homes. At dawn José was outside Oscar's house and was about to knock when his friend opened the door.

'Hey, José, I was just heading out,' said Oscar.

'Where? To hack the other leg off the mare?'

Oscar ignored this comment. He told his friend that when he arrived home the night before, he had told Malena he intended to give up working in the cane fields and buy a cow. Malena had been inconsolable, had thrown herself on the ground and wept. José knew that Oscar could not bear to see his wife cry. So he told her he would go back to work on the sugar plantation and she calmed down. Then, this morning, just as he was about to meet them at the cart, he had found Malena unconscious on the floor. He had not told José that recently Malena had been fainting often. He threw water on her face, but she did not wake. Then he had gone to fetch Ester, who was inside examining her even now. 'That's why I'm late this morning,' said the Kortico.

José stared at his friend suspiciously.

'Why the hell did you do it, Oscar? I told you if you wanted your money all you had to do was wait until the end of the month. Or was this for the animal sacrifice to revoke Olofi's spell?'

Oscar clearly had no idea what his friend was talking about.

'I'm talking about the mare, you bastard. Don't play me for a fool, just tell me the truth!'

'The mare? What's happened to the mare?'

José realised Oscar really knew nothing about what had happened. He scratched his neck and glanced around, studying the undergrowth. He thought he saw a tree moving swiftly, but no wind was shaking its branches and besides trees do not wear hats.

'Has someone killed the mare? Tell me, José.'

'You know what, Oscar . . . I think someone doesn't like you.'

Oscar asked more questions but José had already turned on his heel and was walking quickly back to his house. At that moment Ester's voice came from inside the shack.

'Six weeks, Oscar.'

Both men turned.

'Congratulations,' said Ester.

Oscar's Nightmare

The two men rushed inside and found Ester washing her hands and Malena with a smile on her face.

'What does she mean?' said Oscar.

'You know the old saying: it's too late to eat green guava when you've already got the shits,' said José, laughing.

Oscar nervously asked Malena how she could be pregnant and demanded that Ester check again, explaining that Malena had taken to fainting a lot recently and that besides her predictions were frequently inaccurate. Ignoring Oscar's concerns, Ester walked to the door. 'Take good care of her. She'll need it. I recommend she eat lots of meat and vegetables to increase her blood supply because we never know how much she might lose. You'll find me at my house when you're ready to pay.'

'Wait there! I'll pay you right now.'

Oscar went out into the back yard and grabbed the chicken he had bought a few days earlier to make sacrifice to Olofi. Looking into the midwife's eyes, he said that he hoped she was certain of her divinations because this was a very serious matter, and if this were a joke he would not let it pass. Ester nodded, grabbed the chicken by the legs and left. Oscar stared after her, dazed, as though her coal-streaked smock were some spectre disappearing into the underbrush. Then he stumbled back into his shack, its walls green with moss and mould, still in a deep trance.

'Cheer up, *hombre*, it's not the end of the world,' said José. 'Eventually we all die, and that's the end. Everything we are dies with us. Some day, even your name will have vanished from the earth. "Oscar Kortico?" people will say. "Who the hell was he?" When you think about it, children are the only proof that we ever existed. You'll see, you'll come to love being a father.' Oscar ushered his friend out, saying that he and Malena had a lot to talk about. José walked down the path, skipping for joy, greeting everyone he passed along the way. He had completely forgotten about the dead mare, her tongue poking out. Oscar and Malena were going to have a child, that was all that mattered. A child would bring the two families even closer together and would finally root out the bitterness lodged in his friend's heart. This is what children did, they brought happiness into a home, something Oscar had rarely experienced. That day, the Mandingas celebrated Malena's pregnancy in secret while the Kortico cabin remained shut up as though there had been a death in the family.

Unlike Betina, who scarcely believed in her own shadow, Malena was fiercely devout and visited the church of Our Lady of Charity in El Cobre at least once a week in addition to the three prayers she made daily. I know this doesn't mean anything because there are lots of people who claim to be Christians when actually they're complete bastards who would sell their own mothers. But Malena was not like that. Oscar thought that perhaps this was why the gods had bestowed on her the gift of pregnancy because, truth be told, during their marriage they had had sex only once a month and each time he had tied a string around his enormous penis in accordance with the traditions of his forebears.

'Tell me the truth, Malena, have you slept with another man?' he asked her over and over. But every time Malena would cross herself three times, swearing she had done no such thing, and every night she offered up a prayer for her husband who, though he was a good man, was sometimes possessed by demons.

Oscar, who always saw his wife as sacred, knew that she was sickly by nature; she was often woken by a recurring nightmare: a man raping her, pinning her against the timber floor. Sometimes, in the early hours, when he heard her scream in terror, he would run and fetch a damp cloth and press it to her forehead but when he asked what had frightened her, she always answered: 'It's just a nightmare.' The same nightmare had tormented her for years. Oscar never believed that these moans and tortured cries were simply the result of nightmares. And so he became jealous. Sometimes he would follow Malena all the way to El Cobre to discover that there was indeed something else, but he never saw evidence of anything unseemly. He would study her in the presence of other men, he even watched how she behaved with his friend José, and finally he was forced to admit that Malena was a saint, a pure woman, utterly devoted to her husband.

But Oscar was highly strung by nature. If he had never

dreamed of getting married it was because he was convinced that no woman could ever love him. Being four feet tall and with a dark-black complexion, he felt sure it was impossible, since Negro women dreamed of tall, handsome men, mulattoes preferably, with whom to bear children. Racism was commonplace among Negroes. Oscar was one of the darkest, and probably the shortest slaves, which was why the first time Malena told him that she loved him, he ran away, unable to believe that this cruel woman could dare mock him to his face. It was only thanks to the persistence of José, who invariably dragged Oscar along on his visits, that he finally realised Malena was serious; that she genuinely loved him.

Even so, Oscar had no idea how to make a woman happy. José, who was an expert on the subject, gave him tips on how to treat the fair sex. He suggested Oscar bring her flowers, make her laugh, massage her feet and her back, and recommended lots of sex on the grass and in the mud. Oscar picked romerillo, hibiscus and wild roses to which he added stems of sicklebush and wrapped this bouquet in a banana leaf to give to Malena who immediately pricked her fingers on the spiny sicklebush and began to laugh uncontrollably. Oscar sucked the blood from her fingers for a moment, and Malena went on laughing as he joked and perfomed silly tricks, then Oscar sent her sprawling face-down in the mud.

'What on earth are you doing, Oscar?' said Malena. By now Oscar had already climbed up on to her back and was kneading her neck and shoulders like a baker. According to José, this was how women were conquered; little different from a sow or a nanny goat, and this, therefore, was how Oscar treated her. After all, where goats and sows were concerned, Oscar was an expert. Have you ever tried to massage a sow? I didn't think so. Well, Oscar had. He had given Malena flowers, had made her laugh, and massaged her shoulders. All that remained now was José's final recommendation. Oscar turned Malena on to her back. Her vision was blurred from the mud and so when Malena saw Oscar holding a black cudgel thick as a mango sapling, she thought for a moment he was about to beat her.

'Throw down that stick, Oscar . . .' said Malena. 'What are you doing!' She quickly wiped the mud from her eyes. Only then did she realise what the thick cudgel actually was. She jumped to her feet, ran off and shut herself in her house for a week. Oscar went back to consult his friend, explaining that the last phase of his plan had failed.

'That's because you've got a prick like a horse,' said José. I don't know if people said 'prick' back then, but never mind. Anyway, José advised that from now on Oscar should treat Malena with love and tenderness. This he did. Though Malena refused to open her door to him, he would lay his bunch of wildflowers on the doorstep. He did so every day for months, and the outcome was always the same: still Malena remained silent, shut away in her shack. Until one day, after working in the vegetable garden, tired of waiting for her to respond and wounded by the lash of her indifference, he told José that it was all his fault.

'All my fault? What's all my fault?'

'You put ideas into my head, you gave me hope.' Oscar went on to explain that he had been perfectly content fighting wars and killing Spaniards, it had been José who had steered them away into this domesticated life, and all it had brought Oscar was pain. He had done everything José had told him to do, he had dared to hope, and it was all for nothing.

'What am I supposed to do now?' asked the Kortico.

'What do you do now? You do what everyone else has to do. You accept the golden rule: sometimes life is fucking terrific, sometimes it's terrifically fucked,' said José, clapping him on the back. They talked for a little longer and in the end decided never to mention the subject again. Oscar picked up his sack of vegetables and went home. When he got there, Malena was waiting for him. They both stood frozen for what felt like a century. They were speechless. Like two sleepwalkers sharing the same dream, they moved to the bed and undressed. Oscar tied his penis with a length of twine and Malena's eyes widened, unable to take in what they saw, but she said nothing.

For the first time they discovered each other's bodies; came to know them by heart. Oscar penetrated her and Malena drew him in, her legs hooked around his waist, her mouth half-open. Afterwards, with Malena's face resting on his belly and his hands stroking her still-trembling breasts, Oscar realised that she was the love of his life, that he would marry her and together they would fashion a new life. The rest you know. The couple settled in Pata de Puerco and lived happily for a while in that little hamlet. Which brings us back to where we left our story.

Now I'll tell you something you don't know, starting with the fact that from the moment Malena fell pregnant, Oscar became a dutiful husband, attending to his wife's every whim with an almost religious devotion. Malena had only to lift her finger and already he was by her bedside waiting for her orders: a sweet grapefruit, or maybe she wanted him to boil water on the fire so she could take another bath – the third today. He massaged her feet and her hands, he went with her everywhere, he bathed her, dressed and undressed her, brushed her hair, took her out walking, put her to bed and woke her in the morning. Anyone would have thought his fondest wish was to have a child. He realised he could change the gruff manner many had criticised, and one morning people discovered that Oscar had teeth, that he was capable of smiling. 'He has teeth as white as coconut flesh,' they said.

Very soon the bellies of both women began to swell. Day after day, Betina's belly came to look more like a watermelon, a vast vaulting bulge jutting out from beneath her clothes. Malena's belly was almost the same size, something no one could explain given that she had become pregnant six weeks later. José taunted his friend Oscar, saying that he had clearly unleashed twenty years of seed, that he was a prize stud. 'With a prick like that you could impregnate a cow.'

Oscar laughed. He didn't draw his machete as he used to do; nothing seemed to bother him now, nothing could make him lose his temper. He had become helpful and obliging to his neighbours; he even ran errands for the Santacruz family. He helped Evaristo make kites which they gave away to the children every week. José had persuaded the other men that Oscar had not killed the mare, that he himself had seen some local thug running away, someone he did not recognise in the darkness. The men believed him.

That same day, the two friends apologised to each other

and they did not go back to working in the eastern cane fields. They spent their mornings working their little plot of land and making wooden toys for the children. In the afternoons the two couples would go strolling through the village hand in hand, happy and content. Oscar would kiss Malena, hug her, massage her feet, her shoulders; this he did every time his wife had walked ten paces. José and Betina simply laughed at him. It was as though he had suddenly gone mad, but with a harmless, contagious madness, one that was utterly hilarious.

One day during their afternoon stroll, the Kortico broke with his usual routine. Leaving his wife sitting with her sister on the grass, he took José aside and said, 'I never thanked you, José.'

'Thanked me for what?'

'For Malena. You were right. She is the only good thing that has ever happened to me.'

'Thank you, too,' said José.

'Me?'

'Yes. Thank you for rescuing me when I was wandering the streets.'

Oscar smiled, showing the brilliant white teeth he had recently discovered in his mouth.

'You know something?' said José. 'If you carry on like this, you're in danger of becoming a good man.'

The two men hugged. Oscar wrapped his arms around the Mandinga's waist, and his friend bent down to complete the embrace.

11 April 1898

Time, as it always does, continued to pass and so arrived the year of 1898 which began with an incident that was to change for ever the history of Cuba. I'm talking about the battleship USS *Maine* sailing into Havana harbour.

After thirty years of war against Spain, people had become immune to threats of annihilation. By now, both Martí and Maceo were dead and the population of Cuba was barely one and a half million. They say the centre of the island and all points east had been completely destroyed, that it looked like a vast rubble heap. February came and the yellow press began to speculate. Some said the warship had come to help us, others that it had come to overthrow us. On 15 February, the world exploded and shards of the battleship were scattered everywhere. Some two hundred Americans died: the United States blamed Spain; Spain blamed the United States. Eventually the USA, deciding to enter the war, began to arm the fleet and . . . What the hell am I doing talking about the USS *Maine*? Sorry, sometimes when I'm on a roll I get muddled and end up talking shit. It tends to happen when I'm hungry, because food, for me, is sacred. I swear, I'm

44

capable of killing someone for food; I'm serious. It's like that time back in primary school when I wrung the neck of that fucking cat for eating my lunch. But anyway, back to the story . . .

In April, while the whole thing about the USS *Maine* was still kicking off, Oscar and Malena were preparing for the momentous changes in their future. Malena was only seven months pregnant, but her belly was huge; she looked as though she might give birth at any minute. This in fact proved to be true, though no one knew it then. So, on that April morning, José and Betina set off walking to El Cobre with little Gertrudis, without the faintest idea of what the coming hours would bring.

The sun had risen early, lighting up the hills, the red earth of the Callejón de la Rosa, and the shacks of the little village. The day was set fair and the child of Oscar and Malena seemed ready to be born since, from early that morning, it began to kick and prod, desperate to get out of its mother's belly. Oscar immediately went to fetch Ester the midwife who arrived within five minutes, nervous and agitated, her eyes sharp and shining. She kneeled between Malena's legs, slipped a hand inside her and whispered: 'The baby's coming. Fetch some water.'

Ester shooed away the cockroaches crawling over the bed, the wooden floor and in the dark corners while Oscar dashed out with a bucket to the village well twenty yards from his shack, and he could still hear his wife's howls of pain as he ran. Within ten minutes he came back to find the midwife not where he left her, but standing at the head of the bed. Ester was still shaking nervously.

'What's happening?' asked Oscar, setting down the pail of water.

'Nothing, I was just wiping sweat from her forehead. Bring the pail over here.' Ester washed her hands. She seemed awkward, as though this were her first childbirth. 'Push hard,' she said. Malena began to push, screaming so loudly the walls of the shack trembled. She was poorly nourished and her body shuddered with every push as though she were losing slivers of life. The baby's enormous, bald head popped out, eyes tight shut, and clearly in distress.

'Come on, push!' screamed Ester. 'He's coming!'

The broad-shouldered baby did not seem to want to come out. Oscar did not have the courage to say anything. He simply stood, as though hypnotised, staring at his child's head between his wife's legs; he clutched Malena's hand and did his best to ignore her blood-curdling howls. Ester pulled the baby by the head and Malena writhed in agony until, in a final effort, they managed to get the baby out.

'It's a boy!' the midwife said with a smile. 'It's a boy, Malena. A healthy baby boy, and big too. The worst is over now.'

Ester was about to cut the umbilical cord. 'Not yet, Ester. Leave him attached to me a little longer.' Malena held out her thin arms and Ester handed her the child. Still Oscar said nothing, staring down not at his son, but at the dark body of his wife which looked frighteningly delicate framed against the white sheets streaked red with blood.

As Malena held him up to her face, the baby began to wail. Slowly, he opened his dark eyes and looked at his mother who smiled up at him weakly. For what seemed an eternity they stared at each other as mother and child met for the first time. Then Malena glanced at her husband. 'You have to be strong, Oscar. Never forget that I loved you from the first day I met you. When he grows up, tell Benicio to be even-tempered. Tell him that, and let him be a comfort to you too. Tell him avenging past wrongs brings only present suffering. Tell him that.'

Before Oscar had time to take in these words, Malena's voice flickered out as though someone had snuffed a candle; her hands slipped to let her son's body rest on hers. She was dead.

'Malena! No, Malena, no! Please God, no!' Ester shook her, but it was useless. Oscar fell to his knees, still staring straight ahead; he shed no tears. In his place, another man would have roared, tried to revive his wife, thrown water in her face, run for help, slapped her if he had to. But Oscar did not move. He simply stared at the same fixed point: at his wife's eyes, suddenly lifeless.

'I swear I don't know how this happened, Oscar. In all my years as a midwife, I've never seen anything like it.'

'Cut the cord.'

'Oscar, think about what you're going to . . .'

'I don't want to think. Cut the cord right now and leave, I'll take care of everything.'

Ester did as she was asked. Quickly, as though he had suddenly emerged from his trance, Oscar got to his feet and walked Ester to the door.

'Maybe she was undernourished,' said Ester. Oscar was not listening. He paid her for her services, and then coldly told her to leave, saying that he would take care of everything. When Ester was only a speck on the horizon, he went back inside his shack, removed the pig's-foot amulet he had inherited from his mother, and hung it around his son's neck. He propped up his wife's body so that he could continue to gaze into her dead eyes, then lay down next to her, with the baby between them, suckling at Malena's breast.

Some hours later José and Betina arrived back from El Cobre. The blood that had coursed from Oscar's veins now formed a vast pool that spread across the floor of royal palm. The bodies of Oscar and Malena were cold, their skin purplish-yellow; a swarm of blowflies and cockroaches were already feeding on the putrefaction.

One by one the people of Pata de Puerco, heads bowed, dressed in their Sunday best, walked in a slow procession past the house where José and Betina kept vigil in the silence only death can create. Afterwards, the bodies were carried in a cortège to the ruins of the old sugar plantation where Oscar had been born and where, on José's instructions, they were to be laid to rest.

Oscar Kortico and Malena de Flores died on 11 April 1898, the day on which their son – my grandpa Benicio – was born and the very day the United States Congress, in the wake of the explosion of the USS *Maine*, drafted a joint resolution stipulating that, from that moment, Cuba was to be a free and independent nation.

Melecio is Different

And that is all there is to say about Oscar and his wife Malena. So much love and so much pain and all for nothing. These days, no one dies of passion as they did then; in 1995 people get married just for the extra rations of beer and cake, just to throw a party. And I've always said that life does not believe in love, life does not believe in anyone, and that when you least expect it, you find yourself six feet under. Basically, love is something that hurts like fuck and soon becomes a memory, and memories, as we all know, are fleeting and almost always fade. I've only ever been in love once, with a beautiful mixed-race girl called Elena. In fact, she turned out to be a complete bitch. But that's a different story, one that later, if I've a mind to, I'll tell you.

Let's move on. Malena died, Oscar died, the *Maine* was blown up. The Yanks – *Yumas* we call them – joined forces with Calixto García and his troops to kick the Spanish out of Cuba. Calixto blockaded Santiago and the whole surrounding region while the Americans blockaded the western part of the island, especially the port of Havana. A contingent of Americans landed in the east to meet up with

Calixto García and together they agreed to take the small villages around Santiago. First they took San Juan, then El Caney, and then one by one they took every town until they came to El Cobre.

Spain ordered its naval fleet to break the cordon and abandon the port of Santiago, but in less than an hour the American fleet destroyed what had once been the powerful *marina española*. Everyone knows what happened next: the Americans shat on their pact with Cuba and wiped their arse with the joint resolution, the Cuban national anthem was not heard again – instead sovereignty of the island was transferred to the United States and Cuba ceased to be a Spanish colony only to become an American dependency. Then came the Platt Amendment. Anyway, this is what was happening – or rather what was happening in the rest of the island since nothing ever happened in Pata de Puerco.

Demand for sugar increased. More schools and hospitals were built for the wealthy minority. Nobody took any notice of the families of a remote village that kept its existence a secret from the rest of the island. No one arrived to plant sugar cane, to lay claim to the land. No streetlights came. Since the wave of immigration that had brought the Santacruz and the Jabao families, no one left Pata de Puerco and no one arrived and quickly the families began to intermarry: cousins with cousins, uncles with nieces, everything was permitted except brothers marrying sisters which was considered a mortal sin. Over time, it became easy to identify the members of any family by their characteristic features.

When Malena and Oscar died, Betina wept continually for three weeks. She lost her appetite, she lost weight, and neglected her appearance more than ever. José too was much affected, but Betina was in such a state that he had to set aside his own grief in order to care for his wife, who was about to give birth. Several times, he tried to persuade her to take a bath, telling her he could not bear for such a beautiful woman to have a forest of hair under her arms, to smell unwashed, to look like a beggar. The Mandingas had always been a proud family. What would the neighbours say, those same people who had always thought of the Mandingas as the guiding force in Pata de Puerco? What sort of example was she setting for Gertrudis, who worshipped her mother? What had become of the radiant woman with whom José had fallen in love?

Betina talked to her husband about a conversation she had had with Juanita, a *santera* and wise-woman who lived alone and spent her time tending mysterious plants in her garden. Juanita thought of herself as a cynical pessimist, but she had a keen eye capable of diagnosing disease and in Pata de Puerco it was she who tended to the health of the community. More than once she had said that Cuba was a cesspool and she was simply waiting for her plants, her bird-of-paradise flowers and her orchids, to grow so she could die in peace. She invariably wore a housecoat that reeked of alcohol and wandered around with a cigar hanging from her lips.

'Juanita told me that all this time the truth has been staring us in the face, but we would not see it,' Betina told her husband. José said she should pay no mind to Juanita whose brain was addled by the strange herbs she smoked, but instead accept things as they are. Death sometimes comes unexpectedly, he said, and once again reminded her how his parents had perished of yellow fever, adding that his twin brothers had died of that terrible disease. 'You have to remember you are about to give birth.'

This seemed to calm her for a while, but the following day Betina's head was once again plagued with ghosts and suspicions; Malena had not been herself for a long time, she insisted, her sister had become more withdrawn as though afraid to speak, afraid to look her in the eye. Betina had known something was wrong, but every time she raised the subject her sister said she was imagining things.

'Malena died in childbirth, *mi amor*,' said José. 'You know how delicate she was.' But Betina, with the wilfulness of pregnant women, insisted no one died in childbirth just like that. To calm her, José went to fetch Ester so the midwife could tell her exactly what had happened.

'I warned Oscar. I told him that Malena needed to eat more red meat,' said Ester.

'No one could have eaten more red meat than Malena did,' said José.

'In that case, I don't know what happened,' said Ester.

Neither the midwife's statement nor her husband's comforting could sway Betina. José had no choice but to allow time to do its work. Months passed and slowly Betina began to forget, though every week she made the pilgrimage to El Cobre, bringing sprigs of fresh roses to the church in memory of her beloved Malena and Oscar.

Melecio was born precisely four weeks after Benicio. José and Betina watched over him in the weeks and months that followed, eagerly waiting for his first word. Gertrudis's first word had been 'mamá'; Benicio, to be contrary, had said 'papá'. José and Betina wondered what Melecio's first word would be; it was a matter they took very seriously.

One day, Melecio looked up into his parents' eyes and said, 'Architecture!'

'Architecture? What do you mean, architecture? What does he mean, Betina?'

Betina folded her arms but could not say anything. A little later, they both came to the conclusion that it could mean only one thing: Melecio was the strangest child in the world.

Physically, the two boys were similar in complexion and in size, and both had a thin mop of hair; but in character, they were utterly different. Melecio liked to sleep. He was a quiet child who never woke his parents in the middle of the night; nor was he a guzzler like Benicio – because unlike his half-brother, my grandfather was born with the appetite of a lion, suckling Betina's breasts until they were wizened dugs.

A goat had to be bought because Betina could not provide milk enough for both children. Juanita the *santera* advised them to take care, warning them that mixing milk could make a newborn ill. Neither boy fell ill; both grew up hale and hearty.

'They're not boys at all,' said Juanita six months after Melecio was born, 'they're a pair of mules,' adding that José and Betina had no need to worry about their health. Juanita, in her role as sorceress, had recently consulted her cauldron and for now the future seemed clear and cloudless. Smiling from ear to ear, she told José and Betina that Melecio had a brilliant future ahead of him but that they should keep a close watch on Benicio because, she said, he was different. 'Of course he's different, Juanita. We are Mandingas and Benicio is a Kortico,' said José. The *santera* explained that she had good reason to say what she had said and once again advised them to keep a close eye on the son of Oscar and Malena.

José and Betina's first strategy was to ask their neighbours to say nothing to my grandpa Benicio about his real parents until he was old enough to understand and not become confused. Until that time, Benicio was treated like another member of the Mandinga family, although his surname was Kortico.

Benicio slept in the bed next to Geru while Melecio had his own room. Grandpa used to say that at night he and his sister curled up in the old bed made of tree branches and told each other their deepest secrets. Geru wanted to be a *santera* like Juanita, but said that no one was allowed to know. My grandfather had no dreams, no aspirations. He was mischievous, as children are, but he was affectionate with his brother, his sister and his parents and in his first seven years did nothing that marked him out as different from other children in the village as Juanita had foretold. Melecio on the other hand had been born with an insatiable curiosity, eager to learn everything – something curious and strange in a child his age. He spent hours poring over Betina's old magazines or peering at the cans of tomatoes that came from the store, trying to read the words without knowing how. There was nothing unusual in a boy wanting to know how to build a cart, to fish and work the land; skills proper to a man. But Melecio also wanted to learn to cook, to sew and clean the house as his mother did, while Benicio and Geru preferred playing games with their little friends. By the tender age of seven, Melecio had learned to slaughter a pig and wring a chicken's neck.

One day Geru and Benicio headed off to the Chinese store on an errand for Betina, who was going to El Cobre to lay flowers at the church for Oscar and Malena. José was out working in the field.

When they got to the store, Geru and Benicio joined the queue. They asked for two pounds of rice, two pounds of black beans, three pounds of chickpeas and jars of cumin, oregano and salt. Li, the Chinese shopkeeper, poured the beans and pulses into the sacks they had brought and parcelled everything else up with paper. Benicio paid the three *reales* and brother and sister set off home. On their way to the store they had met a fat woman with huge breasts wearing a smock smeared with coal dust and a brightly coloured head-scarf. The woman looked about fifty, though from the expression in her wounded eyes she could have been much older. She stood staring at Benicio and her face slowly seemed to age. 'You are a sad child, Benicio,' Ester told my grandfather with a thin-lipped smile. Then she quickly hurried away along a narrow winding path that led into the mountains, vanishing into the undergrowth until she became just one more leaf in a sea of plants.

'Who is that woman?' Benicio asked. Whoever she was, Gertrudis said, she wasn't right in the head; the whole area was full of lunatics. Her answer did little to convince her brother. Grandpa set his sacks on the ground and went back to the store to ask Li. 'I think she lives in Pata de Puerco,' Li said. 'But run on home now. You are too young to be sticking your noses in other people's lives.'

As they headed home, Grandpa Benicio could not get Ester's face out of his mind and her words echoed inside his head. When they came within ten metres of their house, both children smelled something strange. Surely Betina could have arrived back before them, unless someone had given her a ride in their cart. Pushing open the door, they found Melecio in the living room, hands stuffed in the pockets of his shorts, smiling a mischievous dazzling smile, as though he had just done something naughty.

'Is Mamá home already, Melecio?' said Gertrudis, setting her bags down on the wooden table. 'She must have been inspired today because it smells even more delicious than usual.'

'Mamá's not here. But it does smell delicious, doesn't it?'

'What are you talking about?'

Geru and Benicio ran to the kitchen where they found rice and a chicken Melecio had cooked, and a lettuce and tomato salad. There was a vast quantity of food. Melecio tried to explain that he had taught himself to cook but Geru and Benicio said he must have gone mad, that cooking was woman's work and José would beat him to within an inch of his life.

They were right. Five minutes later José arrived and, when he found the mountains of food, gave Melecio such a beating his screams could be heard as far as Santiago. 'Who told you to cook for the whole village, huh? You know very well that chicken was to commemorate Malena and Oscar's anniversary. I swear I'll kill you.' José went on beating Melecio, shaking him like a rag doll. Benicio tried to intervene, grabbing his father by his belt.

'Get out of here, Oscar,' roared José and gave him a clout.

'I'm not Oscar, I'm Benicio and she's Gertrudis.'

'You're right, you are Benicio and she's Geru and you . . . you're Melecio, the little bastard who just cooked a whole month's worth of food. Out of my sight, the three of you, and Melecio, I don't want you setting foot in the kitchen again, do you hear? Now get out!'

When Betina got home, she scolded Melecio some more. She didn't know how she was going to feed her family the following week since they did not have a peso and the beans and pulses Benicio and Geru had just bought would barely last three days. What Melecio had cooked was bound to be inedible, but they would have to make do, or sell it to a neighbour as pig fodder.

Betina and José were the first to taste the food. As the fragrant flavours of Melecio's cooking melted in their mouths, they were overwhelmed by an indescribable feeling. José got up from the table, rushed to find Melecio, fell to his knees and said, 'Forgive me, *hijo* . . . I promise I'll never beat you again. You can cook all the chickens you want.'

José wept as Betina rained down blows on him, calling him an ill-bred lout for doing such a thing to his own son and swearing that the next time she caught him beating Melecio she would cut his balls off. Benicio sat, his spoon hovering before his mouth, unable to believe what he was seeing. Melecio himself did not understand what was happening. He sat in silence trying to work out which of the spices he had used could have produced such an effect.

Too late Grandpa Benicio screamed, 'Noooo!', but Gertrudis had already put a spoonful in her mouth.

'From now on I'm not going to share a bed with you,' his

sister immediately announced and ran from Benicio's side to sit next to the little chef. 'I'll only sleep next to my brother Melecio.'

Benicio and Melecio were the only ones who did not eat. They decided that they would never speak about what had happened and that Melecio would never cook again. They made this vow in silence, locking their lips with invisible keys they tossed over their shoulders towards the mountain. The following day when they woke up, José, Betina and Geru remembered nothing. Geru woke up next to Melecio and ran to ask Benicio why she had not slept next to him as usual. Benicio suggested that perhaps the food had disagreed with her, but privately vowed that this could not happen again.

The following day was *El día del Nacimiento* – the Festival of Birth – something celebrated every Sunday in the village. Fathers would set out stools and earthenware bowls filled with food beneath the flame tree, garlanded with flowers, a table would be set with a tablecloth and the place turned into a rustic tavern with drums, cans, dogs and people who came along with the sole intent of forgetting their constant gloom and celebrating their miserable lives. José and Betina told their neighbours about the bad luck they had been having, how two nights earlier a wild animal crept in and devoured their only chicken, leaving bones and feathers strewn all around.

'We don't have anything to bring. We're sorry,' said José, ashamed. Abel Santacruz said it did not matter, that in Pata de Puerco the Mandingas were almost a royal family, and Evaristo the kite-maker immediately sat them next to Silvio and Rachel Aquelarre from where they had a perfect view of the faces of everyone in the village, with the exception of El Mozambique and Ester the midwife who never joined in these feasts.

'Today's game involves telling tales. Old and young alike are welcome to take part. The person to tell the funniest story will be the winner,' said Evaristo, sitting in the crook of the red flame tree where everyone could see him.

'What kind of stories?' asked Pablo el Jabao.

'Any kind of tale at all,' Evaristo replied, 'anything that will make people laugh.'

'In that case,' said Epifanio Vilo, 'I'll start.' He stood up on his stool and began. 'A tomato was walking with a lettuce along the Callejón de la Rosa. "Hurry up, tomato, there's a cart coming," said the lettuce. But the tomato, being stubborn, refused to listen and the cart rolled right over him. "Tomato!" yelled the lettuce, but it was too late. As the cart trundled off into the distance, the lettuce looked at the red splodge on the road, walked over to his friend and said, "I told you *ketchup*!"'

There was general hilarity. People slapped their thighs and doubled over with uncontrollable laughter.

'That's nothing,' said Justino the coal merchant, and clambering on to his stool he began: 'A little black boy wanted to know what happens to Negro children when they die. "They go to heaven, where God gives them a pair of wings and they become little black angels," his father told him. The little boy thought for a minute and then asked his father curiously, "And what happens to white children, Papá?" "Exactly the same," his father replied. "They go to heaven, God gives them a pair of wings and they become barn owls."'

This time the laughter became hysterical. Betina clapped her hand over her mouth. José laughed until he cried. Some people collapsed on the ground and were writhing with glee. 'That's a good one, Justino.' Evaristo raised a hand to calm the bedlam. 'Let's see if anyone can beat it. Who else has got a tale to tell?'

'I do,' said Juan Carlos el Jabao, the eldest of Pablo and Niurka's children. He was a tall lad with hair as red as fire. 'A man went to the doctor complaining that his son had died from a strange fever that made his face turn yellow. The doctor, who was a drunk, looked at him and said, "There's no need to be sad, señor, at least he died with a beautiful colour."'

Juan Carlos's joke did not elicit the same reaction. José did not laugh at all. He felt his muscles tense and from that moment on he bore Juan Carlos a grudge. The next person to speak was Ignacio el Jabao, the brother of Juan Carlos, and the rudest, most foul-mouthed boy in the village.

'A little boy was sitting under a tree crying and a drunk stopped and asked him what was wrong. The boy said his papá had fallen out of the avocado tree, landed on his dick and now he was in heaven. The drunk looked at the boy, then the avocado tree, then looked up to heaven and said, "Fuck! Your papá must have had a dick like a spring."'

Niurka el Jabao leaped from her seat, grabbed Ignacio by the ear and dragged him off, slapping and kicking him. Pablo apologised, explaining that the boy was the spawn of the devil. He asked Juan Carlos to look after the rest of the Jabao brood and make sure they behaved themselves then followed his wife home, cursing his son Ignacio. 'Boys will be boys,' said Evaristo. 'Justino the coalman is still in first place. Would anyone else like to beat him?'

Now it was Melecio who spoke up.

'I'd like to tell a story,' he said, getting to his feet. 'What story, Melecio?' said Betina. 'You're a little young to be telling stories.' She gestured at him to sit down again. The kite-maker said it did not matter, that the game was for all ages. 'It's true, Betina,' said José. 'Let the boy tell his joke. Maybe he inherited my sense of humour.' Betina rolled her eyes to heaven. 'Let him, señora . . .' everyone chorused, 'let the boy tell his joke.'

Betina had no choice but to agree. Melecio clambered on to his stool, stuffed his hands in the pockets of his shorts and in a thin, falsetto voice began:

> *The squalid reality is the oblivion which enfolds our village*
> *The squalid reality is that no one cares about the squalid reality*
> *The squalid reality is hunger, it is the everyday suffering of the*
> *   outcast, the true existence of the negro*
> *The squalid reality is Pata de Puerco, the starvation ingrained in*
> *   the skin of its people, the endless begging*
> *The endless waiting, the pain of Pata de Puerco: the squalid reality*

There was a ghastly silence. No one knew what was happening and though many did not understand Melecio's words it was clear that his story had delved into their souls. No one laughed. On the contrary, many of those present began to sob and went on sobbing long after Melecio's little mouth was closed.

'Where did you learn that? Who taught you that? Tell me!' Betina demanded, shocked.

'No one, Mami. I just thought it up right now. Why is no one laughing?'

'It's the saddest thing I've ever heard,' said Abel Santacruz, 'and it's true. We can't go on like this. We have to improve our lives.'

Everyone agreed; everyone except for Evaristo who carried on insisting that this was a celebration and that they should not allow their joy to die. But no one had the heart to go on celebrating. Their joy, like a rickety shack dragged along by a storm, had been knocked out of true.

José thanked the kite-maker and all those present, saying that the food and everything had been wonderful but that it was time to go home.

'Don't go now, *caballero* . . .' Evaristo protested. 'Have you heard the one about the deadly avocado?' But José, Betina, Gertrudis and Benicio had already set off, carrying on their shoulders little Melecio as though he were some treasure that had suddenly been revealed to them. The wind blew gently, whipping away the dry dust only to bring more, suffused with the smell of horseshit common to country paths. And so night began to draw in, and Pata de Puerco sank into utter silence.

A Trip to El Cobre

One day, José borrowed the old mare belonging to Evaristo the kite-maker to take his children to El Cobre. Evaristo begged him to bring the mare back with all four legs and José assured him that he would not allow God Himself to touch the old nag's tail. He yoked the beast up to the cart and they set off while the dawn sky was still dark and the dew still settling.

It was a long journey. Geru's little cotton skirt embroidered with flowers grew damp with dew, as did Benicio's shirt and his patched shorts. Benicio tried to touch Melecio's shorts to see whether they too were wet, but his brother quickly covered himself with his hands.

They stared at the cows, at the mud-caked farmers tilling the earth, at the steep mountains of the Sierra Maestra which looked like giants standing guard over the valley. Butterflies and dragonflies were beginning to flutter across the lush green plain. It was a glorious day and, for the first time in a long while, José and Betina seemed happy.

'Hey, Benicio, you see those canebrakes over there on the left? That's where we used to work, me and your fa—' Betina gave José a clip round the ear. 'You and who?' my grand-father asked. 'Me and a good friend.' It was a terrible job, José added, telling his children that when they grew up they should plant crops or raise animals, because working on a sugar-cane plantation was backbreaking and badly paid. They would soon be adults and it was time for them to think about what they were going to do with their lives. At this point, Melecio said he wanted to be a cook. Grandfather protested that the kitchen wasn't his and pinched his arm.

An hour later, the family found themselves in the little square of a small town with stately detached houses, most of them built from stone. In earlier times, El Cobre was known as '*el barrio negro*' – the black neighbourhood. The area had been populated by 'the king's slaves', some of the few slaves in Cuba to receive an education. Most of them worked in the copper mines, and they were educated because the work required a greater level of knowledge.

The Americans had taken control of most of the strategic sec-tors of the Cuban economy. In addition to sugar production, they held sway over the mines, public services, banks and much of the land; they also owned the Cuban Electric Company and the Cuban Telephone Company, and much of the power industry including coal, oil and alcohol. The first thing José, Betina and the children noticed when they arrived was the number of white men, all of whom spoke a strange language.

'Look, Mamá, milk men,' shouted Melecio.

'They're not made of milk,' said Benicio. 'They're white because they come from a faraway place where the sun doesn't shine.'

Geru pointed out that the sun shone everywhere, so that

could not be the reason they were white. In the end, they asked Betina who said, 'Where do white men come from? Juanita says they come from Alaska.'

'Alaska! What's Alaska?'

Betina explained that, according to Juanita, Alaska was a place where ice came from, where everything was white and it was always very cold.

'Well then, that's where these men must come from,' said José, 'because they're the coldest people I've ever met.'

'So they come from Alaska,' Melecio concluded and Betina nodded slightly.

None of the children had ever seen anywhere like this: concrete houses, cobbled streets; here was a town with no grass, no trees, no animals. They studied everything with great curiosity. José tried to recognise some of the places he had haunted years earlier before Oscar rescued him and signed him up to the war, but all of the old taverns were gone now, as were the markets and the grocery stores. The town was brand new with signs everywhere in English. 'It's time to go,' said José and turned the mare towards the outskirts of the town where the old church stood.

When they reached the cathedral, José tethered the horse to a tree fifty metres from the church courtyard. Benicio, Geru and Melecio's eyes grew wide and their mouths gaped to see such a vast building with its towers and its belfry. Five black carriages drawn by white horses drove past and stopped at the entrance to the church. They watched as impeccably elegant ladies and gentlemen alighted and made their way into this palatial building.

The Negro coachmen, wearing frockcoats and derby hats, parked off to one side and waited for their masters. Ragged mendicants, all of them black, some missing parts of their bodies, begged for alms. Soldiers chased them off with kicks and insults. There were many of them. Men with no feet, no hands, children no older than Melecio, Benicio and Gertrudis. These people were forbidden from entering the church.

Ignoring the entrance, the Mandinga family walked to the balustrade surrounding the basilica. From here, they could see the grounds of the cathedral which seemed to include the whole valley. In the distance, they could make out huts and shacks just like their own and next to them a vast gaudy tract of land ringed by lush jungle. This tract, José explained, was the municipal rubbish tip. In the midst of this pestilential riot of colour, scurrying frantically up and down, were tiny coffee-coloured specks. 'It seems incredible,' said José, 'but Oscar was right. Thirty years of war and all for nothing. Everything is still the same.'

They stood looking at the men scavenging through the garbage and Betina put an arm around José's shoulders. He flinched and then sighed, then suddenly he began to laugh. The last time he had laughed like this was when he smashed the kitchen table at home, hurling it against the door. But Melecio did not care. Pointing to the largest, most elegant carriage, he said, 'I know what I want to be when I grow up. I want to be like that man.' They all turned to look in the direction he was pointing.

'A coachman?' said José. 'Over my dead body.'

'No, Papá, not a coachman. I want to be like the other man, the milky man getting out of the carriage.'

Melecio was referring to the white man in a black suit descending the steps of the most opulent of the carriages. He was a thin man with an aristocratic face. People crowded round to welcome him and as he passed men and women greeted him with the same admiration they might a hero. José bent down so he could look his children in the eye.

'Listen carefully to what I'm about to say. That man is not one of our kind. Our kind are over there foraging in the garbage dump. These elegant people, with their horses and whatnot, these are the people who started the wars, the ones who cut the arms and legs off those children, the ones who invented black coachmen and slaves . . . don't you understand? He is our enemy and should be feared. If one of them should come up to you some day, the best thing you can do is run away, do you hear me? Run anywhere, run as far from them as possible, to somewhere where there are only people like us or plants or animals. Do you understand?'

The three children nodded though none of them had understood a word José had said. One of the Negro coachmen from the imposing carriages came over to them. He was dressed in a red jacket with a long tail at the back, belted at the waist. He doffed his large black hat and the sun glittered on his bald pate, emphasising the broad scar across one cheek.

'Excuse me, I couldn't help hearing you laughing and I thought to myself "at least there are still people who can laugh". You know, with all the terrible things you see these days, it's rare to meet someone cheerful. Today is your lady's birthday, is it not?'

'No,' José replied.

'One of your children then, surely?'

'No, I only laugh like that when I'm angry.'

José turned away from the man and back to his children. Betina stood staring at the coachman. Not prepared to give up, the coachman exclaimed that he had seen so many strange things in his life he had almost begun to think he had seen it all. Life was wise, he said, and constantly managed to surprise him and in the end many end up a fool. José turned back to the coachman, his face now was calm.

'Tell me, señor . . .'

'Aureliano. Aureliano Carabalí, at your service.'

The coachman bowed and smiled, showing a yawning gap where four of his teeth were missing.

'Tell me this, Señor Aureliano, slavery has been abolished, has it not?'

The man nodded. José said that if this was true, how could Aureliano bring himself to serve a white man after all the terrible things they had done?

'The terrible things they did? I don't understand, señor . . .'

'José. José Mandinga.'

'Could you explain to me exactly what you mean, *amigo* José?'

José said there was no need, because the coachman knew very well what he was referring to. White men had spent their lives exploiting Negroes. They were to blame for the poverty, the misery in which the black man lived. For thirty years war had been waged with the sweat of the Negroes of this country, with slaves and those who were already freemen; that it had been the Negroes who had truly triumphed with their machetes. But even now, José went on, there

68

were no white coachmen and Negroes were still in the same shit they had always been in while white men enjoyed every luxury. Of course there were exceptions, men everyone knew about, José Martí, Máximo Gómez, but in general, José concluded, that was how things were.

The coachman listened intently, all the while baring his broken teeth. 'I can tell you are a man of passion and that you speak from the heart; this is why I am going to give you my honest opinion on the subject. I never talk about such things with anyone, certainly not with someone I have just met, but I feel I can trust you.'

The coachman told José his story. He had lived in slave quarters on a sugar plantation near Santa Clara, one of the most vile, where the food was poorer than the slaves themselves. They were never allowed to stop to rest, not even for a moment, because the overseer was always there with his whip ready to beat them. Aureliano hated the whip, but many times he bridled because he was stubborn. He was put in the stocks and was whipped until his back was lined and furrowed like a rice field. On other occasions he was shut up for weeks in one of the tiny recesses set into the walls, and when he was finally let out the pain in his back from being forced to squat for so long, unable to stretch his arms or his legs, was unbearable. And yet there came a time when he was to suffer a punishment far worse than whipping.

'A punishment worse than whipping? What can be worse?' asked José.

'To be betrayed by those closest to you,' said Aureliano.

These were the lashes that truly hurt, the coachman said,

and he had endured them all his life. His sisters, his mother, everyone had betrayed him. When not robbing him, they were playing some other dirty trick. A boyhood friend had slashed his face. Another raped his wife. The worst thing of all was that they never justified their actions but went on living cheek by jowl with him, their consciences clear, as though nothing had happened. This was why when slavery was finally abolished he went far away, where no one would ever find him. This was how he had come here. He was lucky to find the man who engaged him as a coachman, who taught him to read and write, a white man, the most generous man he had ever known.

'As you can see, *amigo* José, my troubles have always been with black men, for whether you believe it or not, in my darkest hours when I found myself with nothing, with no one, it was always a white man who offered me his hand.'

'What about slavery?' asked José indignantly.

The coachman replied that slavery was as old as mankind itself; that it had also existed in Africa, and not just slavery but human sacrifices and even cannibalism.

'Slavery existed long ago, it is with us today, it will always be with us.' These were not his words, the words of an ignorant man, but what was written in books and therefore the best thing to do was believe the great thinkers who asserted that in reality there are no colours: no black, no white, no red, no yellow. That colours exist only in the eyes and are interpreted by the brain.

'That is rank hypocrisy,' said José. Many white people affirmed such things, he went on, claimed all men were equal, but not one of them would sit down and break bread with a Negro. 'If I tell you that you are as worthy as I, but brush you aside and live as far from you as possible, am I not a hypocrite? White men are like palm trees; they never bend their trunks to offer you a palm fruit. Not like mango trees that bow down to the ground so you can gather their fruits. White men live their lives looking down from on high and we are the worms wriggling in the mud waiting for some crumb of earth to feed on. They do not share with us, they do not mix with us, they are like damned palm trees, Aureliano. I don't know about you, but me and my friend Oscar — may he rest in peace — did not fight so that we could go on living in slave quarters or garbage tips. Besides . . .'

At that moment, José's dark eyes became two huge, luminous spheres.

'Melecio! Where's Melecio?' Melecio had disappeared. They frantically rushed around, looking everywhere for him. 'Betina, where the devil can that blessed boy be?'

They divided up into groups. Betina and Benicio headed towards the valley while José and Geru ran back to where they had left the cart. The coachman, seeing the group had dispersed, walked slowly back to his carriage.

The earth had opened and swallowed up Melecio. No one had seen him, no one had spoken to him, no child had played with him. They wandered far beyond the railing to where the valley began, but there was no sign of him. Back at the church, a voice hailed Betina and Benicio as they were walking towards the cart: 'Would you perchance be looking for this little man?' Betina turned and found herself face to face with the white gentleman wearing a black suit and tie and a bowler hat, the very man Melecio had pointed out only minutes ago. His noble, almost aristocratic expression radiated authority.

'Excuse me, señor. Melecio, where did you get to? I told you not to leave my side. What were you doing bothering this gentleman?'

'Not at all, señora. Your son was not bothering me. In fact, he has clearly had a fine education,' said the gentleman, doffing his hat.

Betina looked warily at the man. José and Geru rushed up a moment later, pouring with sweat. 'There he is. Melecio, what did I tell you . . .' roared José but the other man broke in again. Although he did not know them, he said, from his brief conversation with this young gentleman, Melecio, he was convinced they were people of learning, something rare in these parts. He talked about an elderly Englishman who was convinced that the maxim 'appearances are deceptive' was simply a crude aphorism. '"Appearances tell us everything, Emilio," the Englishman used to say, "they are a true reflection of what is within us. A man who looks like a collier has a heart of coal. That is the truth of the matter, everything else is folk tales." I wonder what he would say if he were to meet Melecio here.'

José and Betina stared at the man, trying to discern the hidden intentions in his gentle, easy-going face. His manners were too seemly to be genuine. No white man had ever been polite to José and Betina, much less a rich white man.

'I'm grateful to you for finding our Melecio. Now we have to go and find our cart,' said José.

'I understand. And believe me, the pleasure was all mine,' said the man and bowed graciously. 'But before you go, I wonder if you might satisfy my curiosity and tell me who educated you in the poetic arts?'

'We cannot read or write, señor. Now, by your leave . . .'

'What do you mean you cannot read or write? That's impossible. Are you telling me that your son made up the splendid poem he just recited to me?'

'Poem? What poem?'

Melecio took a few steps back so that everyone could see him, and with his head turned heavenwards, waving his hands, he recited:

> Sky, who takes away the bitterness
> Of my imprisoning fears,
> The threshold to my refuge
> My hopes, my yearnings.
> I fall insensate on my bed
> And yielding to despair I dream
> A wintertime of emptiness
> A lifetime of dread.
> Tell me, eternal sky, who I am
> Where did I come from, where am I going?
> Your breath alone my consolation,
> Your voice alone my voice.

'Who taught you that, Melecio?' asked José.

'Answer your father, Melecio, where did you learn to talk like that?' said Betina.

Melecio looked up into the faces all around him, shrugged his shoulders, incapable of explaining whence this curious ability had come.

'Well, well, he has recited a different poem,' said the white gentleman, applauding and patting Melecio on the head. 'This boy really is a phenomenon.' He apologised for not having introduced himself. His name was Emilio Bacardí, he owned a modest rum distillery on the outskirts of Santiago which had afforded him sufficient money to build a successful business. He went on to say that he did not know what José and Betina's plans were for Melecio, but that whatever they were he would like to help.

'We do not need your help, thank you,' said José brusquely.

'I can understand why you might not accept. I know that past deeds linger on, that spilled blood is still fresh, but perhaps you might do for me as I did for your son, by which I mean do not assume a collier has a heart of coal. I know that it is difficult to believe, but perhaps you might try to see beyond the white man who stands before you and not assume that I wish to exploit you, though well you might after so many centuries of . . . Well, as my father used to say: opportunities are bald and you have to grab them by the hair. Believe me, I am thinking only of your son's talent, but I realise you have many other things to think about.'

'The only thing we need to think about right now is finding our cart and heading back to Pata de Puerco,' said José abruptly. 'So if you'll excuse us . . . Let's go.' Betina hesitantly turned towards the man. José gave her a gentle shove. The man continued on his way and once again people swarmed around, eager to greet him. The coachman with the scar across his face, who had been talking to José only moments earlier, courteously opened the carriage door.

74

'Melecio, if I catch you talking to a white man again, I'll split your skull,' said José.

'Opportunities are bald, Papá, and you have to grab them by the hair.' Melecio stared at the cloud of dust left by the carriage as it passed.

When they came to the place where they had tethered the cart, they found the mare lying dead on the ground, her tongue sticking out, her body twisted like a hank of barbed wire. One of her legs had been hacked off.

'What do you mean, someone killed the mare?' Evaristo clapped his head in his hands. José said he was sorry. Evaristo worriedly asked how José planned to pay for the beast, since it was the only horse he had. 'Before the month is out I will buy you a new mare,' said the Mandinga. Someone had done the same thing to Oscar, José went on, and one day he would get his hands on the son of a bitch and string him up by his balls from the nearest pine tree. The strangest thing was that he had had a premonition. From the moment they arrived in El Cobre and seen the soldiers bustling about, the Negroes begging and the rich white people glaring at them scornfully, José had sensed it was not a good day to make this trip. And to make matters worse, one of the rich bastards had had the nerve to pester them, offering to help Melecio. 'Can you imagine, Evaristo? A white man offering to help us! There he was wasting my time while some *bandido* was hacking off the leg of your mare. If it hadn't been for this Emilio Bacardón, or Bacardín . . .'

'Emilio Bacardí?' said Evaristo.

'That's the man. If it hadn't been for him, right now you would have your mare here exactly as you lent her to me.'

'Wait a minute. You're telling me you talked to Emilio Bacardí, the mayor of Santiago?'

'*Chico*, I don't know if he was a mayor or a priest. Besides, they all speak some strange language round those parts, it's like a different country. But the fact is this Bacardí held me up talking about how Melecio had a gift for poetry and how he wanted to help. The things you have to listen to. Thirty years we fought these people and now they want to *help* us!'

'What are you talking about, José? Don't you know that most of the rifles we had during the war of independence were bought with this man's money? Don't you realise that Bacardí's own son fought shoulder to shoulder with Maceo? You must have met him. He stood right there right next to you wielding his machete.'

'Only two or three white men fought alongside Maceo. And the only one who proved himself a good soldier, not afraid of bullets and bayonets, was a scrawny lad with a moustache they called Emilito.'

'That's him. Emilito was the son of Emilio Bacardí.'

José walked slowly back to the fence that surrounded his neighbour's shack. He stared out at the infinite expanse of green that looked like an undulating emerald mantle. In the distance, he could make out pine trees, poplars and the tangle of vines that choked the pathway leading into the Accursed Forest which, in the gathering shadows of dusk, looked like tall windmills.

'Give me a month and I'll pay you for the mare, Evaristo,' he said. Then he walked back to his house, head bowed, deep in his own thoughts.

Ignacio's Idea

To continue. Someone had cut off the leg of Evaristo's mare. There was something else José needed to do, something more pressing, and that was to visit the wise-woman Juanita. Her shack was little more than a hovel, set apart from all the others, which reeked of damp, dried plants, alcohol, cumin and tobacco. A narrow room crammed with cauldrons filled with husks, mysterious roots and snails of every colour, a single room with a privy in the back yard and a fire on which she cooked.

The *santera* opened the door and, for the first time, José and Betina saw her without her housecoat. Her hair was a hank of dry, dishevelled straw that smelled of rancid oil. They went inside, sat on a pair of stools next to a *santería* altar and told Juanita about their worries and their doubts.

'So you think I was mistaken . . . ?' said Juanita. José and Betina protested that, though they did not doubt Juanita's gifts, they were confident Benicio was completely normal. He was sometimes naughty, as any child might be, he played war games and climbed trees. But there was nothing unusual about that. It was Melecio who was different. And this they found worrying. They reminded her about the poem he had recited beneath the red flame tree, told her what had happened in El Cobre. When they had asked the poor child, he himself did not know where he had found these words he had never heard before in his life.

'Maybe the day you told us about the boys' futures you'd smoked too much and made a mistake,' said José, smiling. Juanita looked at them gravely. Her eyes narrowed like those of a Chinaman. She was not mistaken, she said; it was true that she liked alcohol and tobacco and the herbs José had mentioned, but he could rest assured that in matters of magic she was never mistaken.

'Why then did you not tell us what was going to happen to Malena and Oscar?' asked José.

'Because it is impossible to change a person's destiny and, alas, there was nothing that could be done,' said Juanita, then served them some coffee in two polished cans.

They sat there for a little while, talking about Gertrudis, who had grown up to be a sensible girl who did not have to be asked twice to wash clothes in the river or clean the house; they talked about how much they still missed Malena and Oscar. They speculated about the future of Pata de Puerco, about whether it would one day be a town with cobbled streets like El Cobre and other cities around the country. Then Juanita walked them to the door and they made to leave.

'Not you, José. I'd like you to stay a little longer. There's something I want you to see.'

Betina protested, asking why she could not stay too, and Juanita explained that what she had to say concerned José alone, that no one else could be present. Grumbling, Betina headed down the dirt path to their house.

'Sit over there,' said Juanita, gesturing to a stool next to the altar. The seat, carved out of wood, was sculpted in the form of an Indian, almost life-size, wearing a headdress of eagle's feathers, surrounded by cauldrons filled with river stones, metal artefacts, pieces of dried coconut rind, a pair of maracas and a dozen candles. The *santera* lit the candles, grabbed a flask of rum and drank straight from the neck then spat at the figure of the Indian. She picked up the five dried coconut rinds and with a flick of her wrist tossed them on the ground.

'What is already known should not be asked,' she said aloud.

'What is already known should not be asked?' repeated José.

'Five coconuts face up, not one face down. This confirms that I was right. Every time I have asked about your future I have received the same answer: five coconuts face up. It means there will be war.'

'Another war? But what has that got to do with my future? Don't tell me I am to be drafted to fight in another war.'

'No. This war will be fought in your house, and it involves Benicio.'

Once again José insisted that Grandfather was a good boy and said he believed Juanita's saints had a grudge against poor Benicio. Juanita threw the coconuts again, and once again they fell face up.

It was dark by the time José got home, pale and silent as though he were in another dimension.

'What happened? Why the long sad face?' asked Betina.

José looked at her as though for a moment he did not recognise this woman who had opened the door to him. His expression changed suddenly. He hugged Betina and said that he was hungry. He asked after the children. Betina served him a plate of yams and rice and then they went to bed.

In the days that followed, José thought about their visit to El Cobre, about the American soldiers who now occupied the zone, about Emilio Bacardí and his coachman. He thought about how times had changed, and more than ever he realised that time did not exist in Pata de Puerco, neither the hours, the days, nor the months. Those who lived here were invisible, impervious to the march of progress. He felt sad to realise that in the grand scheme of things, the village was not even a dot on the map, and that the lives of the villagers did not even make up one melancholy moment in the immensity of life.

During those days, he talked a lot to Betina, who told him that she agreed with the white man who had offered to help Melecio. It was clearer than water that nature had bestowed their son with a gift, she said, a gift that needed to be nurtured, and that they could not help since their knowledge was limited to working in the fields. 'Pata de Puerco is not right for Melecio, José. We have to get him out of here.' José repeated his old arguments about how white men were to be feared. Bacardí, he said, probably wanted Melecio so he could turn him into a coachman. But above all, José spent his time brooding about Grandpa Benicio. The more he watched him, the more certain he was that Juanita's *orishas* were mistaken.

On Sunday, as usual, the village celebrated the Festival of Birth. Evaristo gave every boy a kite and every girl a doll he himself had carved from dried coconut. This time, José and Betina brought sweet cassava, potatoes and lettuces they had picked from their vegetable garden. Miriam, the wife of Justino the coal merchant, cooked the stew. To it she added bacon from the Santacruzes, yams from the Jabaos and the chicken brought by the Aquelarres. Juanita the sorceress and Epifanio Vilo agreed to cook the rice, and the whole village had enough to eat. The boys flew their kites while the girls drove their coconut dolls around in toy carriages that were little more than broken branches snapped from the trees by the wind.

When the food was ready, José gathered all the villagers beneath the flame tree. 'Pata de Puerco cannot carry on like this. If the country is not prepared to look after us, we will have to do it ourselves,' he began. He suggested that together they make a collection in order to send someone from Pata de Puerco to school in El Cobre where they could learn to read and write so that they could pass on this knowledge to the rest of the villagers. While studying, the chosen candidate would stay with grandparents of the Carera family who had recently arrived from El Cobre.

'It is a little late for education,' said Epifanio Vilo.

'For us, perhaps, but not for our children,' said José. 'We have to think of them.'

There was a great debate. The Jabaos said they agreed with the idea and suggested sending their son Juan Carlos, who had shown a remarkable intelligence and refined manners. Juanita the wise-woman suggested they send her, since given her skills in the dark arts, she could learn to read and write in only a week. Her Angolan orchids had still not blossomed, the wise-woman added, which clearly meant that the hour had not yet come for her to die, that being so her dearest wish was to contribute to the prosperity of the village.

'My daughter Anastasia is intelligent too and she is the best laundress in Pata de Puerco,' said Silvio Aquelarre. 'I think she should be the one to go.'

In the end, all the villagers wanted a member of their family to be the one to escape this desolate life of trees and animals for civilisation. José explained that they did not have to decide immediately and suggested that they postpone the decision for three weeks while they considered how best to choose. Everyone agreed that on the third Sunday they would settle the matter of who was to be the future village schoolteacher.

While the meeting was winding up, Gertrudis, Grandpa Benicio and Melecio had been playing with their kites and coconut doll, but after a while they had grown bored and started competing to see which of them could make the loudest, smelliest fart.

'Look who's coming this way,' said Gertrudis. Melecio and Benicio ran over to Ignacio el Jabao, who suggested they go and taunt El Mozambique: throw stones at his shack to make him come out.

'What's the matter?' he taunted. 'Are you scared? I always knew you were just a bunch of fucking pussies.'

Obviously Ignacio wouldn't have used those words back then. He probably said something like: 'You're just a bunch of lily-livered chicken arses, little babies scared of El Mozambique.'

Melecio insisted that they were not scared, but the fact was that El Mozambique had seven dogs as big as lions. Nonetheless, all three turned on their heels and began walking towards the dreaded house. Ignacio brought up the rear.

'What has El Mozambique ever done to you that you want to pick on him?' asked Geru.

'He's never done anything to me, but he's eaten a lot of people,' said Ignacio.

'What if he eats you?' said Grandpa Benicio. Ignacio el Jabao stopped in his tracks.

'You see? I was right. You're all shitting yourselves, especially you, Benicio. A lot of good it did you having a famous father! My mamá says your papá Oscar was a real brave man who wasn't scared of nothing or no one. And my papá says that one time working in the cane fields he got mad at El Mozambique and nearly cut his balls off. José and your papá were known as the Duo of Death because they killed more Spaniards fighting with Maceo during the war than anyone else. And just look how his son turned out – a gutless wimp with no balls.'

'I don't know who this Oscar is,' said my grandfather. 'My papá's name is José Mandinga.'

'That's not what my mamá says. Don't make no difference anyhow, you're still a gutless wimp with no balls.'

Benicio hurled himself at Ignacio. Gertrudis and Melecio waded in to separate the two.

'You are too a wimp. If you're not, then prove it. Go and throw a stone at El Mozambique's shack,' said Ignacio el

Jabao. Benicio felt his ears getting warm, and his judgement becoming clouded.

'Don't do it, Benicio, don't do it,' said Geru and Melecio, but Benicio ignored them and walked down the Callejón de la Rosa as far as the path leading up to El Mozambique's place.

No one ever saw El Mozambique. Much was talked about him, but no one knew anything about his past, where he was from or when he had come to the village. Some people claimed that he had always lived here in this tumbledown shack, set apart from the others on the outskirts of the village; they said he had arrived shortly after the Mandingas and the Korticos. But no one dared walk past his house or along the pathway. He was a violent man; Epifanio Vilo was the first to suffer his wrath when he organised a meeting one day to try to have El Mozambique thrown out of the village. This happened not long after Oscar and Malena died. José told Epifanio to leave El Mozambique in peace; we all have our faults, he said. But Epifanio was a mule-headed individual and he had made up his mind. So they called the meeting and after an hour it was unanimously decided El Mozambique should move far from Pata de Puerco and leave the villagers to live in peace.

'The very mention of your name terrifies people, Mozambique. They can't sleep for thinking about your dogs and the hides hanging in your back yard that look like the skins of murdered children pickled in alcohol. You're not wanted here, so get out,' Epifanio announced, acting as spokesman for the crowd of twenty neighbours gathered outside the despised creature's house.

El Mozambique, a giant of a man, tall and hulking as a palm tree, silenced his dogs with a wave of his hand, then he picked up Epifanio's thin frame and tossed him on to the ground in front of everyone – including Epifanio's children – as though he were nothing but a piece of wood.

'I would not give you all the satisfaction. You'll just have to kill me or wait for me to die, and I warn you: the next person to walk up my path, I'll rip him apart – I'm always in need of fresh meat for the dogs.'

Epifanio Vilo and the other villagers took to their heels and vanished. From that day forward, no one ever walked down El Mozambique's path or exchanged a word with him. They left him to himself, living with his dogs as though he were a stranger. Only Ester regularly visited, bringing provisions from the grocery store. Before the confrontation with Epifanio, the neighbours had spoken to her, begging her to persuade El Mozambique to move away, but Ester ran off before they could explain their reasons.

As he crept up the path to El Mozambique's shack, Benicio passed an avocado tree, a sweet apple tree and a ruined water tank that was utterly useless. He looked to one side then to the other but saw no one. Only the figures of Ignacio, Melecio and Geru far behind on Rose Alley. The wind began to blow, churning the earth into mud which it spattered against the branches of the trees. It was daytime, but the whole area was swathed in fog thick as an avalanche of spirits.

Benicio picked up a smooth river stone that lay, almost waiting, next to his feet. He walked as far as the fence of barbed wire and timbers studded with vicious nails. Just as he was about to throw the stone, the door to the shack flew open. Benicio felt a shudder of terror as he saw the burly giant, his bullish coarse face, square jaw, pale eyes, step out into the daylight. His face looked as though it were incapable of any expression beyond the undying hatred for the world he wore like a mask. Seeing Benicio, his frown softened and his lips parted to reveal fangs as sharp as those of his dogs.

'Someone has finally come to visit me. And not just anyone, a boy no less. I knew some day my luck would change,' said El Mozambique with a noble expression that for a moment caught Benicio off guard. 'Come on, come in. Don't be afraid, I'm not as black as people paint me.'

'I'm sorry, señor. I wasn't going to throw the stone at you, I was going to throw it into the thicket. I'm going now.'

'What do you mean, you're going?'

El Mozambique's eyebrows resumed their original scowl. Benicio could see the thick veins pulsing in the man's throat. His arms were strange too, as though he had no forearms, just two huge biceps extending from shoulder to wrist. 'That's no way to greet someone. What am I supposed to do with the orange juice I've made? There's far too much to drink it by myself.'

My grandfather had no choice but to obey. Before he did so, he glanced back at Melecio, Geru and Ignacio el Jabao standing rooted to the spot, hands clapped over their mouths, watching everything.

The dogs looked at him mistrustfully but did not make the slightest sound. Inside, the shack was dark and shadowy as a cave and the smell of rotting wood hit Benicio. Pinned to the walls were rags to stop the light stealing through cracks in the boards. There were other smells too, the stench of old, dirty clothes. From the walls hung countless curious objects: machetes of every shape and size, garden tools, rag dolls that smelled of coal dust; a number of *santería* cauldrons filled with metal objects were dotted around the room and there were bowls of rotting fruit that teemed with ants and blow-flies. Through the noxious odours came the acrid, unmistakable smell of blood. The shack seemed like the very fount of stench and putrefaction.

'There you go,' said El Mozambique, handing Benicio a rusty can filled with orange juice. He apologised for the pestilential smell, explaining that he had never seen any need to clean the house since he lived alone and, until now, no one had ever visited. And so he had grown accustomed to the smell of shit and rancid blood.

Benicio stared at the contents of the tin can and saw eight or ten ants and a dead fly floating on the yellow liquid. His stomach heaved but, seeing the eagle eyes of his host widen, Benicio drank the contents, ants, flies and all, in a single gulp. El Mozambique smiled in satisfaction. He took the can from the boy's hand and set it on a wooden table on which stood one of the countless bowls of metal objects. Then, cradling his face in his calloused hands, he proceeded to stare at the boy as though studying some precious long-buried artefact.

'There is nothing more glorious than the innocence of youth. I had it once, you know, that innocence. Long, long ago. But then someone taught me hate, and since that time everything I have known has been coloured by that word.' An expression stole across the face of El Mozambique like that of a lost child desperate for affection. He tilted his head to one side and closed his eyes as though listening to distant voices, to thoughts from times long gone. 'But then I discovered that hatred can be a wonderful quality if directed as it should be. For example . . .' He got to his feet and grabbed a sharp machete from the wall. Benicio swallowed hard.

'People always wondered how I could cut so much sugar cane, how I could hack away all day and never tire. I'll tell you: hatred. It was hatred that drove me to be the best. With every swing of my machete, I vented my fury; I imagined the sugar cane was my enemy and so I hacked at it and sometimes howled with rage and I went on swinging late into the night, long after the other *macheteros* had gone home. Still the hatred would burn inside me and I would carry on until dawn; this is how I came to be the best. Do not fear being hated; hatred is not such a bad thing; it means people leave you in peace.' El Mozambique put the machete back where he had found it. Benicio felt himself relax.

'But we are not here to speak of unpleasant things, are we? You are wondering why I invited you into my house. Firstly, because no one ever visits me and secondly, because we have a mutual friend. Did you know that?'

'A friend, señor?'

'Indeed. It was she who said I should meet you. You know Ester?'

'No, señor.'

'Of course you know her! Ester, come out of the kitchen!'

The midwife stepped into the room. She was wearing the clothes she had been wearing the first time Grandpa Benicio ever saw her. She stopped, arms folded, right between them, and from the timid way that she moved it was clear she too was scared.

'Do you recognise her now?'

'Yes, señor. I know this lady, but I've only ever seen her once: the time she told me I was a sad child.'

El Mozambique let out a bear-like roar and doubled over. Benicio and the midwife flinched, then Ester smiled and Benicio noticed that all her upper teeth were missing. El Mozambique could not stop laughing. 'So you told the kid he was a sad child? The things you came out with, Ester. What do you know of sadness? Pay her no heed, Benicio, the weight of her tits has left her addled in the head. We like Ester when she keeps her trap shut, don't we, Benicio? So not another word out of you, Ester, do you hear me? Now go back to scrubbing your pots, we men have things to discuss.'

The midwife pouted and gave Benicio a miserable look. Then, head down, she trudged back whence she had come.

'Tell me a little about you,' said El Mozambique.

'About me?'

'Indeed.'

'Well, I have a sister and . . .'

'And a brother named Melecio who recites poetry. All this I know already. Tell me about . . .' The man's eyes had alighted on the amulet around Benicio's neck. He walked over to the boy, took the pig's foot in his hand and did as he had when staring at his face: he studied it as though he were a detective.

'I should have expected it. Who gave this to you?'

'It was given to me by my papá, José. I've had it since I was born. My father says it brings good luck.'

'Given you by your father José? Don't make me laugh. It's very handsome. Why don't we trade? I'll give you one of my puppies in exchange for your necklet.'

'I can't, señor.'

'What do you mean you can't?'

'I told you, it was a gift from my parents.'

The murderous expression returned to the face of El Mozambique. He grabbed the necklet again and began to tug. Benicio started to scream, flailing his thin arms, biting the giant's hand, struggling to stop him from taking the amulet. Just then the dogs began to bark.

'Benicio! Benicio, are you in there?' called a voice from outside. With a fierce wrench, Benicio managed to prise the giant's hand from the talisman and, like a flash of lightning, bolted outside where he found the whole village gathered. Melecio, Ignacio el Jabao and Geru were standing in front; behind them stood Epifanio Vilo and his brood, followed by a throng of people crowded around José, waiting impatiently for something they had spent years hoping might one day happen.

'Benicio! What possessed you to go bothering El Mozambique?' roared José, breaking through the crowd encircling him. The dogs were still barking. Abruptly, they fell silent as the imposing figure of their master pushed his way past and faced down the crowd.

'Uh . . . Mozambique, I apologise for Benicio's intrusion . . .'

'There was no intrusion. I was just telling him how much I admired his amulet.'

'He's lying, Papi. He tried to steal it from me,' wailed Benicio in despair.

Among the crowd, indignant voices began to clamour.

'Did you hear that, José?' said Epifanio Vilo. 'It's like we've been telling you for years. This man is a menace.' The assembled crowd chorused their support. The clamour rolled around the woods like a thunderclap.

'That's enough, señores, that's enough. El Mozambique has not harmed anyone. You may not like the way he lives, but every man has a right to live as he pleases. This is the great principle of freedom.'

'Perhaps, but that same freedom can become catastrophe if not used wisely,' said Abelardo Cabrera. 'Besides, we all hate the man. It is not merely one or two people, everyone despises him, so there must be some reason. As the old saying goes, when the river roars, there are rocks beneath.'

El Mozambique stood smiling at everyone.

'Hatred is a harsh word, Abelardo,' said José. 'When someone hates, he stoops lower than the man he hates, and that is not good. We hate in others that which we hate in ourselves; that is why I believe hatred is too strong a word.'

Everyone fell silent, shaking their heads in disbelief.

'It's true, Papá . . . El Mozambique tried to . . .'

'Shut your mouth, Benicio,' said José, taking the boy by the shoulders and moving him to one side. 'Mozambique, why don't we prove to everyone here that you don't devour people, why don't you come and join us for the feast, hey?'

'Never,' said El Mozambique categorically, 'You all decided long ago that I was the devil himself. Let us leave it so.'

'So you agree with these people?'

'Since when has anyone cared what I believe? I've already admitted that I am evil, and I am not about to try and change anyone's mind since the only one who needs to remain calm is me. I know that they are all simply waiting for me to die and perhaps one of these days I will give them that satisfaction. Who knows? Now get the hell off my property, all of you, before I throw you to the dogs.'

José stood for a moment, brooding over what El Mozambique had said. The neighbours waited, impatient, each wondering how the Mandinga would react.

'You know something, Mozambique? You might not realise it, but if that is how you think, then you began dying long ago. If that is how you want to live, well then wallow in your contempt, but don't say we didn't warn you. All right? Let's go, *caballeros*. Let's go back to the fiesta.'

'But, José,' howled the neighbours in chorus, 'how can you do this?'

'Calm down, calm down,' José said firmly. 'Can't you see the man's a pitiful wretch? Leave him alone, he has enough misery in his life.'

With great misgiving, all did as José insisted. They headed back down the path towards the flame tree and the festivities, shielding their eyes against the dust whipped by the wind. Melecio and Gertrudis hugged their brother.

'We were scared we'd never see you again. Ignacio said children are El Mozambique's favourite food,' said Geru, giving him a kiss. 'So, are you going to tell us what happened or not?'

Benicio told them everything that had happened. Then all

three glared at Ignacio el Jabao, walking hand in hand with his father, laughing as he pointed at them. Lastly, they glanced back at El Mozambique who was standing where they had left him, staring at them with his pale eyes, cackling malevolently and licking his lips.

The Village Schoolteacher

When they reached home, Betina was sitting waiting angrily in the doorway. She asked Benicio what had happened and Grandfather explained that it had all been Ignacio el Jabao's fault for saying he was a fucking pussy if he didn't throw a stone at El Mozambique. Betina's eyes grew wide with horror. José started to laugh. 'Don't laugh, José, this is not funny. Benicio, what kind of language is that? Don't ever let me hear you say a word like that again or I'll cut your tongue out. The only one in this house allowed to swear is me. Even your father would not do such a thing, do you understand? And all three of you are forbidden from hanging around with Ignacio. As punishment, you can all go to your rooms.'

Geru slowly headed for her room but Melecio, considering the punishment was unfair, bowed his head, saying that he was to blame for everything. Benicio planted himself in front of Betina and told her not to listen to Melecio, that what had actually happened was that Ignacio had said he was nothing like his father, some man called Oscar.

'Who is Oscar, Mami?'

Betina and José looked at each other conspiratorially and

Betina told Benicio that he shouldn't listen to that little monster Ignacio and once again told all of them to go to bed.

The children did as they were told, but it did not end there. Every time Ignacio encountered Benicio, under the flame tree, in Chinaman Li's store, or at the Festival of Birth, he repeated the same taunt: 'Your papá's name was Oscar.' This went on, until one day, unable to bear the insults any longer, Benicio threw a stone that cracked Ignacio's skull and the poor boy ran home howling, his head streaming blood. His parents immediately went to see Betina and José to find out what had happened.

'Ignacio won't leave me alone,' said Benicio, sobbing. 'He's telling everyone that you're not my parents and it's driving me mad.'

The four adults decided that the moment had come for the boy to learn the truth. The Jabaos went back to their house and Betina made linden tea for the children and coffee for the adults. Then she sat all the children around the table and told them what had happened to Benicio's true parents.

'So Ignacio was telling the truth, you're not my real parents.'

'Of course we are,' said José, putting a hand on Benicio's shoulder. 'Parents are not those who give birth to you, they are the people who raise you.' The boy bowed his head and pressed the amulet to his chest. It was hard for him to accept that his mother had died at the very moment he was born, and that his real father had chosen to take his own life, leaving him in the care of his friends Betina and José. He wondered how an orphan was supposed to feel. He wondered this and as he did so he felt a sharp pain in his head, a pain that made it impossible for him to clearly see the origin of things. He got up from his chair and ran to the flame tree.

'Let him go, Betina. It's normal for him to feel this way. He needs time to think.'

Betina closed the door. José put an arm around her shoulders and they went to their room.

Melecio and Gertrudis went looking for their brother beneath the flame tree.

'I knew it,' said Melecio. 'You look nothing like me, and besides your bellybutton sticks out. But it doesn't matter,' he added. 'No one can ever say that we're not brothers.'

The three children hugged. Benicio ate the cracker Gertrudis had brought him and a few minutes later in the company of his half-siblings he felt much better. The sky grew thick with dark clouds and, in the wink of an eye, the three figures were gathered into the darkness.

The third Sunday came and, as agreed, the villagers discussed who would go to study in El Cobre so they could teach everyone to read and write. They cast votes, a show of hands for each of the various options: Juan Carlos (another Jabao), Anastasia Aquelarre, Ana Cabrera, Silvia Santacruz and Melecio Mandinga. Since everyone voted for their own family, it was logical that the largest family would win, meaning that Juan Carlos would go to El Cobre.

'One moment, señores,' said José, rising from his chair. 'This is not right.'

Pablo, the head of the Jabao clan, protested that the voting had been fair, that no one had cheated.

'There was no cheating, but in a vote it was inevitable that your family would win because there are more of you. We have to think of another way to decide.'

'All right. Why don't we decide by having a sack race?' suggested El Jabao.

'Pablo, you know very well that your family would win a sack race as well,' said José, and all the neighbours agreed.

Everyone began to advocate contests that their family was likely to win.

'It should be the person who sews best,' proposed the Santacruz family.

'The best storyteller should decide it,' suggested Evaristo.

Juanita the wise-woman continued to insist that she should be the one to go and threatened that a flood lasting three months would descend upon Pata de Puerco if she were not chosen.

Suddenly, a distant rumbling attracted everyone's attention. It sounded like a carriage moving at great speed. The villagers went out on to the Callejón de la Rosa to witness the miracle: a stranger arriving in the village for the first time. The carriage was moving at great speed, raising clouds of dust that made it impossible to see anything.

'Didn't I tell you? I knew that sooner or later it would have to come this way,' said José.

'What are you talking about, José?' everyone chorused.

'At last! The streetlights have arrived!'

People began to jump for joy. According to José, the country had finally realised that Pata de Puerco existed and soon perhaps builders would come to build schools and hospitals which would mean it would no longer be necessary to send Juan Carlos or anyone to El Cobre. Civilisation had finally come to the village.

As the carriage drew closer, the *patapuercanos* grew more and more confused. 'I think you're wrong, José. I don't think it's the streetlights. It's a private carriage,' said Evaristo, stepping into the middle of the Callejón de la Rosa the better to see. The carriage was being driven by a black coachman dressed in red wearing a large black hat. Immediately José realised who it was.

'Melecio, come here.'

Melecio ran over and stood next to José. Gertrudis and Benicio stood next to Betina, watching. Aureliano, the coachman, greeted them with a magnificent bow and, without wasting a moment, stepped down from the carriage.

'I have heard of exotic places, but this truly is a wonder. Green, very green, and not a single lamppost.'

Everyone was staring at the white man stepping cautiously out of the carriage.

'Hello, José. Do you remember me?'

'How could I not remember you? You'd do well not to come any closer; it is your fault that the leg of my mare was hacked off.'

'You don't say! When was this?'

'While you were telling me that my son Melecio was gifted and that you wanted to help him. That was the very moment the *bandido* chose to strike.'

'I beg your forgiveness. It's true I did detain you for some time. Here you are, José.' Don Emilio had Aureliano unhitch one of the thoroughbred horses and handed over the reins. 'Once again, my sincere apologies.'

José looked Emilio Bacardí up and down incredulously and eventually pointed to Evaristo the kite-maker, explaining that the mare had been his.

Evaristo hesitantly stepped towards the white man. 'I . . . I . . . I . . . don't know . . .'

'Allow me . . . Is the gentleman a stutterer?' asked Don Emilio. 'Because I have the perfect cure. It is called Indian honey and is a syrup confected from a variety of psychotropic plants which restores the balance of the central nervous system. The problem is centred in the brain. I shall send you a bottle.'

Evaristo was incapable of responding, his stutter growing ever worse. No one present had ever seen him in such a state, his eyes welled with tears and he trembled with excitement. The villagers had not yet decided whether to trust the stranger. Again and again they weighed him up, inspecting his coachman and his carriage and finally looking back at José waiting for some signal that would tell them how to behave towards the outsider.

El Jabao was first to break the ice. He walked up to Don Emilio and said cordially, 'No, señor, Evaristo is not a stutterer, he is just nervous. Don't worry about what happened just now, he will be fine in a moment. It has been a long time since an outsider has visited our village, so you can imagine how curious we are. The truth is that you could not have arrived at a better moment. What is your name?'

'Emilio! His name is Emilio Bacardí,' Evaristo said finally, without stuttering.

Emilio Bacardí looked at him, smiling. El Jabao went on, 'Well, Señor Emilio. Before you arrived, we were discussing which of the villagers here should go to El Cobre to study and become the future schoolteacher for our village. The options are these . . .'

Juan Carlos, Anastasia Aquelarre, Ana Cabrera, Silvia Santacruz and Melecio took a step forward. One by one Emilio Bacardí studied them, with the exception of Melecio whom he treated as though he did not exist. José realised that the stranger's attitude had changed; he glanced at Betina, but his wife gestured for him to remain calm and let matters play out.

'Now,' said El Jabao, 'I think the best way to decide the future teacher for our village is to have a sack race, but no one will agree. Nor are they prepared to simply put the matter to a vote, meaning a show of hands with the candidate who receives the most votes being declared the winner. And another thing, Juanita, the wise-woman, the woman at the back there, has threatened that if we do not choose her she will bring down a terrible curse on us. Perhaps you could help. What do you think would be best?'

'What I think is that now would be the moment to give you the gifts I've brought,' said Don Emilio and the coachman quickly began to unload from the carriage dozens of baskets of bread, roast suckling pig, legs of ham and earthenware bottles filled with rum.

The inhabitants of Pata de Puerco had never seen so much food. But they remained wary and nobody moved. The coachman told them to go ahead, the food was for them: that if they did not eat it, it would go to waste. José nodded. In the blink of an eye, the villagers fell upon this banquet. Everyone grabbed a leg of ham to take home while stuffing themselves from the other baskets and swigging rum. There was mango juice and guava juice for the children and toys the like of which they had never seen. José watched as Betina, Geru, Melecio and Benicio ate frantically, sampling every delicacy.

In the midst of this ravening ferocity, José walked over to the coachman and said, 'I was told your master's son fought with Maceo. Is it true?'

'Yes, señor. Emilito his name is. I told you, José, Don Emilio Bacardí is an extraordinary man. Not long ago he went to a far-off country called Egypt in mother Africa and brought back a dried-up body more than a thousand years old to put in the museum he plans to build. "If the world will not come to us, then I will bring it here so that my people can know it," he said to me once. And that's what he's doing.'

José listened carefully to Aureliano's words. He spat on the ground and then looked at Emilio Bacardí who was delightedly listening to the tales and stories of the candidates for the post of village teacher. Still he resolutely ignored Melecio.

An hour later, when everyone was sated and drunk, the stranger addressed the assembled crowd.

'How do you feel now?'

'Excellent! *Fenomenal!* This is the best food we've ever had in our lives,' they chorused.

'I am very glad. It has been a genuine pleasure to share it with you and I am grateful to you for sharing your concerns for the village. To turn now to the problem raised by Señor Pablo, I believe that the person best suited to assuming the role of teacher is Melecio. I say this because I had the good fortune to witness the boy's talent and I can assure you it is truly exceptional. Believe me when I tell you this, señores. Moreover, I promised to teach this extraordinary boy everything I know.'

Bacardí hugged Melecio to him.

'Unless of course someone has a better idea. Is there anyone here who disagrees with the idea of sending Melecio?'

'No, sir, you are completely right. From the very beginning I thought as much, but no one would let me speak,' said Pablo el Jabao, staggering around clutching a bottle of rum.

'I agree,' said Juanita, unable to get up from her chair. 'Melecio is our man and if anyone doesn't like it, I swear I'll cast a spell that leaves him bald for the rest of his life. I completely agree with Señor Bacardón.'

Everyone began chanting 'Me-le-cio, Me-le-cio, Me-le-cio . . .', then the chorus changed to 'Bacardón, Bacardón, Bacardón . . .' José smiled to himself, he could not but admire the stranger's cunning. Don Emilio first winked at him and then walked over to where he stood, eyes twinkling, and whispered, 'Well then, José, you decide.'

José Mandinga looked at Betina and could tell by her eyes that she agreed. He looked at Geru, at Benicio and lastly at Melecio who stood, hands in his pockets, nervously awaiting the verdict. Then he turned back to Don Emilio.

'I have never trusted a white man, but I suppose there is a first time for everything. And as someone from El Cobre once told me . . .' José turned to look at Melecio who was smiling excitedly '. . . opportunities are bald and you've got to grab them by the hair.' Bacardí gave a satisfied smile.

'But listen to me, Señor Bacardí. I want my Melecio to come back with all four limbs because if he doesn't, I promise I will come for you with a machete and for anyone who comes between us. I want him back in perfect condition, is that understood?'

'You have my word as a Cuban,' said Don Emilio simply, then held out his hand which José took and shook warmly.

'*Bacardón! Bacardón! Melecio! Melecio! José! José!*' everyone bellowed, tossing chicken bones, hunks of bread and pieces of ham into the air – these are the bits of the story I really like, all the stuff about ham and chicken . . . but anyway, I'm getting sidetracked.

The shimmering June sun was already beginning to set. All the villagers bid farewell to Melecio, hugging and kissing him. Betina shed a few tears as she reminded him to brush his teeth every day and make his bed every morning. José read him the riot act and told him to behave himself. The last to say goodbye were Gertrudis and Benicio.

'Promise me you'll take care.'

'Don't be stupid, Melecio, of course we'll take care. Besides, Papá is strong as a ceiba tree.'

'Not Papá, I'm talking about your secret, the one you both carry inside you, it is sómething truly special.'

Geru and Benicio looked at each other bewildered, then kissed Melecio on both cheeks and with tears in their eyes, they watched him set off, thinking that a great part of their lives was leaving with that carriage. José watched in silence as the carriage moved along the Callejón de la Rosa. He always had something to say, some opinion to offer, but at that moment he was speechless, as though his thoughts had been carried off by the gentle breeze that followed behind the carriage of Don Emilio Bacardí.

'Cheer up, *hombre*. It had to happen some day. We bring children into this world, but they are not ours,' said Evaristo, putting an arm around José's shoulder. Then the Mandinga family headed home, not realising that with those inconsequential words the kite-maker was saying goodbye. Had he been aware, Evaristo would doubtless have found something memorable to say, but he could not have known that the following morning he would wake up dead. He had no time to enjoy his new horse, nor to say farewell to everyone.

'Apparently his heart just stopped,' said El Santacruz. Juanita had a different version. She spent five minutes examining him, sucked in a deep lungful of smoke and, rubbing her hands, she said, 'This man has been poisoned.'

José suggested a whole day be spent keeping vigil over Evaristo, without speaking or eating.

'No one can live without eating, José. We'd all die like Evaristo.'

In the end, it was decided there would be eight hours of silence and fasting. Only two people fainted. Evaristo was buried in the same spot as Oscar and Malena. It occurred to several people that since the deaths of Oscar and Malena, no one had died in Pata de Puerco.

And this, according to my grandfather, was the end of Evaristo the kite-maker, one of the most generous men he had ever known.

Three Years Pass

With Evaristo's death, the weekly Festival of Birth became a tedious ritual. Eustaquio the *machetero* attempted to take on Evaristo's role, but he was an oafish man who had spent all his life wielding a machete. Few were surprised when he suggested 'a scything competition', which consisted of cutting back the brushwood in the area and stuffing it into sacks. Whoever filled the most sacks in the shortest time was to be the winner. Eustaquio was of the opinion that not only would this be a good exercise to build up the arms of both men and womenfolk, it would also improve the appearance of the village.

'Thanks, Eustaquio, but we don't want to cut back the undergrowth,' everyone told him. 'The village is fine just as it is.' The plants and the trees were a part of the lives of everyone. They had grown accustomed to dragging around the weight of years in the verdant world that was Pata de Puerco and thus, somewhat relieved of their pain, could stride on towards death. This wilderness was their universe and nothing existed beyond the borders of the Accursed Forest but an infinite emptiness. The modern world they so often heard of was a mirage, a dream, a tale oft told but never believed.

Shortly afterwards rains came that quickly turned into a tornado, winds gusting at more than a hundred miles an hour, ripping trees up by the roots. It was a curious thing, since no tornado had ever passed near Santiago before. Many people were of the opinion that Melecio should not have left, that his departure had brought the cyclone.

The Jabaos' house was swept away by the storm. Every neighbour contributed three or four boards ripped from their own walls or the roofs of their shacks, they made use of pine trees that had been felled by the storm to rebuild the frame, recycled all the dried palm fronds they could find from the old shack, and in less than two weeks the Jabao family had a new house that was sturdier and more comfortable than the old one.

The village was tidied up. Branches and tree trunks were cleared from the paths. The betel palm that had become lodged in the well was removed. They cut back the weeds, the sicklebush and brambles that had grown up during the rains and gradually taken over the area, threatening to create a thorny jungle. The village returned to normal. At Chinaman Li's store, the corrugated-iron roof had been ripped off, but his family – some twenty strong – soon returned the store to its original state.

The days became long and heavy. People ceased to dream about the possibility of progress. By the time they looked up and took notice, it was 1914.

During this time, Grandpa Benicio grew so much that José could not explain the change in him. One morning he simply woke up and he was not the same. José began to watch him closely, to follow him constantly; he even went into the bathroom when he was bathing, something he had not done since Benicio was a little boy. Sometimes Grandfather thought José had gone mad because at night when he was asleep he would creep into Benicio's room, slip a hand into his shorts and measure his *pinga* with a length of string. My grandfather woke with a start, as did Gertrudis, and they frightened him off. It was an obsession.

'I don't understand, Betina. Malena was small, Oscar was scarcely four feet tall and you've told me that your parents were not very tall either, so where the hell does the boy get it from?'

Betina answered that it was simply in the nature of things, but she could not convince him. The truth was that every day José was growing older. He walked more slowly and constantly had to look down, careful not to trip. Overnight, he appeared with a walking stick which he had whittled from the branch of a ceiba. His hair had turned white, his shoulders had begun to droop and something like a hump began to grow on his back.

Yet still he went on working in the vegetable garden every day to feed his family. Benicio helped out as much as he could while Betina and Geru made a little money washing clothes down at the river, or sometimes they would go to El Cobre and sell the skirts and trousers the Santacruzes made. This way they managed to get by.

José began to talk constantly about the past, almost always with a sense of guilt about the death of Oscar. No one could persuade him that he was not to blame for the death of his friend. Over and over Betina had to remind him that Malena had died in childbirth and that Oscar had simply decided to follow his wife into the next world. José would never listen. And so he got into the habit of walking to the cemetery every morning to talk to his friend. He would go very early, when the half-light still veiled the colours of day and the dew heightened the forest smells of the village.

José Miguel Gómez, who had been a general in the war of 1895, was the new president of the country. Everyone in Cuba knows that Negroes were not allowed to join the police force, could not take part in official ceremonies or hold public office; they were not allowed into hotels or anything of that kind. But very soon a wave of protests erupted across the island by unions, veterans of the war of independence, progressive movements campaigning against exploitation. And so the *Partido Independiente de Color* – the Independent Party of Colour – was founded with the aim of abolishing the exploitation of coloured people and the death penalty, while supporting a policy of free education and other civil liberties. The movement grew to become a political party which participated in elections; however the Morúa Law – introduced by Martin Morúa, one of the few black men in the Cuban senate – outlawed political parties based on race. At this point, the sectors of the oligarchy who had always lived in fear of a race war began to sow the seeds of hatred among the traditional parties and the wealthy classes, accusing the PIC of seeking to impose black power in the island and spreading rumours of black men supposedly raping white women.

Matters became heated. The PIC mounted demonstrations in the streets and rose up in arms in Oriente, particularly in Santiago, Pinar del Rio, Havana and Las Villas. These rebel groups did not initiate violent confrontations; they were mobilised simply to put pressure on the government to recognise the demands of their party. The government of José Miguel Gómez responded by sending in the Rural Guard, the volunteers and all the heavy artillery, urged on by retired general Mario García Menocal, who years later would become president of the republic. In less than three months, the 'rebels' and their leaders were all butchered. Three thousand black people died in the massacre.

'I told you, Aureliano, but you wouldn't listen. It's just like the story of the Emperor's New Clothes,' José told the coachman one day. Betina, Benicio and Geru looked at him, puzzled. 'You know the story – the emperor who always wanted to wear the latest fashions and one day, having tried on a dozen outfits and finding none of them suited him, was persuaded to leave the palace wearing a suit of invisible clothes. Everyone clapped and cheered until one little boy shouted, "But the king is stark naked." This is exactly the same. I told you that the white men were a double-edged sword and you went on clapping and cheering just like the people praising the bare-arsed emperor. It took this race war and the mass slaughter of everyone for you to finally understand.'

'I still think as I always thought, *amigo* José,' said the coachman, shaking his head. 'Our mistake was to think like sheep. This is why the Independent Party of Colour failed, because it tried to put all white men in the same basket when there are tramps on the street who are white, there are white people who are oppressed and exploited. But let's not argue, these things are not over yet.'

From the pocket of his red jacket, Aureliano took a sealed letter that smelled of ink and glue. Everyone stared at the yellow envelope.

'But that's a letter,' said Betina, looking into the coachman's eyes. 'What are we supposed to do with a letter since none of us can read?'

The coachman asked Betina to warm a little coffee and said that he would take charge of reading the documents. José suddenly announced that he was going to the cemetery.

'To the cemetery?' said the coachman, surprised.

'Yes. Betina, you can tell me what's happening with Melecio when I get back. And you, Aureliano, could you please tell my son that he has been gone a long time. Just tell him that. And give him a hug from us.'

How to Conquer a Woman
According to María

José left the shack. Five minutes later Betina reappeared with the coffee. Aureliano asked what the matter was with José and Betina told him it was just old age. The coachman began to take sheaves of paper from the envelope; it seemed as though this letter was unending. They realised that it was not just one letter, but all the letters that Melecio had written since his departure three years earlier.

The Bacardís had shown a great affection for Melecio and had accepted him as a member of the family, especially Marina, Lucía, Adelaida and Amalia, the daughters of Don Emilio's second marriage to Doña Elvira Cape.

Don Emilio, a man passionate about poetry and about art in general, patiently taught Melecio his vowels and consonants, the difference between subject and predicate, between adjectives and nouns. In the field of poetry, he taught him about metre, about how some poems rhymed while others did not, all the things Melecio did not know but which he had instinctively applied in the poetic improvisations when words seemed to come to him as though dictated by some supernatural being. Melecio learned mathematics, physics and chemistry. Bacardí was very happy with his results and was constantly surprised by the boy's ability to learn.

Every afternoon, the whole family would sit out on the porch of the majestic house in the shade of the almond trees and admire the talents of the boy from Pata de Puerco: Doña Elvira and her four daughters, the six children from Don Emilio's previous marriage to the late Señora María Berluceau, Don Emilio's brothers José and Facundo and their wives, and the coachman Aureliano. Melecio would delight them with a dozen spontaneous poems, which were all the more powerful now that his vocabulary had been enriched by his classes with Don Emilio. These gatherings invariably ended with Melecio being showered with praise and with kisses, as though he were not just some poor black boy from Pata de Puerco, a village no one had ever heard of, but an exceptional individual or, as they often referred to him, an *illuminato*. Never had Melecio experienced such joy as in these moments. These afternoons beneath the almond trees became an attraction for Don Emilio's friends who included key figures from Cuban society, heads of government, mayors, colonels, even Americans drawn by the legend of this child prodigy of extraordinary sensibility who could recite poems that seemed to emanate from the very heart of God.

One day, after coffee, Don Emilio gave a little speech in front of the assembled company. It was time, he said, to expand his business, to take his rum to all corners of Cuba, beginning with Havana; when this was done, he would take on the world. To do this, he needed a symbol that would give his product weight, a powerful image that would mark the peak of the Bacardí empire, and that symbol, he concluded, should be a building, a building surmounted by a statue of a bat, the animal adopted as the emblem of the Bacardís since the beginning and one which had brought them their good fortune. All those present agreed with his proposals and suggested a number of possible architects, some already established and some who had recently emerged with the new tendencies and demands in the art of construction. There was talk of Rafael Fernández Ruenes, of José Antonio Mendigutía and Esteban Rodríguez Castell, of Govantes and Cabarrocas and the structural engineer José Menéndez.

Melecio listened in silence to the names of these distinguished personalities. Ideas teemed inside his brain, ideas which even he did not understand, ideas that existed only in his mind.

'Where are you going, Melecio?' asked Marina, Don Emilio's daughter, seeing the boy get up to leave.

'I don't feel well. I need to lie down,' he said, and went back to his room.

No one knew what was the matter with him. Every time they knocked on his door to ask, Melecio simply said, 'I just need some time to think.' They tried to open the door, but Melecio kept it firmly locked. There was nothing to be done but leave food on a tray on the floor outside, which Melecio would eat in the early hours when everyone was asleep.

'Melecio, we have guests, why don't you come out and recite something for us? It's getting so we can hardly remember what you look like,' Don Emilio said one day after Melecio had spent three weeks completely isolated from the outside world. Don Emilio received the usual response: 'I need time to think.' That afternoon, as on so many others, the guests had to make do with the tales told by Aureliano the coachman, Don Emilio's stories of his trip to Egypt and Emilito's accounts of the war of independence which invariably featured General Maceo who, Emilito insisted, was mulatto though Aureliano maintained he was a pureblood Negro, and so the chatter went on into the early hours.

One sunny morning, Melecio finally decided to emerge. Having hugged him as though he were a relative recently arrived back from the wars, everyone gathered in the living room. Melecio placed dozens of sheets of paper on the marble table in the centre of the room. They were covered with drawings, mathematical calculations and geometric diagrams of something that looked like a huge box or a house, projected in various dimensions that from some angles looked like crates of rum, from others like coffins or sinister towers. It was so strange that no one present had ever seen its like.

'Who are the coffins for?' asked Don Emilio.

'It's a building,' said the boy from Pata de Puerco, smiling mischievously, his hands, as always, stuffed in his pockets.

The faces around him looked puzzled as they struggled but failed to see anything resembling a building in the sketches. Until Melecio began to colour in a frontal elevation. The marble tiles of the façade were reddish; deep terracotta for the ground floor rising to a soft beige on the remaining eight floors. Each floor had eleven carved wooden windowframes and the central tower was studded with dark crystals and mosaic tiles. Melecio sketched the huge streetlamps that hung from the ground floor like opulent pendants and, on the apex of the tower, he drew a globe of the world straddled by the hairy feet of a bat. Little by little, all these details appeared before the astonished eyes of the assembled company.

Don Emilio summoned his partners to a meeting attended by some of the most esteemed architects in the country and showed them Melecio's designs. The calculations were precise and the extraordinarily ambitious project was brilliantly conceived. But what astonished everyone was the imposing, ornate style, the innovative grace of the brightly coloured embellishments. It was an expression of modern art, of sophisticated elegance unlike anything they had ever seen.

'This architect is either a genius or a fool. And I don't think he's a fool,' commented Señor Rafael Fernández Ruenes, peering at the drawings through rimless spectacles. 'One thing is certain. This man is someone with exceptional talent and considerable experience. I would go so far as to say we are dealing with someone who has created a new style.'

Rafael Fernández Ruenes was referring to the art deco style which Melecio unwittingly invented when designing the Bacardí Building in Havana.

'I'm afraid you're wrong, Rafael. The architect is a boy of sixteen who has never so much as designed a sewage system,' said Don Emilio, patting Melecio on the shoulder.

'Are you telling me that this was not designed by an architect?'

'It was designed by this boy standing next to me.'

Rafael Fernández Ruenes and the others present stared curiously at Melecio as though he were a new species recently mentioned in some zoological treatise. They studied every detail of his clothes, the hands stuffed in the pockets of his shorts, the noble face, the bushy eyebrows, the square jaw, as the boy smiled at them artlessly.

'Dear God, Don Emilio, don't make me laugh. What does some poor Negro boy know about architecture?'

'Watch your tongue, Rafael,' said Don Emilio, suddenly getting to his feet. 'The boy's name is Melecio and he is not some poor Negro boy, is that understood?'

The architect apologised; he had meant no dishonour or insult to Melecio, he said, and promised it would not happen again; he simply found it difficult to believe what Don Emilio had just told them since architecture is a complicated discipline that requires years to perfect. He asked if he might be permitted to quietly study the plans at home and suggested that, in the meantime, Melecio might favour them with another of his designs.

Once again, Melecio locked himself in his bedroom for three weeks. On the third Sunday, he appeared with a sheaf of papers three times larger than the first. In these sketches there were trees, streets, children playing, shops, markets; everyone was flabbergasted.

'But, Melecio, this is a whole city,' said Don Emilio.

'I know,' said the boy. 'I call it Cabeza de Carnero.'

Don Emilio once again summoned his partners and showed them Melecio's plans. No one could believe it. 'You have persuaded me, Don Emilio,' said Rafael, studying the faces of everyone through rimless glasses. 'The boy is a genius. We must do everything possible to nurture his talent.'

And so began the voyages. Melecio travelled and designed; this was his life. He designed a dozen buildings in a city called Santa Clara, a dozen more in another called Camagüey and his fame spread beyond the borders of Oriente, reaching all the way to Havana.

Havana was an awe-inspiring city of thousands of inhabitants which had contraptions known as 'street cars' used to transport people to various destinations. It was a city that never rested, in which there was no place for silence since at all hours of the day and night one could hear the booming voices of hawkers selling their wares on the cobbled streets, the foghorns of the ships coming into harbour. A riot of noise, of traffic, of confusion: this was Havana. And yet the sea was beautiful, crystal clear, blue as the sky; moreover it was boundless, unlike the lakes and the rivers whose banks were always visible and whose waters were dark and choked with water hyacinths, mud and mossy stones. In the dawn light the capital attained a different splendour when only the buildings were visible, guarding the sleeping city like faithful watchmen. At this hour peace reigned, a silence akin to what Melecio had known in his little village.

It was about this time, having returned from his travels to various cities, that Melecio met María, a beautiful black girl, radiant, coy, with a cheerful disposition and a boldness that, from the first time he set eyes on her, Melecio found unbearable. She was eighteen, two years older than he, and worked in the Bacardí distillery in Santiago. She had a glorious mane of hair – glossy and curly rather than dry and dull – that fell over her shoulders and she used it principally to flirt, winding a finger through her thick curls as she knowingly closed her eyes or, as circumstances dictated, opened them wide like two full moons.

She lived alone with her mother because her father had died during the Great War. More than once she confessed to Melecio that he looked like her father. Perhaps this was the reason she was attracted to him, some subconscious need to find someone to fill the void left by the death of the only man in her life. Melecio, barely seventeen, was already six feet tall and threatening to grow to seven; like his father José, he was sturdy. But he was too shy to speak to María, so it was she, with her typical boldness, who came up to him one afternoon in the distillery while they were working on creating a new *añejo*, a new blend.

'When making rum, you have to fire it up to remove the impurities. Just like a woman. You have to fire her up if you want to conquer her,' said María, twirling a finger through her curls. Melecio looked at her and scratched his head. If he was a genius in certain matters, he was utterly incompetent in others. 'You mean to conquer a woman you have to burn her?'

'Not burn her, you brute. You have to caress her. That's what fans the flames. Come here and I'll show you.'

María took hold of Melecio's large powerful hands and moved them over her face, her small, pointed breasts, her firm buttocks. For the first time Melecio could feel the fire María had spoken of. He felt it burning him up, blazing through his body which was unable to resist. 'Burning! I'm burning! I need water!'

'Come here, boy, don't be so dramatic, it's no big deal,' said María in an attempt to stop him. But Melecio was already dashing from the factory at breakneck speed back to the Bacardí house.

The factory supervisor gave María a stern talking to, accusing her of upsetting the smooth running of the workplace. María apologised and promised it would not happen again. It made no difference. The next day she was fired for being a bad influence on a child prodigy who needed to keep a clear head in order to complete his designs.

When Melecio discovered what had happened, he spoke to Emilio Bacardí and told him how much the girl meant to him, told him about the fire he had felt and said he could not bear for María to walk out of his life when she had only just arrived. He asked Don Emilio to give her back her job.

'Consider it done. Without love there can be no architecture, there can be no magnificent poetry,' said the great man.

The following day, just as Don Emilio had promised, María was back at work. Melecio tried to get close to her but María refused to say so much as a word. During the break, he tried again, but María ignored him and walked away, leaving Melecio racked with shame and guilt. He told the coachman about what had happened and everything he was going through.

'Grovel at her feet,' Aureliano suggested. 'The best thing you can do is let her see you as a fool.'

Next morning, Melecio went to the distillery prepared to do anything.

'María didn't come to work,' he was informed.

The same thing happened the next day and the next. It was then he realised that María was not coming back. He searched for her everywhere. He did not find her at her house, at the factory, or at the park where she always spent her afternoons. As the days turned into weeks and he still had no idea where she was, he began to think he had lost her for ever. He locked himself away in his room. He stopped reciting poems. He stopped drawing. He lost a lot of weight. It seemed pointless even to leave his room to see the sun.

'María is down on the riverbank,' read the note slipped under his door one afternoon after he had spent weeks shut away. Melecio dressed frantically and rushed to find the girl.

'Can I talk to you?' said the *patapuercano*, staring into her huge eyes.

'Talk to me? About what?'

'I have a gift for you.'

'Thank you, but I don't want any gifts.'

'I promise that after I've given it to you, I'll never bother you again.'

'Never?'

'Never.'

'Get on with it, then.'

María twirled a lock of hair around her finger and stared up at the sky and then back down at Melecio, kneeling in the mud, searching to meet her eyes. He began:

> *I wish that I could reach across this distance,*
> *this fatal gulf that keeps we two apart,*
> *grow drunk on love inhaling the sweet fragrance,*
> *mystic and pure, that your fair self imparts.*
>
> *I wish that I could be that tangled skein of grace*
> *that binds us in the shadows when you're near;*
> *and somewhere in the skies of your embrace*
> *could drink the glory of your lips so dear.*

I wish that I were water, I were wave,
so you might come and bathe within this torrent,
and I, as in my lonely dreams, might brave
a kiss, everywhere and always in one moment.

I wish, oh how I wish, that I could lure
you into me as cloud into a flame,
not cloud as in its lonely way endures
merely to burst and melt away in sheets of rain.

I wish I could your soul to my soul bind,
distil your essence, carry you within,
and this same essence, filtered and refined,
refashion as a scent to breathe you in.

Unblinking, unmoving, María sat and stared into Melecio's eyes. Her heart was pounding and beads of sweat were pearling on her cheeks.

'Did you like it?' asked Melecio.

Still María stared, lost for words.

'It's the most beautiful gift anyone's given me in my life,' she said when she could finally speak.

'I'm glad.' Melecio got up off his knees, brushed away the mud and walked away.

'Wait,' called María. The boy turned. 'You know you're the weirdest person I know? I swear. No one in the world is weirder than you.' Melecio smiled broadly and looked down at the ground. 'Come here, and this time do me a favour, don't run away.'

'What do you mean?'

'I mean I want you to be still. No drama, no weirdness. This time I want the fire to blaze until it burns itself out. Is that all right? Leave it to me and I'll show you how it's done. This time we'll burn together.'

Melecio came back and kissed her tenderly, then passionately. And then it began. María grabbed his hands and moved them all over her body, over her breasts, her arse, took Melecio's muddy fingers into her mouth and their bodies began to blaze. They didn't care that it was the middle of the day. They stripped off their clothes and rolled in the mud; María climbed on top of him and they fucked right there . . . I mean that, right there, Melecio lost his virginity.

Hormones are unstoppable. I don't know about you, but just thinking about the scene is giving me a hard-on.

The Transformation

By the time José got back from the cemetery, Aureliano had already left. Betina told him about everything Melecio had written in his letters. 'That boy fell to earth with an angel. Now let's talk about what you two are going to do. Geru, you're a young woman now, you have to keep your eyes peeled because the sharks will start circling. I don't want you having anything to do with the Jabaos, do you hear me? The man you will be promised to must be pure inside, and black.'

That night, Grandpa Benicio could not sleep. He lay curled up in bed thinking about Melecio's letter. He felt a little envious, a harmless jealousy that he did not have a fraction of his brother's talent. Neither José nor Gertrudis ever talked about Benicio's qualities though Melecio was not the only one who had changed in the past three years. Benicio too was almost as tall as José and had grown into a handsome lad with a strong, chiselled, muscular body that had not gone unnoticed in the village. Betina was the only one who would walk around the village with him, slipping her arm through his with typical maternal pride. Geru always preferred to follow at a distance and she never responded when old crones and some young women told Betina what a handsome lad Benicio was, a fine specimen of a Mandinga.

'That's because you're jealous,' Benicio said to his sister.

'Me, jealous? Of who? Of some little *chiquillo* who thinks he's the centre of the universe?'

'You're jealous because Jacinta is my girlfriend.'

Geru burst out laughing and said witheringly, 'Don't you think that for her to be your girlfriend, she should know about it first?'

She was right. Jacinta did not know she was my grandfather's girlfriend. How could he let her know? The only person who could teach him how to court a woman was José. But recently his father had seemed distant and barely spoke to him. Benicio felt José no longer loved him; after all, unlike Geru and Melecio, Grandpa was not his real child so there was no reason for him to show him the same affection. Even so, it was worth trying to ask him for advice.

'You've come to the right person,' said José. 'It was I who taught your father and look how well that turned out. The first thing you need to do is . . .' José gave Benicio the same advice he had given Oscar years before: flowers, make her laugh, massage her feet, her back and . . . 'Absolutely no sex. You don't want to get the girl pregnant and screw everything up. You're both too young and we're too old to be starting the whole rigmarole of babies again.'

Jacinta was the elder sister of Ignacio el Jabao. She was sixteen, the same age as Benicio, with a beautiful body and pale skin. Betina had once suggested to her children that they advance the race, that they go out and find mulattoes or pale-skinned blacks, and Jacinta fulfilled this requirement since she was an octaroon – a mixed-race girl with blonde hair and a pinkish complexion. Grandfather liked her, in spite of Geru saying that she was an ugly, freckle-faced freak with a shock of lank blonde hair she never washed.

One morning, Benicio went to see Jacinta and brought her a gift José had suggested.

'That's no way to treat a woman. What are you thinking, giving me a bunch of thorns?' said Jacinta, licking blood from fingers that were swollen from the bouquet of sicklebush wrapped in banana leaves Benicio had offered her. Crestfallen, Benicio went home and told José what had happened.

'Don't worry, *hijo*,' he said. 'These things happen. The next step is the most important. If you can make her laugh, you're halfway there.'

Grandfather went to see Jacinta again the following day.

'Two skeletons were out for a walk and one of them lit up a cigar. The other skeleton looked at his friend and said: you do know that smoking can kill you?'

When he finished telling his joke, he waited for Jacinta's reaction. She stared at him, as though she could not believe her ears.

'It's a joke. Don't you think it's funny?'

'Funny? It's the dumbest thing I've ever heard in my life.'

'I'm not much good at telling jokes. The only thing I'm good at is climbing trees. Do you want me to climb one for you?'

'Climb a tree? What for?'

Time flew by, March rolled around and with it a heatwave so intense it felt like summer. Then something strange happened.

One morning while working in the vegetable garden, Benicio suddenly felt short of breath. It was not the breathlessness he often got when tilling the ground, nor was it because of the midday sun which sometimes makes you want to peel off your own skin. It was a weird feeling, as though his lungs were blocked. He saw José working out in the back yard and, for the first time in his life, he experienced something he recognised as hatred. An overpowering hatred for this man who had raised him, for his family, for the whole world. Benicio loved José very much, much more perhaps than even he could imagine, but in that moment he wanted to strangle him. 'It's this damned sun,' he said, staring up at the sky.

The following day the same thing happened, but this time with Betina when she came to wake him for breakfast. 'Shit, Mamá Betina! Leave us alone, can't you see we're still asleep.' Gertrudis immediately jumped out of bed and Benicio sat staring at her, not knowing how to explain what had happened. Betina roared into the room like a hurricane and gave him a slap across the face that left him reeling. 'Speak to me like that again, and I'll rip your head off!' Grandfather and Gertrudis did not move. Betina turned on her heel without a word and went back to the kitchen.

'How could you talk to Mamá Betina like that?' said Geru, getting to her feet. Grandfather bowed his head while Geru lectured him about how you had to respect your parents, and not just parents but people in general, going on to say that he had to learn to control his temper. Benicio said that he didn't know what had come over him, but that it would never happen again. But still these flashes of fury kept coming, this murderous desire to throttle everyone, the foul-mouthed

126

impudence to Betina's orders. His family no longer recognised him; even Benicio himself could hardly believe the filth that came out of his mouth.

One day, Benicio went with Geru to bathe in the river and seeing his reflection in the water, noticed for the first time that he had changed and now had a thick bull-neck and powerful veiny arms. He also realised he was more than six feet tall.

'Geru, have you noticed anything weird about me?' he asked his sister. Gertrudis told him that he had grown into a giant; she had been meaning to mention it for some time but that she had not wanted to embarrass him. On their way home, they met a boy from the village bringing a bunch of flowers for Geru. Ignoring the look on Benicio's face that glowered, 'How dare you?', the boy offered the flowers to Geru who never even managed to accept them since, as she reached out her hand, the boy keeled over. The blow had been swift and powerful and the lad dropped to the ground unconscious. Benicio hurled himself at the boy and continued to beat him until Geru screamed something that brought him to himself.

'Benicio, you're going to kill him!'

Only then did he stop, but by now the boy's face was a bloody mess. At his sister's insistence, he picked the boy up like a dead cat and carried him home. When asked what had happened, he lied. 'A coconut fell on his head,' he said.

That night the parents of the injured boy went to speak to José and Betina.

'Out of the respect I have for your family and the past that we share, I am not going to kill Benicio yet, I will give him an opportunity to leave the village,' said the father. Mortified, José and Betina swore that they would punish their son and this they did. Benicio was locked in his room for a week. When eventually he was allowed out, he grabbed every boy he met by the throat and forced him to strip in front of everyone to humiliate him; the adults he encountered he shoved brutishly aside like rag dolls, such was his phenomenal strength.

'You can't go on treating people like this, Benicio. You have to control your temper,' said Geru, but Grandfather simply said, 'I can't help it.'

Every night he would weep helplessly, cursing every inch of the person he had become. Gertrudis too would cry and dry his tears. In her eyes, Grandfather was still the noble Benicio no one ever saw, like a prisoner condemned to live in some cramped space inside his chest. Gertrudis's sweet smile reminded him that life was not about assaulting people, throwing stones at cows, or wringing the necks of the neighbours' chickens in order to start a fight; it was not about finding some excuse to vent his fury, pounding someone's face to a pulp without caring how much that person might mean to his family, without thinking of the ties of friendship between them since everyone in Pata de Puerco had watched Benicio grow up.

'That boy is a menace. He is worse than El Mozambique,' the villagers complained to José and Betina. The Mandingas did everything they could to calm them, promising to buy another chicken, or buy clothes for their child, promising to make sure it would never happen again.

One morning Geru and Benicio went off to buy groceries at Chinaman Li's store and, on their way back, they ran into Jacinta and her brother Ignacio. Ignacio el Jabao had also grown, but he was still shorter than Benicio. He was beginning to grow a blond beard which made him look much older.

'*Hola*, Benicio,' said Jacinta. 'We're heading down to the river later, do you want to come?'

'To the river? Um . . .'

'No, Benicio, you have too much work to do,' said Geru coldly. Benicio looked at her angrily. He did not want to argue, so he signalled to Jacinta, to let her know that he would come down to the river. Then Ignacio stepped forward and said, 'Geru, I know you'll think this is just me being dumb but I got a present for you a while ago and I was hoping to give it to you this afternoon.' My grandfather's ears began to burn and flushed a deep red. As he raised his fist, Gertrudis pushed him aside. 'You keep your nose out of other people's business, Benicio,' she said, then, 'Thank you Ignacio, that's very kind of you.'

'Have you gone mad, Geru? Remember what Papá told us: no Jabaos and no white people.'

'Jacinta is a Jabao too. Anyway, I'll do what I want. It's my life and I won't have Papá or you making my decisions for me.'

'Wicked!' said Ignacio, or whatever kids said back then. 'So you'll come and get the present?'

'Of course. Together to the end of the world.'

Geru slipped her arm through Ignacio's and together they walked back towards the village. Benicio watched them walk away and said nothing. Jacinta pressed her lips to his ear, whispering that Geru was a bore, that he should forget about her, while she had just made some delicious *pan con tomate*. 'Maybe you could tell me one of your jokes.'

Still Grandpa Benicio said nothing, he simply stood staring at Geru as she walked arm in arm with Ignacio. Jacinta went on talking, but her voice reverberated in his ears like a faint echo.

When they got to the village, Ignacio gave Geru a huge bunch of beautiful flowers unlike anything anyone had ever given her: roses, hibiscus, orchids; no one knew where Ignacio could have found such things. Grandfather witnessed the presentation.

'Pretty, aren't they?' said Ignacio, smiling, and Geru kissed him on the cheek before they wandered off together up the hill. Jacinta asked Grandpa Benicio what was wrong, but the truth was even he could not explain. He said perhaps they should go to the river some other day and then rushed home and shut himself in his room.

In his letters, Melecio had not described what it was like, the fire he felt when his hands moved over María's body. He had simply said it was intense and that it burned. He did not say he had trembled, that it was not just his skin, but his insides that burned; nor that his heart had hammered against his ribs and he had found himself weeping with sheer help-lessness and rage; he had not said it was a feeling that went far beyond desire. For this was how Benicio had felt as he watched Geru's pursed lips graze Ignacio's cheek.

Many years later, Grandfather would consider himself a lucky man that he could pinpoint the precise moment when he knew he was in love. It happened on that day, in that unforgettable moment when El Jabao took his sister by the arm and walked her back towards the village. This was the first time Grandfather wept for Geru. And yet he did not know when it was he had come to love her in this way. Many years later, remembering the past, he came to the conclusion that he had been in love with her all his life. He had always been captivated by her delicacy, though José and Betina thought of her as a daisy surrounded by thorns because, according to them, she was sickly like her Aunt Malena.

Grandfather had slept beside her every night while she had suffered her various illnesses; he had even been there the night she became a woman. When she woke up the next morning in a pool of blood, Geru's first reaction was to check that Grandpa Benicio was not hurt. The blood was coming from between her legs, a sight that she found spellbinding, since her favourite colour had always been red. Neither of them understood what had happened. Benicio looked at Geru's delicate face in terror, but his sister laughed, revealing those teeth that were the sun itself.

Benicio would always remember the night when Geru hugged him so hard he could not breathe. He might not have been as clever as Melecio, but he knew the meaning behind those hugs, Geru's sweaty fingers and her pounding heart against his back. He did not need to be told, since he felt exactly the same. From the moment they could express their thoughts, they had shared with each other their innermost secrets, their dreams, their confidences; there had always been a special chemistry between them. He never had the courage to tell her that he loved her more than anything, that to him she was the most important thing in the universe.

He answered her with his silence, with deeds rather than words, as do those who truly love, and the passing time simply strengthened the bonds between them.

That afternoon Benicio wept inconsolably, imagining Geru kissing Ignacio's freckled lips. Betina came into his room with a jug of linden tea, stroked his head and said nothing. She knew all too well what was happening. For some time now she had seen in her children's eyes the defiance and the arrogance of passion. By the time Geru came back from her walk with Ignacio, Benicio was asleep.

'Wake up, Benicio.'

'What is it?'

'Nothing. I just wanted to say I'm sorry.'

'Sorry about what?'

'About what happened this afternoon. The truth is Ignacio and his flowers mean nothing to me. I only did it to make you jealous.'

Benicio choked back his words and, as always, answered only with his silence.

From that day, they became inseparable. Benicio watched Geru blossom into a woman whose beauty and radiance were obvious not only to him, who loved her already. Everyone in Pata de Puerco was bewitched by her beauty, because Geru was radiance itself. She had inherited the honey-brown eyes and purple lips of Betina but she was taller and more slender and her jet-black hair had a natural shine that lit up her face. Everyone believed that the closeness between them was that of brother and sister. Only Betina noticed another bond between them, something more passionate, more dangerous.

Benicio knew that his feelings would have grave consequences, that it would be difficult for others to understand
since, at the end of the day, they were brother and sister.
Though they were not related by blood. This was in their
favour. Even so, José would see their relationship as a curse
from the saints, a dark, bitter card that fate had dealt him;
one he did not deserve since in spite of his failings he had
been a good father, a good friend, and an excellent
neighbour.

'Papá, I need to talk to you,' Benicio said to José one day
when they were working together in the vegetable garden.

'Of course, son. If it's about you being in love with Jacinta,
don't worry, she likes you. It's just a matter of time. Your
sister is a different matter. I've seen that little bastard Ignacio
hanging around her recently. That really is worrying, because
the first boy to touch Geru, I'll cut his balls off.'

Benicio changed the subject. He talked about the
weather, about how they had had no news from Melecio,
about how much he missed his brother. When they had
finished digging, he went into the living room and found
his sister coming out of her room. Geru looked different,
there was an intensity about her and in her eyes he thought
he could see that the same secret was eating away at both of
them. José came into the house, took off his boots, kissed
his daughter and went into the bedroom where Betina was
already sleeping. They stood frozen, love driven like a spike
into their hearts.

That night neither of them could sleep. Neither dared to
move a muscle. Benicio remembered what José had said and
the words drummed inside his head but, weighing the

betrayal of his father's trust against what he felt for Geru, he came to the conclusion that his love for his sister was stronger than what he felt for José.

'This is unbearable,' he thought. He loved Geru more than he loved José and Betina who had raised him, given him a home. He spent the next week swimming against the tide of his conflicting feelings, feeling bitter at life when he thought of his incongruous situation. He tried to distance himself from his sister as much as possible, he moved out of the bedroom and began sleeping in Melecio's room; whenever he saw Geru coming he ran the other way; he even tried seeing Jacinta again, to make up for lost time, but none of these things worked: still the love lingered like a threat within his breast.

José and Betina were asleep the night that Geru came to him with tears in her eyes and confessed: 'I've been feeling different about you, Benicio. I don't know how to explain it.' Benicio looked up into her face but he could not think what to say. He did not have the courage to tell her he felt the same, that the feeling slowly eating him up inside was not the ordinary love between brother and sister.

It began to rain. Still Geru stared into Benicio's eyes then, bowing her head, she left the shack and headed for the flame tree, soaking her thin cotton dress. Benicio watched as her slim figure melted into the rain, as the dress clung to her skin, emphasising the curve of her breasts, the beauty of her exquisite body. Like a sleepwalker, he followed her. He watched as rain lashed her face, washing away her tears of frustration. Stepping beneath the branches of the flame tree, they sought the warmth and shelter of the trunk. Geru and

Benicio kneeled down. He took her in his arms, felt her warm breath against his throat.

'We are no longer brother and sister now,' said Geru.

'Why do you say that?'

'Because I want you to do with me as you will.'

His dreams were soaked by the rain. Geru pulled him to her nervously, opening the doors to his imprisoned desires. They rolled on the ground, heedless of the flame tree's roots which tore at their skin until they bled. Their screams were howls of freedom, of pain and pleasure. Benicio, who did not know what he was doing, let his intuition guide him, kissing Geru's body, pressing her to his chest as though she might pierce his ribcage and remain inside him for ever, and he went on hugging her to him until orgasm came, hard and shuddering like a white-hot explosion. They tried to lie still, to recover from the pain, the frustration, the breathlessness of enchantment and pleasure, but it was impossible; their bodies continued to spasm as though they had a will of their own.

'Who's there?' said a gruff voice, booming like a thunder-clap against the tree sheltering them. They knew the voice. 'What's all that screaming? Whoever you are, come out of there!' It was pointless to run; they would be recognised. Their hearts began to pound once more and Benicio, seeing the terror in Geru's eyes, stepped out from the shade of the flame tree and faced the man. 'It's me, Papá José,' he said standing in the moonlit clearing. 'Benicio. What was all that howling? You sounded like an animal.' Benicio watched as José's face grew harder, his brows knotting into an expression of concern. 'What . . . what are you doing out here naked?' Silence. 'I don't believe it. So you finally managed to conquer Jacinta?'

Geru emerged from beneath the tree, her shoulders bare, her clothes clasped over her breasts. Her face wet, she stared shamefully at the ground. For the first time in his life, José did not know what to say. He stood, paralysed, staring at them as though they were ghosts, as though they were two phantoms returning to the forest from the river. There was not a single star in the sky although the night was cloudless: he could see every detail, every contour of even the smallest thing as though some angel had gifted him with night vision.

José said nothing. He did not howl with rage, nor did he beat them with the walking stick he had whittled from a ceiba branch. He tormented them with his silence, with the look of pained disbelief in eyes that flashed in the moonlight. Then he turned his back on them and, shoulders stooped, he hobbled away, drained of his customary vitality. Around him reigned an utter stillness, an emptiness.

When Benicio and Gertrudis arrived back at the house, José was sitting in his chair, and there he sat until the morning. He did not look at them now. His eyes were cast down. Betina did it for him, her glassy stare stabbing at her children's eyes. There was no place for Geru and Benicio in this room. Shamefaced, they retreated to their bedroom, Benicio hugging to him a sobbing, half-naked Geru, who buried her face in his chest as in some dark refuge.

The following morning they found José where they had left him, his mouth twisted to one side, his eyes filled with tears and clotted with sleep. Betina was hunkered on the floor next to him, her hair wild as though she had just escaped from an asylum. 'He's paralysed all down the right side of his body,' was the diagnosis of Juanita the *santera*. 'But don't worry, he'll recover quickly.'

Betina and Juanita took José by the shoulders and managed to lift him out of the chair. When Benicio tried to help, José jerked at his arm and mumbled something unintelligible.

'*Owww* . . . Oww of my hhhouse.'

Grandfather took a step back. He looked at Geru. They both stood, frozen. The silence was agonising and seemed to go on for ever. Grandfather could not bear it. 'To hell with it, I'll go then. After all, it's not as though you are my real parents.'

Tears streamed down Betina's face. José's shoulders began to pump like pistons and the good side of his face shrank a little more, then he gave a curt wave of his hand to signal to Benicio to leave. Grandfather took some things from his room and left the house. Geru followed him.

'You know that what you just said will make them miserable for the rest of their lives,' she said, remaining a little distant.

'It will make me miserable too,' said Grandfather.

Once again there was silence, broken this time by a northerly breeze.

'I don't know if this will help, but I will say it anyway. I once knew a boy who saved a young ram that had been bitten by a dog. The poor animal was lying in the road and whimpering with fear. The boy picked it up and brought it home. He fed the ram until it could walk again. A lot of people would have raised it, fattened it up so they could kill and eat it. But this boy took it out into the Accursed Forest and, halfway up the hill, he set it free.'

'That was me,' said Benicio.

'Exactly. That was you. The real Benicio.'

And then they embraced. It was only in these moments of profound remorse that the good in Benicio resurfaced. But by then it was invariably too late.

'Think about that,' said Gertrudis again.

Benicio kissed her passionately then set off down the path towards the Callejón de la Rosa heading nowhere. Geru stood for a while longer, watching as he slowly melted into the verdant sea of plants and trees.

Mangaleno

On the Callejón de la Rosa, Benicio encountered Ester the midwife who looked as though she had been waiting for him for some time. She was wearing the same clothes as when Grandfather had first met her outside Chinaman Li's store. In a faltering voice she begged him to go with her to her house, insisting that he had to come right now. Having nowhere to go, Grandfather agreed and followed the midwife back down Callejón de la Rosa in the opposite direction to El Cobre.

They went into her house. Ester gestured for him to sit down on one of the four makeshift wooden chairs set around the table. The room was dark but this was partly because the day was overcast. There were two east-facing windows in front of which stood a table covered by a sun-scorched red tablecloth and a kerosene lamp. There were two more windows facing directly west. The bleached tablecloth was proof that Ester opened these windows every morning and her room was scourged by the sun from the moment it rose until the moment it set. This idea made Benicio think that, contrary to village gossip, Ester was a cheerful woman after all, or had been at some point in her life.

Ester reappeared with a can of guava juice, handed it to Benicio and then anxiously sat next to him, staring at him intently.

'You're the spitting image of him,' she said, with a look that was more sad than surprised.

'Of who?'

'Of your father.'

'You know my father?'

'Of course. These hands . . .' Ester held out her calloused hands in the lamplight. 'These hands were the first that ever held you.'

'If you were there when I was born, then you must have seen my parents die.' At this, Ester felt a lump in her throat, a lump that twisted her words, forcing her to swallow hard. 'My family would never tell me what happened. Papá José used to talk to me about his friend Oscar, but he never talked to me about Oscar being my father. They told me my mother's name was Malena and that she died giving birth to me. Were you there when my father killed himself?'

The midwife hesitated a moment.

'No, but I know what happened.'

'What did happen?'

'He cut his wrists.'

'Cut his wrists! That's a coward's way out.'

'Not everyone has the courage to go on living.'

They sat in silence for a moment. Grandfather did not want to keep digging up the past, he wanted to bury it. Now that José and Betina had thrown him out of the house, he felt as though he too were buried. It was perhaps the only thing he shared with his real parents.

'I had a premonition it would happen,' Ester went on, 'I knew it would happen sooner or later. I wanted to tell you that you are not alone.'

'What do you mean I'm not alone?'

'I mean you've got us.'

'And who exactly is "us"?'

'El Mozambique and me.'

Grandfather burst out laughing and got to his feet.

'Don't make me laugh, Ester. El Mozambique? The most hated man in these parts? I still haven't forgotten how he tried to rob my amulet. That man has never cared for anyone in his life.'

'You're wrong. Nobody knows him as I know him. Believe me when I say that you and he have a lot more in common than you might think. Starting with the fact that you're both utterly alone.'

'I'm not alone. I have Geru.'

'You have Geru, that's true. But absence makes the heart grow cold. You'll see how things change, now you've been thrown out of the house. At first, you'll see each other every other day. Then days will turn into weeks until lack of physical contact chills your bodies and one day, when you least expect it, you'll find yourself no longer caring and in time forgetting. Give El Mozambique a chance, everyone deserves that. Besides, I know he likes you because you are the only person he has ever allowed into his house. The only one. That's why I think there's still a chance.'

'A chance?'

'To save you both.'

'Listen, Ester, I'm not going to waste my time on El

Mozambique. You said I was the spitting image of my father, so I assumed what you had to say to me was about him. So, are you going to tell me the story or not?'

'When he was ten years old,' Ester began, 'Oscar was sold to the owner of a large plantation named Giacomo Benvenuto. In 1868 war broke out. Oscar and José joined the *mambí* army under the command of General Antonio Maceo and, a few years later, they met Malena and her sister Betina. They pledged undying love beneath an avocado tree and, as time passed, Geru, Melecio and you were born.'

'I know all that, Ester.'

'Do you want me to tell you how . . .'

'No, I want you to tell me everything.'

'Everything?'

'Everything.'

The midwife took a deep breath, so deep that for a moment she seemed to suck all of the oxygen from the room.

'Very well, Benicio, I shall tell you everything. Macuta Dos, Oscar's mother, was as short as he was. She had two older brothers. Their parents had long since passed away long ago and had to be buried together because they were both found dead one morning with their arms so entwined around each other no one could prise them apart. When she was a little girl, Macuta Dos was convinced that the edge of the earth was somewhere on the outskirts of Pata de Puerco, that beyond the bounds of the slave quarters there was nothing but shadows and forests of flame. The idea had come to her in a dream she had while afflicted by a strange rash that almost killed her. Her dreams began with this mysterious disease which some people blamed on the urine of a large yellow hutia that appeared one day in the slave quarters and was never seen again. Others claimed it was the result of some magic by the Efik people with their ganga drums or the machinations of the Mayombe tribes, because it was not just Macuta Dos, but a dozen other slaves who fell ill, all of whom were immediately placed in quarantine to be cured of the rash, the itch and the fever brought on by the disease.

'In her fever dreams, Macuta Dos saw the past and the future, and sometimes she saw secrets and mysteries entangled in the trees of Pata de Puerco. One of those who appeared to her in these dreams was a *wije* – a spirit – named Bonifacio who wore a loincloth and claimed to be her guardian angel. No taller than a gnome, with frizzy hair and gleaming teeth, the *wije* Bonifacio knew everything: he revealed to her the precise day on which her brothers – who since the age of ten had been her only relatives – would die, and everything about the slave revolt which would bring about ruin on the Santisteban sugar plantation. He told her that she had something evil in her belly, that she would never know the love of a man and that her life would be empty and meaningless. All this Macuta Dos learned, just as she learned that she would live to see all those she loved perish and that before she got to heaven she would endure hell.

'On the very day she became a woman, the *wije* vanished from her dreams. Macuta Dos would talk to him in dark corners when she was alone, though she could not see him and did not expect him to trouble to reply, but the world is full of miseries, after all, compared to which her wishes were insignificant. She had but one wish in life: she wanted a child.

'She began working on the plantation, feeding the animals, cleaning and drawing water from the well. Since she was a strong, muscular Negress, they set her to cutting cane with the menfolk and gave her so many backbreaking chores that often she worked twenty-two hours a day.

'On one of the countless days that Macuta Dos prayed and hoped the *wije* might hear her prayers, in one of the countless murky corridors on the plantation she encountered a small black man she recognised as the *wije* Bonifacio. He smelled of charred forests and he wore the same loincloth and had the same frizzy hair and gleaming teeth as when he appeared in her dreams. The *wije* told her he had been sent to her by Yusi the Warrior since God did not intend to answer her prayers. Bonifacio told Macuta Dos not to worry, because he would give her a child. He gestured for her to come close and whispered, 'Tombo,' then he kissed her gently on the lips. The moment she touched the *wije*'s thin lips, which tasted of ripe mango, Macuta Dos knew that she would bear a son to a man named Tombo, but she had no idea who this man might be.

'One week later, a new consignment of slaves arrived at the plantation. Among them was Tombo, a pureblood Kortico four feet tall with velvety black skin and an impulsive character. The attraction between them was almost instantaneous and nine months later Macuta Dos gave birth to Oscar. Just as the *wije* had predicted, there was no love between them. Tombo was cruel and quick-tempered and the few times they had sex, he would cover her head with a sack or push her underwater so that she could not breathe. But Macuta Dos expected these things because the *wije*

Bonifacio had forewarned her. Just as she knew that Tombo's days were numbered.

'"Oscar, say goodbye to your papá," Macuta Dos said to her son on the last night they spent together as a family. Tombo picked the boy up and kissed him on the cheek. The child wailed, he could sense something; but his parents simply looked at him in silence. The following morning at dawn, Tombo escaped into the hills. He was brought back that same afternoon dead, the skin flayed from his body, his face unrecognisable. They dragged him from the dense scrubland and strung him up in the middle of the plantation to serve as a lesson to others. Then they buried him in a secret place halfway up the mountain to obliterate any trace of him. Never again would anyone mention the name of the Kortico Tombo.

'Time passed. Macuta Dos went on with her backbreaking chores and Oscar went on growing. Every night, Macuta Dos would shrug off her tiredness and tell her son stories from her native Africa, about how the Korticos were a tribe of fearsome warriors who knew the secret ways of plants. She told him that in Africa, even boys hunted with spears, though during their training many ended up in the maws of lions. Macuta Dos raised Oscar until the day she was locked away in a dark room with Tampico, a man who had the misfortune to have two metal bars by way of arms and a pillar of chiselled black marble by way of a torso. His legs were thick trunks of ebony, the very sight of him instilled terror.

'On the Santisteban plantation, Tampico was the man who turned the wheel for the sugar mill and the coffee mill. This task, which usually required three or more slaves, he did alone. He could carry fifty buckets of water a day, in addition to cutting cane. He was a clumsy, gruff, slow-witted Negro like a sleepy giant and he stammered when he talked. But he was very useful, according to Don Manuel who, from the moment he first bought the slave, recognised that Tampico had been born into this world to toil and sweat until he died. And so this muscular Negro lived his life exhausted and in pain because of his work on the Santisteban plantation.

'Manuel Santisteban had bought him in Havana; he had bought only Tampico, not his wife or his children. When he arrived in Pata de Puerco, Tampico found that everything was barren and desolate. No one knew him, no one spoke to him, people looked at him fearfully and in the slave quarters kept as far away from him as possible. And so, gradually, he began to grieve for the life he had left behind before he had been captured and shipped to Cuba.

'In the first few weeks, he obeyed every order and was meek as a lamb. But precisely a month after he arrived, he suffered a bout of depression and began to strangle any living thing that crossed his path. The steward and the overseers believed he was possessed, but on the strict orders of Don Manuel no one dared lay a finger on him. "We must find him a mate. Lock him in a dark room with Macuta Dos," suggested Don Manuel, and this they did.

'As she was torn away from Oscar, Macuta Dos realised that her dreams of shadows and forests of flame were nothing more than shadows of her own life. Nothing could compare with the pain of losing her beloved son Oscar. This is why she did not flinch when the giant Tampico pinned her to the wooden floor, nor when he straddled her like a rutting bull, biting at her breasts and sucking at her neck like a vampire. She allowed herself to be dragged along by the whim of destiny and nine months later a son was born.

'"We'll call him Satanás," suggested one of the female slaves. Macuta nodded her head in approval. "Satanás is the name of the devil. Damián is nicer," said another woman in the barracks. Again Macuta nodded in agreement. In the end the dozen or so slave women, fighting to pick an appropriate name for the boy, decided upon Mangaleno. For the fourth time Macuta gave her consent. She did not care because she already sensed her own life ebbing away. Reluctantly, she suckled the child, feeding him her frustrations and her pain at having lost her beloved son Oscar.

'Mangaleno grew up in the shadow of his brother. He knew no love, except for the love his mother daily professed for Oscar. She would talk about Oscar to herself and sometimes referred to Mangaleno as Oscar so that from his earliest childhood he learned to despise the name. "I'm not Oscar, I'm Mangaleno," the boy would say furiously, but nothing changed.

'So it was that Mangaleno grew up longing for a life he never lived, a life that for him could never exist. He had no choice but to rise from the ashes of his miserable existence and add more suffering to the suffering he had already amassed.

'At the time the Slaughter of the Santistebans took place, Mangaleno had just turned thirteen. The blockhouse was one of the first places torched by the slaves and in all the chaos and all the shouts of joy and freedom, no one realised that Macuta Dos had deliberately remained inside. But Mangaleno knew she was in there and ran to rescue his mother. He dashed through the flames, oblivious to the pain as they burned his skin, and he searched among the rubble until, beneath a burning beam, he found a bundle that had a human form. His mother lay dying, her frail body half-charred, her head a mass of red and black blisters that spread all over her skin. Mangaleno doused the flames and lifted her up, wrapped her in his shirt, cradled her in his arms and clutched her to his chest as though she were a newborn, then he ran straight at the nearest wall which offered no resistance, it crumbled, and Mangaleno kept on running frantically as far as the river, hoping with every step that he might still save not only his mother's life, but his own.

'"Don't leave me, Mamá, don't leave me alone," he begged, pressing her to him. "I love you, Oscar," were the last words Macuta Dos ever spoke as she stared into the eyes of Mangaleno: two dark pools, a vast universe of hatred and bitterness.

'From that day, Mangaleno had only one goal in life: to track down this man he hated more than anyone on the face of the earth, this man who had stolen his mother's love, who had ruined his life, this man he had never met but whom he dreamed about every day, thought about every minute, this ghost of a man named Oscar. His was a simple life. Other people had to worry about learning to read or write, about being loved or admired, about acquiring a trade or being loyal to their family. Not he. He had been put on earth with the sole purpose of using every ounce of strength to make Oscar suffer.

'But to wound, to wound deeply, one must be patient. This was something Mangaleno understood even as a child.

And so he waited until he had grown into a man. In the year 1878 Mangaleno was twenty-five years old and his body was a lethal weapon, not simply because he shared his father's genes, but because he had spent his every waking hour exercising, carrying logs, cutting cane, dreaming of the day when he would be avenged. It was in that same year that Oscar and José, with their respective wives, settled in Pata de Puerco. Mangaleno was already here, waiting for him. He assumed that since he was hatred incarnate, then Oscar must be his antithesis, meaning someone who felt fulfilled, happy, in other words a romantic, and romantics invariably returned to their birthplace. This was why he had spent years here in a remote shack he had built with his own hands, patiently waiting like an alligator for its prey.

'But Oscar did not come alone. And what is the most effective way to make a man suffer? To hurt that which he most loves. This is what Mangaleno planned to do. He devoted himself to hounding Malena. He found out everything there was to know about her; that she fell ill at least once a month, that she was quiet and reserved, that she often made a pilgrimage to the church at El Cobre. He knew that in the church she prayed for everyone, for her family, for her friends, for strangers and even for a world ravaged by poverty, which proved that Malena had the temperament of a saint; she was a woman who preferred to conceal her pain so as not to hurt others, a woman who had long since learned to suffer in silence.

'The most important fact was that, after she had prayed for the world and its misfortunes, Malena always concluded with a dozen prayers for her soul and that of her husband Oscar, the love of her life, the one man who had taught her how to love. Mangaleno could not believe it could be so easy. He licked his lips, realising that in Malena he had found the perfect means of destroying the life of his mortal enemy.

'On one such afternoon, Mangaleno lay in wait on the Callejón de la Rosa. Malena appeared looking happy, radiant. The sun had set by the time Mangaleno confronted her, grabbing her by the throat as though she were a meek dove. She tried to resist, began to scream only to be silenced by two blows to the face that left her dazed. Mangaleno covered her mouth but he did not cover her eyes so that she would be able to see his spider's soul and his overflowing hatred. He bit her neck until blood began to spurt from her veins, he covered her breasts with bitemarks, blood-sucking bruises that would never fade. Then he thrust into her, again and again until he saw her eyes well with tears of pain and rage. Having satisfied his ancient and twisted desires, he tossed her into the grass. Then he buttoned his breeches and walked away smiling, leaving Malena's groans behind, groans that seemed to come from a mouth with no tongue, no lips; it was the sweetest revenge he could have had. "The happiest day of my life," as he would describe the moment years later.

'Yet still he continued to spy on her, slipping among the trees, and did the same to Oscar as he worked in his vegetable garden; he even followed him when he went to Chinaman Li's store. He quickly realised that Oscar knew nothing of what had happened, that Malena had buried her secret even as her belly was already beginning to swell with the fruit of lovelessness and hatred.

'"He who does not see, does not know. He who does not

know, does not suffer." Oscar was not suffering. Mangaleno realised that Oscar was living his life as through nothing had happened and that was something he could not allow. He writhed to think that the man he most loathed was living a life without pain. He spent a long time looking for some way of hurting him more effectively. He tried to discredit him with the other *macheteros*, hacking off the leg of their mare, but nothing worked. Oscar carried on with his life, his idyllic life with Malena, as though nothing had happened, while Mangaleno carried on raging that he could not find a means to bury him.

'When he heard gossip that Malena was pregnant, he went to check. He hid behind some trees and watched the couple argue. Oscar could not understand how his wife could have become pregnant. He gesticulated wildly, and the more he waved his hands, the more Mangaleno licked his lips. This, he saw, was his sweet revenge, something that would make his half-brother writhe in pain and remorse, a pain that would dog him like a shadow to the end of his days. Mangaleno had only to wait for the child to be born. Nine months later, you were born. What happened next, you already know.'

Grandpa Benicio sat, slack-jawed, confused, pressing the amulet to his chest, not knowing what to do, what to say.

'But . . . but what does it all mean?'

'It means that Mangaleno raped your mother,' the midwife said simply.

'But . . .'

At that moment the door flew open. Benicio and Ester leapt to their feet.

'Mangaleno!' cried Ester, her voice tremulous with fear.

Turning his head, Benicio found himself face to face with El Mozambique.

'Thank you, Ester. Now go into the kitchen, my son and I need to talk.'

'Don't you dare call me that,' said Benicio.

'What would you like me to call you? Don't be stupid, Benicio. Did you really think a four-foot pygmy could have given you that body of yours? Don't make me laugh.'

Benicio did not say anything, he could not understand anything. He glared at El Mozambique, eyes blazing, then looked to Ester as though waiting for her to say that it had all been a joke.

'Don't believe me if you don't want to. Check for yourself. Ester, fetch the tin,' ordered El Mozambique. Ester went into the kitchen and brought back a sheet of nickel-plated tin like a mirror. She handed it to El Mozambique who stepped closer to Benicio, smiling viciously, and pressed his face against the boy's.

'Tell me then, what do you see?'

Benicio stared at the two faces. He saw the same thick veins in the neck, the same square jaw, the same flat nose. His lips were slightly thinner and his cheekbones slightly less pronounced, but Benicio still had a lot of growing to do.

'It doesn't matter what you say, you're not my father. I'm not your son, and I never will be.'

'This isn't about what you want and what you don't want,' said El Mozambique, handing the tin plate back to Ester. 'My blood runs through your veins. I'm sure you're thinking, "*Carajo*, first I was told my father is José, then I

152

was told it's Oscar and now it turns out to be neither of them but the man despised by everyone." I know what that's like, and I don't expect you to accept me right away: I am the living face of hatred in this village. But as I told you once, hatred is not so bad. After all, it was hatred that conceived you. I don't think anyone can understand you as I do; I know what it is like to live with no one for company, to be spurned like a plague while having the person you most loved in all the world taken from you, as has happened to you, now you've been thrown out of your home and robbed of Geru simply because you feel for her something more than a brother's love.'

'Who the hell are you to talk about love?' said Benicio, and for the first time his eyes paled, like El Mozambique's.

'Me? No one. But if you think I don't know what it is, you are making a terrible mistake. Love is something that cannot be forgotten. This is why I raped Malena. An eye for an eye, I told myself. I could not bear the thought that the man who robbed me of what I most loved should go on living, feeding his soul with the hope of life eternal. All I wanted was the one thing I had never had because of that bastard Oscar. This is why I raped Malena, why I beat her, I did it to teach him about the pain he never knew.'

'You're a murderer, that's what you are.'

'A murderer? Let me think . . . It's true that I hacked the leg off Oscar's mare, and Evaristo's horse. But for all that, if we compare, I still come off the worse.'

Benicio fell silent. For an instant it seemed to him that the faces of Ester and El Mozambique belonged to a different species.

'Well, now you know. You are my son, whether you like it or not. My door is always open to you. But take your time. In the meantime, you can stay here with Ester. Besides my hounds will take time to get used to you.'

With that, El Mozambique set off back down the path. Benicio felt the air grow heavy, an air that did not smell of the countryside, did not smell of anything in nature. It was a rainstorm so heavy he could not breathe and for a moment he thought he might drown. Watching the figure of El Mozambique disappear into the distance, he thought this was the end. He was wrong. In fact, it was the beginning of a new life under his true identity.

Further News of Melecio

Gertrudis was the only one in the family who knew what had happened. When Benicio explained that Ester had told him El Mozambique was his real father, Geru told him not to listen, that Ester was half-mad; besides he knew who his father was. The argument was always the same.

'It's like Papá José told you: your parents are not those who gave birth to you, but those who raised you.'

'Parents don't throw their children out of the house,' said Benicio.

They would always make peace, with Benicio telling a joke or performing some trick with his hands that ended up with Gertrudis rolling on top of him and sending unforgettable feelings thrilling through him.

José and Betina knew nothing of this, but the other villagers quickly began to talk. Some said they had seen Benicio by the river with a heavyset man who looked a lot like El Mozambique. Others were not sure whether it really was Benicio or some relative of El Mozambique, since the resemblance between the two men was astounding. Still others went round to José and Betina to tell them rumours circulating about their son. Before long word spread that José had thrown his son out of the house, a story confirmed by the fact that Benicio and El Mozambique were often seen together.

The Santacruzes and the Aquelarres felt that even if Benicio was no longer the boy everyone had loved, it was their responsibility to watch over him and muttered darkly that his association with El Mozambique would have irreparable consequences for his education. The Jabaos for their part said that they had long since seen this catastrophe coming, that they knew better than anyone how much the boy had changed, but they agreed with Silvio and Rachel Aquelarre: Benicio should not be left to himself.

'Since you care so much about the boy, why don't you take him in?' said José simply. He wanted nothing to do with Grandfather. Benicio, he said, was a grown man who knew what he was doing and he was not about to give himself another stroke attempting to reason with him. Life in Pata de Puerco, had become a living hell, a theatre of furtive glances, glowering faces and awkward silences. For a long time, Benicio and Gertrudis felt their souls were unquiet, as though night would not come and bring them rest. Their sole consolation was the love that bound them and even this they had to temper so as not to grieve their parents even more.

Every morning, Gertrudis set off early to fetch Benicio from Ester's house and together they would head down to the river so that, when Betina rose to make breakfast, she did not have to deal with the awkwardness of finding her daughter at home. There in the dark waters beneath the sheltering canopy of green, they sought solace. Often they made love and the more they did so, the deeper grew this passion that left them gasping for breath, as though someone had poured a pitcher of water into their lungs. When they returned late at night they would sometimes see José sitting on the porch, his lips twisted in a grim rictus, a terrifying expression on his face. He would stare out at the horizon, gazing past them as though they were not people but merely dark shapes or shadows moving along the path.

Grandfather would turn on his heel and go back to Ester's house. So the days passed, and even when José's twisted grimace had been healed by Betina massaging his face daily, still he sat with that terrible look of disbelief, a look that it seemed might always be there.

Neighbours visited him, brought him gifts in the hope of lifting his spirits. José would thank them, nodding his head and withdrawing to his room where he could be alone.

'He is still not himself,' Betina would explain, and those who came to visit would nod. She would show them to the door and the following day the scene was played out again – gifts were brought, José nodded his thanks and Betina watched the neighbours leave: it was a ritual. It was thanks to these gifts that the Mandinga family managed to survive these difficult times.

Aureliano the coachman was the only person with whom José spent time, the only one to whom he would listen. Aureliano still visited regularly, bringing news of recent events across the country.

'Good afternoon, Aureliano. It is a pleasure to have you in our house again,' Gertrudis greeted the coachman on one of his visits.

'Our house! This is *my* house,' spluttered José, spraying spittle. '*I* built it.'

The coachman noticed the tension in the air. Betina looked at him and then scowled at José.

'The thing about you, José, is there's no stopping you,' said Aureliano. 'Anyone else might have become bitter at being paralysed, but not you. You've still got your sense of humour. You're always teasing the children, always joking. You haven't changed at all.'

'And how is Melecio?' asked Gertrudis.

'The young man is doing splendidly. María has taken him in hand, but that is a good thing. The other day he seized me by the arm and confessed that he is in love. Can you imagine? As though love were something he had just invented. I told him I was happy he had finally realised something the rest of us have known for an age. He asked whether it was really so obvious and I said that lovestruck man always has puppy-dog eyes – you know what I mean, those pleading, soulful eyes. "So I've turned into a dog," he said miserably. "Indeed you have, some time ago," I told him. Now let me just be clear, I think María has been the making of him; before she came along Melecio scarcely knew how to wash his own balls – if you'll excuse my language. These days he's always clean, his hair is combed, and I don't mean that tousled mop that looked like a bird's nest. I tell you, women truly are men's salvation! Am I right, José?'

'Or their damnation,' said José, glaring at Gertrudis.

'Exactly. One or the other. But in Melecio's case, as indeed in mine and in yours – because your wife here is truly an angel—' the coachman gestured to Betina who smiled, 'they are the best thing that could ever have happened.'

'The same is true for me,' said Gertrudis. Betina and José stared at her coldly.

'For you?' said the coachman. 'We were talking about women. Surely you're not saying that . . .'

'No. I am talking about a man. A man with many flaws, but his love for me is not among them.'

José got up from his chair. 'I've told you, out there the two of you can do what the hell you like. But this is my house and I make the rules here.'

'Ah! So little Gertrudis is in love!' said Aureliano. 'Why did no one tell me? Come now, José, it had to happen some time. I'm sure the boy is not so bad. Besides, as Señorita Gertrudis says, nobody's perfect. Don Emilio maintains that man is made up of mind, body, imperfections and extremities, and I believe he's right. And what is this about this being your house, José? Don't make me laugh. It belongs to Gertrudis too, and to Benicio. Where is young Benicio, by the way?'

'Benicio is no longer welcome in my house,' roared José.

Aureliano looked at Betina's face and saw Gertrudis begin to cry. Betina scolded José for treating his daughter in such a manner in front of Aureliano.

'Now I understand,' said the coachman, 'This is what brought on the paralysis. But you're wrong, José, not to accept your children for who they are. We cannot crawl inside our children's minds and force them to think as we do. They're in love? So what? In my family brothers marry sisters, cousins marry cousins, there's nothing wrong with that. I tell you I wouldn't be shocked if men married goats. If someone came to me and told me he was in love with a gorilla, I would say, "My best wishes to Señora Gorilla, I hope you have many baby gorillas; after all, deep down man is just another animal."'

'Whether deep down, in the middle or on the surface, I will not tolerate it. Is that understood?'

'José, don't upset yourself,' said Betina.

'Fetch me my walking stick, Betina, I'm going to the cemetery,' said José. He grabbed his ceiba cane and, muttering to himself, he left.

'Don't listen to him, Aureliano. He has suffered more than anyone from the two of them falling in love.'

'And what do you think?'

'Me? Obviously I agree with him.'

'But we're not really brother and sister, not by blood,' protested Gertrudis, drying her tears.

'You might just as well be. It's disgusting.'

'They're not related by blood?' said Aureliano. 'Well in that case I'm sorry, Señora Betina, but don't you think perhaps you are overreacting?'

Betina continued to insist that the relationship between Gertrudis and Benicio was disgusting while Aureliano insisted that they should not have thrown Benicio out of the house, that adolescence is a time of confusion during which it was crucial that parents practise tolerance.

'Well now, I think that is enough discussion for today,'

said the coachman, 'Why don't you make me a little coffee and I'll read you Melecio's letter?'

Five minutes later Betina returned with the coffee. Aureliano took an envelope from his jacket pocket and began to read to her about the exploits of her gifted son.

Melecio had begun to travel abroad. He had visited a place called San Juan in a country by the name of Puerto Rico, which was very much like Cuba. Puerto Rico had a Morro Castle with a lighthouse just like Havana. Melecio designed a building there, and another in a city called New York a long way north of Cuba in the United States, a cold country where snow fell from the sky.

As Aureliano read on, the letter took a darker turn, Melecio was unhappy. There was a strangeness in his tone: a longing, a confusion; something was not right. It was as though he had left adolescence behind and become a man who shared with Melecio only his name, his face. The other Melecio, the one they all knew, had stayed behind in Pata de Puerco. These were his words. He was tired, he wrote, of living another's man's life, far from his birthplace, far from this village built without a single brick, where concrete was unknown, exiled from the far-flung place that was his true home.

He could hardly complain, he wrote, since the Bacardí family had lavished such generosity on him, something he felt he ill-deserved since deep down he sensed that he was not quite normal. Melecio had got it into his head that he was a cross between a human and some other animal, a dolphin, perhaps, given his love of the sea. He lived his life hoping for something, something that had not yet arrived.

Sometimes he wondered whether the stillness that consumed his days, this peace that filled his mind was what people called happiness.

He sometimes argued with Bacardí's architects and associates because, he said, they regarded him not as a person but as a dollar sign (the dollar he explained was the money used in the United States and had recently begun to circulate in Cuba). Someone had told him that talent was not what was important in life, that talent was irrelevant: the most important thing, what conferred power, what governed everything, was money.

'OK, why don't *you* design some buildings? Let's see how much money they make,' Melecio told the man. Afterwards, people came running after him to apologise, as though they had suddenly lost the source of all this money everyone was constantly talking about. Melecio was tired of all the hypocrisy.

On several occasions, Bacardí took him to the Teatro Tacón. Never had Melecio felt more ill at ease. People looked him up and down, unable to believe their eyes: a Negro in evening dress at the theatre, and in the company of Don Emilio Bacardí no less! Emilio always introduced him with great ceremony as though Melecio was the most extraordinary creation in the universe and everyone would smile their plastic smiles and go on looking him up and down, watching as he walked, whispering among themselves or suddenly bursting into laughter, something Melecio could not bear.

In his years away from Pata de Puerco, Melecio explained, what had meant most to him was not the culture or the wisdom he had assimilated, but the sex he had with María. It was something extraordinary; they did it all the time, rolling about in the grass, in rivers, in banana plantations and the act itself was a mingling of the poems he recited and the songs María sang melding together in whimpers of pleasure, howls of pain, and everything in between, into a strange, deep deliciousness more intense than anything he had ever experienced. Melecio added that he was not mad and he did not expect anyone to understand, but he knew what he was talking about. This part of the letter made everyone laugh. But afterwards the letter returned to his melancholy, his homesickness, to a trace of regret that shrivelled the hearts of Betina and Gertrudis to the size of a kernel of corn.

One day he set aside his drawings and his books of poetry, went to the supervisor who oversaw architectural projects for the Bacardí family and told him he no longer wanted to design.

'Why not?' asked the man worriedly.

Melecio answered that he had worked out something which he called the Brick Theory, according to which the brick was the most devilish thing in existence. Not that he expected anyone else to understand, he stressed, but nonetheless he was no longer prepared to design.

'Brick Theory? What are you talking about, Melecio?' said the man. 'Bricks are used to construct buildings and hospitals.'

'True,' replied Melecio, 'but they are also used to build the opulent houses of the rich, the men who control parliament, the lawyers and the landowners.'

'Bricks feed people's dreams, mostly feverish dreams of

power, of wanting to possess. People start off wanting a small brick house, then they long for a mansion and since it is in the nature of man to always want more, when they have finally acquired luxurious carriages and ships, acquired a family and all the comforts that a family requires, they find themselves wanting to possess other people. The easiest way to do this is to take possession of a country. And so a man runs for president, holds meetings, throws cocktail parties where he serves exquisite delicacies to those who belong to the elite, by which they mean his friends, those people who also live in mansions built of bricks, those people who share his interests. Once elected president, men pass laws in order to protect their property and that of those faithful friends without whom their rise to the presidency would have been impossible. They build roads in the name of prosperity and embezzle millions of pesos in the process. They build hundreds of hospitals, as you said, and dozens of schools but they build them for the benefit of their sons, their nephews, their brothers, their uncles, all those who, like them, are privileged to live in brick houses. And this is where bricks stop. They never reach the villages of mud and ditches and timber shacks, villages like the one where I was raised, those places where most of the citizens of this country live. With every brick I lay, I feel I am contributing to the starvation and the misery of my own people and, what is worse, I am adding to the wealth of the corrupt. That is my Brick Theory. It's something I don't expect you to understand, but from today, for me those dreams of concrete and cement are over.'

'But where will you go?' said the supervisor. Melecio left

him hanging and went to explain his theory to Don Emilio Bacardí. Don Emilio replied that his proposition was somewhat curious but accepted that Melecio had a perfect right to hold it.

'Curious in what way?' asked Melecio.

'It is curious because human cruelty was invented by our ancestors,' answered Bacardí.

Melecio did not understand.

'The Greeks and the Romans were the first to invent evil. From them, over the centuries, it was handed down from generation to generation. And where did our forefathers come by evil? Well, if it is true that God made man, then the answer lies above. What I mean by that is that man is possessed of all manner of impulses, good and evil, greed and good sense, jealousy and generosity. The best we can hope is the good in man represents the greater part. If you don't like this life, if you don't enjoy living it, you have every right to reject it, but the fact that a man might be greedy, jealous and sometimes even murderous should come as no surprise to anyone.'

They stood for a long time looking closely at each other. Then Melecio hugged Emilio Bacardí long and hard, the embrace of a son for his father.

'If that's true, then you should know that the lion's share of my gratitude I owe to you,' said Melecio at length. Then he explained that he needed to change his life because he felt unhappy; that if he did not he would become miserable. 'All I see around me here is wickedness,' he said. And then, without another word, he embraced Emilio again and walked back to the house.

He went to look for María.

'I have to keep my promise. It is time for me to go home.'

'Let me come with you.'

'No, if I am alone, I can teach more quickly. I will come back and fetch you. Wait for me.'

'I'll be here.'

So concluded his encounter with María.

José still had not returned from the cemetery by the time Aureliano had finished reading the letter. Betina prepared some food. Gertrudis excused herself, explaining that she had something she needed to do, then she ran to Grandpa Benicio.

'What did Papá and Mamá say?' asked Grandfather.

'Nothing you want to hear.'

'I know that they don't love me.'

'Of course they love you, but they're too old to change. You have to be the one to change.'

'Melecio is right to stay away. Everything here is dead.'

'Nothing here is dead. What happened to the Benicio I fell in love with?'

Grandpa Benicio hesitated a moment and looked up into the sky: a deep, intense blue crisscrossed towards the east by a convoy of clouds like carts heading towards Santiago. Finally he sighed and said: 'He died. The Benicio you fell in love with is no more.'

'What do you mean?'

'I mean I want you to leave. Go. Go and leave me in peace.'

'But—'

'Go, Gertrudis. Live your life. Forget about me.'

The desolation Gertrudis felt in that moment made her think of the desolation of the village. She thought about the prospect of living without Benicio. She thought about how much she missed his body in the night, she thought about her parents, about Melecio. And, as the tears trickled down her face, all these things illuminated by memory seemed desolate.

'So that's it. You never want to see me again.'

Grandfather nodded.

'As you wish, Benicio, I am not going to force you. Just remember one thing: you are not that monster's son, even if what he told you is true. When you feel unsure, when you don't remember who you truly are, come and see me and I will remind you.'

Gertrudis did not wait a second longer but turned and slowly walked home. Benicio watched her go, unable to believe the words that had just come from his own lips. He felt that his life had lost all meaning. He stood, mute, watching as the figure of Gertrudis grew smaller and the hatred in his breast grew. Above all, he even hated himself. When his sister had shrunk to the size of a dwarf, Geru turned and shouted, 'One last thing. You're wrong about Melecio. He's not going to stay away. He arrives home in Pata de Puerco at noon tomorrow.'

The Broken Family

An hour after his arrival the following day, having bid farewell to Aureliano the coachman and greeted the neighbours, Melecio stepped into his house. In the five years he had been away his parents had aged a great deal. Betina's hair was streaked with grey, she even had grey hair under her arms. But José looked worse. He was stooped now, almost hunchbacked, there was no other way to describe him: he looked old. Melecio had left behind two strong, healthy individuals and had come home to find two weak and wizened old people.

The new village schoolteacher said that he had missed them terribly, that he should never have abandoned them, but it was impossible now to turn back time. He brought his fingers to his temples as though he were suddenly getting a migraine.

'You didn't abandon us,' said Betina. 'You went to learn so that you could teach us all to read and write.'

'It's true, Melecio,' said Gertrudis. 'What is important is that you are here now.'

Melecio looked up and for the first time noticed his sister.

He was thunderstruck. She had always been beautiful, but he had never imagined Geru would grow into a nymph.

'A nymph?' Gertrudis said curiously.

Melecio explained that there was something called Greek mythology, a collection of stories, myths and legends about the Greeks, people who live in Greece, a distant country as old as the world itself. In these stories, he explained, nymphs were spirits of nature, beautiful maidens who tended to the gods and dwelled in mountains, rivers, woods and springs. Gertrudis was pleased by Melecio's description.

'So I'm a nymph?'

'See for yourself.' Her brother gave her a box that contained an elegant cotton dress and a pearl necklace. Then, from another box, he took a flat object he called a mirror. Gertrudis's mouth fell open as she studied herself in the mirror.

'You see what I mean?' said Melecio. 'A nymph.'

Meanwhile, Betina opened the transparent container, the 'cut-glass bottle' as Melecio called it. She brought it to her nose and shuddered.

'What a wonderful thing,' she said. 'It smells like rose wine.'

'It does. But don't even think about drinking it, it will give you an attack of the shits that could kill you,' explained her son. 'That is perfume. You wet your fingertips and dab it behind your ears and on your neck.'

Betina applied a few drops of this strange liquid to her throat and went over to show José. José said he did not need to see it, that he knew what perfume was, that the Santistebans had used perfume all the time and it was the most repulsive thing he had ever smelled.

'Don't be jealous, old man,' said Betina.

'Jealous of what? You're not the only one who got presents.'

José tried on the black suit his son had brought him and looked at himself in the mirror. Betina threw her arms around him saying he was the handsomest old man she had ever seen and José prised her off muttering that he was not an old man, that he was still fighting fit. Melecio said he looked a little like Brindis de Salas. 'What's that when it's at home?' asked José. Melecio explained he was a black Cuban violinist who had played at the German royal court over in Europe, a continent thousands of miles from Pata de Puerco.

And so they went on for a while, trying on their gifts and looking at themselves in the mirror, happy and contented. Betina asked Melecio about María. Her son told her that he would go back and fetch her one day, as soon as everyone in Pata de Puerco had learned to read and write.

'So where's Benicio?' asked Melecio. The faces of Gertrudis and Betina became hard.

'Where's Benicio?' he asked again.

'Your sister can explain it to you,' said José.

So Geru took her brother out into the back yard and told him everything that had happened. An hour later, they came back into the house.

'This thing about them falling in love is hardly news,' said Melecio. 'Benicio and Gertrudis have always been in love. You didn't need to be able to read and write to see that. It is a blessing. Can you imagine how wonderful it must be not to have to waste time searching for the love of your life? Imagine how glorious it must be to know, even as a child, that you have already found them? If everyone were like that, it would save much of the time and energy wasted on trying to solve mankind's great riddle, the question that constantly haunts us: where am I going? I understand them. Just as I understand why Mamá and Papá don't approve of your relationship, because they're old. What I don't understand is why Papá José threw Benicio out of the house.'

'I didn't throw him out of the house. It's easy for you to say that,' said José.

Then he began to scold Geru for not telling her brother about how he had been paralysed, how Benicio had turned into a monster, how he had beaten a boy half to death one day. This was not how he and Betina had raised their sons, José said, and then asked Geru why she hadn't told Melecio about Benicio hanging around with El Mozambique.

'I don't have to tell him anything, because Benicio and I are not together. So congratulations. You finally got what you wanted,' said Gertrudis and began to sob.

Her tears were not enough to stop Melecio. He asked where Benicio was and Gertrudis explained he was living at Ester's house. Melecio rushed for the door but Geru put a hand on his arm to stop him and said that José was right, that Benicio was no longer the person he had been, that he had changed utterly. She suggested Melecio wait until she had had a chance to talk to him, because it was impossible to know how Benicio might react.

'What do you think he's going to do to me?' said Melecio, jerking his arm away from Gertrudis. 'Benicio is my brother. He'll welcome me with open arms.'

Then he set off running, ignoring the greetings from the

171

villagers he encountered along the way. When he came to Ester's house, he did not need to knock. A giant of a man matching his sister's description was digging over the small plot of land next to the shack of timber and daub. He had the glossy blackish complexion of a fat Negro although in fact he was thin, chiselled and unshaven.

'Benicio,' called Melecio. Benicio first heard the cry in his neck which immediately jerked upright. The first thing Melecio noticed was the leather band from which hung the shrivelled pig's-foot amulet. He watched his brother's broad glistening back as Benecio rose to his full height and, without turning, said, 'I'd recognise that voice anywhere. It may have changed, but it doesn't fool me. It has to be the voice of the talented Melecio.'

'How have you been, brother?' said Melecio.

'Brother! I'm surprised to hear you call me that. Or haven't you heard?'

'They've told me everything.'

Benicio's relationship with Gertrudis was not news to Melecio, he had been told about José's paralysis and he knew what Ester had told Benicio about El Mozambique. All these things were trivial, Melecio concluded.

'Is it trivial to be thrown out of your own house?' asked Benicio.

'Every cause has an effect. You slept with Papá's golden girl. Besides, he will always think of the two of you as brother and sister. You have to try and see his point of view.'

'And who will try to see mine?'

Melecio changed the subject and asked why he and Gertrudis had argued.

'I was tired.'

'No one tires of the love of his life.'

'Well I did.'

'I brought you a present.'

'I don't need anything.'

'Open it. I know you'll like it.'

Benicio walked over to Melecio and took the box from him.

'What is it?'

'It's a toy ram, like the ram you saved when you were a boy, remember? It's the most noble thing anyone could have done. I always tell people my big brother has the compassion of a god.'

'Well, your toy is no use to me. Your big brother has changed a lot since he discovered his real father.'

Melecio said that did not mean he had to punish Gertrudis.

'I am not punishing Gertrudis,' said Benicio. 'She is punishing herself.'

Melecio talked about the weather and began comparing it to the other countries he had visited.

'What the hell do I care about the weather?' said Benicio.

'You should come to my classes, brother,' said Melecio.

'I'm not one for learning,' said Benicio. 'And let that be the last time you call me brother. And next time you see me, don't come too close or it'll be the worse for you.'

'Well get used to it, brother. Because that is what you will always be to me.'

This was the extent of their reunion; there were no hugs, no kisses. The two men stood in silence for a long time and Benicio assumed there was nothing left to say. He turned and went back to digging the ground. It seemed to Melecio that his brother's every word, uttered through gritted teeth, had nothing but contempt or indifference. Having exhausted all his subterfuges he headed home.

When he arrived back he gave his parents a modified version of his encounter with his brother. His parents said again that Benicio was irredeemable and advised him to leave his brother in peace.

'He's lonely,' said Melecio.

'Some people are happy that way,' said Betina.

And that was all he told his parents.

The full account of the conversation he related only to Gertrudis, who cried when Melecio reached the part where Benicio had said she was punishing herself.

'Don't take it to heart, Benicio is confused,' said Melecio. 'But I've got a plan to bring him back to himself. Trust me.'

Classes started the following day. The Jabaos were the first to arrive at the flame tree, besieging it with the stools and tables they had brought. By the time the Aquelarres, the Cabreras and the Santacruzes arrived there was barely room to sit so they asked Pablo and Niurka to get their family to budge up since otherwise everyone else would have to stand. Eustaquio the *machetero* was next to show up, and then Epifanio Vilo and his family. Melecio, Gertrudis, Betina and José were the last to appear.

Melecio set a blackboard against the trunk of the flame tree and then handed out pencils and sheets of blank paper. 'In today's class, we will learn about vowels,' he explained, then wrote out the vowels on the slate and asked the villagers to repeat them aloud with him. He pointed to them in turn and they repeated the sounds Melecio made. So passed two hours. At the end of the class the teacher gave out homework and the *patapuercanos* did everything that Melecio asked of them. Melecio offered gifts as a reward for paying attention in class or for completing homework.

The following week they continued with the whole alphabet. By the third week, the *patapuercanos* had learned to combine vowels and consonants. Mathematics worked in the same way. People learned to count, to add, subtract, multiply and divide. They learned for the first time that the earth was round and that it was divided into seven continents separated by seas and oceans inhabited by giant animals known as whales. They learned of the existence of something called philosophy and ancient, long-dead philosophers named Plato and Aristotle; they learned that there was something else called science which claimed man was descended from apes and had not been created by Changó, or Orula, or Olofi, or even by God; that there were tiny organisms called bacteria and that art was something complex but very beautiful. That centuries ago there had lived a musician named Mozart. They discovered what a violin was. In short, overnight the Festivals of Birth had become Festivals of Knowledge. Gone were the sack races, the tales, the childish games.

Silvio and Rachel Aquelarre were surprised when their daughter Anastasia won a competition that entailed reading *The Odyssey* and answering questions set by Melecio. She beat Ignacio el Jabao, who did not mind losing because, according to him, Odysseus was a homosexual. Everyone was surprised, not so much by his suggestion but because for the first time in his life Ignacio did not use the word 'faggot'.

'I tell you, señores, Odysseus was a coprophagic homosexual. What other explanation can there be for him leaving Calypso to return to Ithaca after seven years in that fabulous grotto where he could have sexual intercourse as often as he wished with two or even three women at a time? I sincerely doubt Penelope was prettier than Calypso, who was a demigod. Consequently I can see no other possible explanation for his behaviour. Odysseus turned fagg . . . I mean Odysseus decided he was homosexual. This is why I stopped reading the damn book, because every time I thought about it, I felt an ineffable heat surge through my spinal column all the way to my pituitary gland.'

Everyone was astonished by Ignacio's orotund manner of expressing himself. But Pablo and Niurka, who could not bear to lose anything, not even a spitting contest, were furious about the result of the competition. However, their anger did not last long, since the poetry competition was won by their older son Juan Carlos with his poem 'Girls':

> *What exactly are girls?*
> *A rainbow that feeds roses,*
> *A soft breeze that blows*
> *With a sweet scent of jasmine.*

> *What are girls? Let me say*
> *They are whorls of bright coral,*
> *A leaf of swamp laurel*
> *And the perfume of youth.*

176

And if pressed I would say
They suffuse every season
With love and with reasons
That make life worthwhile.

And this poem is to say
In my faltering way
How girls make me feel
And what makes me smile.

Pablo and Niurka rushed over and covered their son with kisses. The rest of the Jabaos leapt to their feet, excitedly celebrating this victory as though Juan Carlos had just won the Olympics.

'Well, well. Your poem is better than the ones that I recite,' said Melecio happily. He looked around him and saw how things had changed. There were children wearing white shirts, women sharing out food, men chatting so quietly they were barely audible, people laughing joyfully, a scene that he had pictured in his dreams and which, now it was real, was all the more moving. Everyone was discussing weighty matters, using words that until recently not one of them had ever heard, casting off the chains that had shackled them for years, the chains of ignorance. 'This is good,' thought Melecio. Still he sat perched on his stool, engrossed by his work, present in every article of clothing, every pair of shoes, every new word learned.

Never before had he so powerfully experienced the happy satisfaction that is the fruit of one's efforts; it was something akin to the love he felt for María and for his family. But very quickly he realised that something was amiss. Melecio scanned the happy faces of the Jabaos, the groups of people chatting, others practising their handwriting, and noticed that none of his family were present. He went home. Opening the door, he found José in one corner of the room, Betina in another and Gertrudis sitting on the floor. All of them were staring at the ground. He did not need to ask them what had happened. The answer was written in the stooped shoulders of José and Betina, in the misted, half-closed eyes of Gertrudis. In that moment he realised that he could never be satisfied by the fruit of his efforts, because in a broken family there could be no happiness. This is what Melecio thought, and José was the living confirmation of it. His father did not move, did not blink, as though he were inwardly appraising himself and realising that behind his stubbornness, his bitterness, his incomprehension, what weighed most heavily were his regrets. 'I have to solve this problem,' thought Melecio. By now everyone in the village knew how to read and write. It was time for him to deal with things at home. To set things right.

He went to see Benicio again.

'I didn't see you at any of the classes,' he said.

'I told you, I'm not interested in your classes. Education is for faggots.'

'That's not what Gertrudis thinks.'

'Who is Gertrudis?'

'She's the love of your life.'

'Gertrudis always was a fool.'

'I can't believe you don't miss your family.'

'Ester and El Mozambique are all the family I need. They don't throw me out, they accept me for who I am.'

'This is not who you are, brother. Don't shut yourself away.'

'If you call me brother again, I'll split your skull.'

Melecio swallowed hard. He went back to discussing the weather.

'If you've got nothing else to say, then fuck off, but don't come talking to me about the weather,' said Benicio.

'What did you do with the toy ram I gave you?' asked Melecio.

'I burned it.'

Benicio turned away and went back to digging. Melecio stared at him, stifling the urge to weep.

'You know something, broth—'

Benicio did not let him finish. He picked up a rock and hurled it and, had Melecio not ducked, it would have split his skull exactly as his brother had foretold. Once again, Melecio trudged home.

The following day, he gave the villagers a whole week's study matter and, leaving Anastasia Aquelarre in charge, excused himself saying he needed time to think. He did as he always did: he locked himself in his room, but this time he took spices, eggs, sugar, spoons and saucepans. When Gertrudis asked what he was doing, he asked her to give him a little time, that what he was doing was necessary and she would find out soon. And so Melecio resumed the role of chef, something he had not done since he was a boy. He spent two days cooking in secret. On the morning of the third day, Señora Santacruz knocked at the door and haltingly told José that Ester the midwife was locked in her house screaming like a madwoman, pounding on the walls and yelling that if anyone other than José came in she would drive a stake through their skull. From his bedroom, Melecio overheard what was said; still he did not come out.

'You stay here,' said José and went outside.

It was a chill morning, the sky was leaden and the wind bit hard. José hobbled past the houses of the Aquelarres and the Jabaos, ignoring the looks and the sibilant whispers from the dark interiors that smelled of kerosene and coal. As he reached the fence around Ester's shack, he could feel the roars, the howls of remorse sprouting from his body, displacing every organ inside his ribcage. José crept towards the door and glanced around. There was no sign of Benicio or El Mozambique.

'Can I help you with something?' asked Epifanio Vilo.

'Go fetch Juanita the wise-woman and tell her to come here straight away,' said José. 'Run.'

'It sounds to me like someone possessed. José, wouldn't it be better to send for a *babalao* or a *santero*?'

'No, Juanita will know what to do.'

When Juanita and Epifanio arrived back at Ester's house, they found the whole neighbourhood gathered, faces gaunt with fear. José was cradling Ester in his arms in one corner of the room; she was naked, sobbing and shaking with fear. The house was in ruins, the walls stained with excrement. Juanita quickly analysed the situation and with a wave she signalled to José to lay Ester on the bed. A moment later, Melecio arrived carrying the cake he had just made. He set it down on the table, the only piece of furniture that had remained intact, and rushed to help carry the stout body of Ester, who was writhing and wailing as though a piranha were devouring her insides.

'My God, what's wrong with Ester? What happened?' said Silvia Santacruz, standing in the doorway shaking her head. Without a word, Juanita checked Ester's pupils, took her pulse and began to prepare a herbal remedy.

'This will make her sleep,' she said.

José opened Ester's mouth to make her drink the dark, foul-smelling brew. The midwife's body convulsed, but a moment later her eyes misted over and she fell back on the bed.

'She's sleeping now,' said Juanita, examining the deep scars crisscrossing Ester's fat body. 'Whoever did this thing is a beast,' she muttered, shaking her head.

'What made those scars?' asked José.

Juanita did not look up. Still shaking her head, she pulled a sheet up to cover Ester's body.

'They are whip marks. This woman has spent her life lashing herself for failing to keep her promises, or someone else has been torturing her.'

Ester slept for several hours. At about two in the afternoon, she woke up and could remember nothing except that she had heard Benicio say he was going down to the river and she talked about a dream she had had the night before. Having considered the matter for a few moments, she changed her mind: what she thought had been a dream was not a dream at all, she said, she deserved to die.

'What are these marks?' asked José.

'It's a long story.'

'We have all the time in the world,' said José. 'This is Pata de Puerco, the one place in creation where time stands still.'

The neighbours settled themselves and Ester began to tell the tale of Oscar's mother and the Santisteban sugar plantation.

'Yes, Ester, but we already know all that.'

'Do you want me to tell you what happened?'

'No,' said José. 'We want you to tell us everything.'

'Everything?'

'Everything.'

The midwife asked if someone could fetch her some water. She drank it. She settled herself back against a cushion, tilted her head to one side as a dog might. She took a deep breath that seemed to suck all of the air out of the shack. Finally, she said, 'All right, José. All right. I'll tell you everything.'

Ester's Confession

'I was a girl, barely sixteen, when I met Mangaleno – El Mozambique as you call him. My parents had died. Both of them had been killed in the war. I had no one in the whole world, all I had were my hope and my innocence. In the hills of Mayarí where I lived, solitude is something that weighs heavily, time crawls. I could not bear the thought of living the life my parents had, a life of grief and pain. Of course, back then I did not know that pain is inherited, that parents hand it on to their children like a suit of clothes that no longer fits. So I did everything I could to block out the pain I had inherited and kept my head above water. From an early age, I learned to take care of a house. I was preparing for the day when the man of my life would appear. I spent a lot of time practising kissing banana trees. I would make a little hole in the trunk and slip my tongue inside; I didn't care that the sap from the trees used to leave my lips and my tongue red raw, like the skin of a dog with mange. I was careful not to let my hands become calloused so that my caresses would be soft as cotton. I did all this and much more waiting for the day when my man would knock at the door and take me away from that godforsaken place.

'And then one day a man did knock at the door. Hatred was ingrained in his very pores and his body struck fear in me. He asked for a glass of water. He asked if I lived alone. Alone, I said. He smiled and thanked me and went on his way. The next day, he came back and asked for a glass of water. This time he talked to me about horses. He told me they were useful beasts. Those were his words. I found it curious, him talking about horses that way, but I said nothing. Then he said I had a beautiful body and asked if anyone had ever told me that before. I told him no.

'"Well it's true, you have a beautiful body."

'Then he thanked me and went on his way. So it carried on for a long time. He would always arrive early with a sprig of flowers and he would flatter my body. There came a time, having spent days listening to his compliments, when I began to miss him. Out of caresses tenderness is born, as they say in these parts, and I learned that this is true. I began to miss his company, his manner filled with mystery and silence. One morning I woke up and I felt something in me was lacking. It was then I knew I had fallen in love, that I wanted to do with Mangaleno what I had been practising on the banana trees. But Mangaleno never laid a finger on me. Still he came and asked for water, flattered my breasts, my complexion, even my hair which is the ugliest thing I got from my parents.

'The waiting seemed to go on for ever. Every night, I dreamed about what my first time would be like. I dreamed of Mangaleno laying me on a bed, gently caressing my body

184

and then tenderly making love to me. I wept with pleasure at the thought of what was to come. But when it finally happened I wept with anger and with pain. One afternoon, Mangaleno knocked on the door. When I opened it, he punched me twice leaving me dazed. He picked me up and slammed me against the wall. No caresses, no tenderness. He made me bleed. He made me weep. Then he tossed me on the ground and left.

'He appeared at three o'clock the next morning to apologise. He brought me a sprig of flowers. He told me he had had a bad day and had needed to vent his rage on someone. I could not utter a word. My face was swollen where he had beaten me. He asked me if I liked meat. He had a cart with him piled high with sacks filled with metal tools, and several dogs that looked savage. I had forgotten what meat tasted like, it had been so long since I had eaten it. So we walked down to the river, taking the opposite direction from El Cobre, then he took a little path over a hill dotted with royal palms and came to a weir. We hid the cart among some shrubs and waited. The night was black as a wolf's maw. There were no stars, no moon, no crickets chirruping, nothing but the dew and the muggy air of dawn.

'Fifteen minutes later, a traveller arrived. The weir was right next to the road that runs between Baracoa and Santiago. Usually, travellers on their way to Santiago would stop and drink a little water before continuing their journey.

'"Champion, Lion, you know what you have to do," Mangaleno whispered to his dogs. There were more than eight of them, all with vicious faces and sharp teeth. He let them off their leash. The dogs crept up silently so as not to frighten the horse and when they were within fifteen feet of the man, they bounded towards him. The man had no time to draw his machete. All he could do was leap into the water and swim as far away as possible from the vicious beasts threatening to eat him alive. Meanwhile, Mangaleno unsheathed his sharply pointed machete.

'"Stay here and leave me to work," he said to me and then crept carefully over to the horse. He grabbed the reins, stroked its mane three times and then slit its throat from ear to ear with the machete. The horse kicked and whinny in pain. It tried to run, but Mangaleno had a tight grip on the reins and went on sawing at the animal's jugular until finally the poor beast, resigned to its fate, collapsed on the bank by the reservoir which by now was a thick pool of blood flecked here and there with gobbets of flesh. I stood, staring at what was happening, my hand clapped over my mouth, cringing in disgust as Mangaleno hacked away, squirming as the poor horse whinnied in pain. All this Mangaleno did with an indifference that did not smack of pride but of a feeling of superiority.

'But worst of all, I had fallen in love with him and he knew it. You all know that when it comes to the whims of love there is nothing to be done and so I learned to endure in the hope that he might one day change and become a good man. I knew that life had not been kind to him and that, like me, he carried with him the pain he had inherited, though more, perhaps much more than me. Every afternoon he would come to eat the food I prepared for him. We sat at the table and ate in silence. He did not like to talk. He had spent so many years in silence. On the rare occasions when he spoke to me it was to ask for water or food, but never again did he tell me I had a beautiful body.

'One morning, I threw up. I felt nauseous and depressed. But in spite of everything, I was happy for though I had no experience of such things, I knew that I was pregnant. That afternoon I waited for Mangaleno, as usual, to give him the news. When he arrived, I told him. That was the first time he whipped me. He grabbed an old whip he always carried and flayed my back red raw. He had me writhing on the floor in pain. I screamed and screamed, but pity was something alien to Mangaleno. He went on whipping until he was unable and I was unconscious. That same night the baby came. It was the most terrible day of my life. I huddled alone in a corner, cradling that bloody bundle, rocking it as though it had eyes, as though it had a mouth, as though it had life. It was the most terrible day of my life but there would be more, many more. More beatings, more miscarriages, more misery and pain.

'Then he told me I had to come with him to a place called Pata de Puerco where his brother lived, the man he most despised in all the world. He told me he had a score to settle with him. He did not ask me, did not give me time to think, to make up my mind. He tossed my clothes into a cart and dragged me like a dog on a leash until we arrived here. Back then, no one lived in the village. José and Oscar had just started building their shacks. The solitude was such that for a while I felt as though I were living in a jungle full of natives wearing loincloths. Full of wild beasts the like of which I had never seen. A place too beautiful to be believed, but after a while I saw other people come with their carts and their carriages, then more and more until Pata de Puerco was no longer a jungle peopled by natives but the thriving village it is today.

'Mangaleno's plan was simple. He wanted to fashion a sackcloth of dust and ashes for his brother Oscar, meaning he wanted to cause him suffering that would stay with him for ever. These, then were Mangaleno's talents: he caused unending pain, just as he had done to me. One afternoon I asked what his brother had done to deserve such suffering. He first told me that his brother had taken from him the only love he had ever known, his mother's love; then he split my lip and whipped me again. In that moment I understood that, though slavery might have ended, it had not ended for me. The worst thing was that I could find no way to break free of him. I was still in love, I tried to justify his actions. I told myself he was to be pitied, that he had never had anyone, hoping against hope that one day I might see in his face something of the good in him. But there was no good in him. Yet still I was in love, as though someone had put a curse upon my heart, and I don't know why, but that somehow made it worse.

'It was he who hacked the leg off the mare you bought with Oscar, José. He also cut the leg off Evaristo's mare that time he followed you to El Cobre. And still he was not satisfied. One afternoon he turned up here smiling and told me he had raped Malena, that he had finally settled his score with his brother Oscar. That day we celebrated, feasting on horsemeat, drinking rice wine. He ended up delirious with joy, and I delirious with jealousy of Malena. How could I not? The jealousy grew in me when I discovered that Malena was carrying in her belly something that belonged, of old, to me. That child should have been mine. After my years of suffering, I deserved it. That's why when Mangaleno asked me to poison her, I did not hesitate; I said yes.

'The day she went into labour, I sent Oscar to get water from the well. While he was gone, I had Malena drink the potion of cassava poison I had prepared. She looked at me with those big eyes as though she sensed what it was I had just done. Oscar did not notice anything amiss. Everything was normal by the time he got back. But a few minutes later, Malena was dead and Oscar fell on his knees. He threw me out of the house telling me that he would take care of everything. Fifteen minutes later the floor of the shack was a sea of blood and Oscar and Malena lay dead just as his brother Mangaleno had planned.

'Even then, it was not enough. His hatred was like a sickness that would not stop until it had consumed everything. He had avenged himself, but it was not enough. The Festivals of Birth brought joy and happiness to everyone but to an embittered man that was unbearable. Mangaleno came up with another plan. God knows I fought with every fibre of my being when he asked me to poison Evaristo. A thousand times I refused, but the beatings were too much and I had no choice but to send the kite-maker to heaven. That's why I must die, why I deserve to die. I realised that, having spent so long with him, I too have become an animal; it is as though Mangaleno has passed his evil to me. A person is known by the company he keeps; no proverb was ever truer. My only hope is that, having heard all this, you will have the decency to kill me, so that once and for all I may be rid of these sins that will not let me sleep. I cannot bear to hear Malena's voice again telling me avenging past wrongs brings only present suffering. I cannot bear to hear her voice again. I cannot go on with the lying, the beatings; let Satan take me now so that I may finally be free.'

When Ester finished her confession, no one moved to kill her. Betina was weeping, but she did not move, nor did José. The neighbours stared at her but not in anger, more with surprise and pity. Juanita the wise-woman held her hand as the midwife sobbed.

'Kill me, kill me, José,' Ester begged.

'No one here will lay a finger on you,' said José and turned to look at the crowd. 'Everyone stay here.'

'No. Don't go, José. Stay,' said Juanita the wise-woman, taking his arm. 'Stay. I know what I'm asking of you.'

José would not listen. 'Melecio, make sure that Ester has everything she needs,' he said and, drawing his machete, he set off for the house of El Mozambique. Everyone ignored his order. Hardly had José stepped through the door than the whole neighbourhood followed him like a herd of mustang.

The Long-awaited Confrontation

As José arrived at the baleful shack of timber and palm fronds, he looked around and noticed that the dogs were chained up. And Benicio did not seem to be around, which made him think El Mozambique was expecting him. With the agility of a sixteen-year-old boy, he vaulted the fence, and gave the door a kick that took it off its hinges.

'That's what I like to see. Someone with balls coming to take me on,' said El Mozambique, getting up from his chair to face him down. José did not let him finish, but leaped at him swinging his machete. The giant stopped him in his tracks, grabbed the arm holding the machete with one hand and with the other dealt a vicious blow to the Mandinga. José staggered back and crashed against the wall.

'Kill him, José! Kill that son of a bitch!' shouted Epifanio Vilo and his family, the fifteen Jabaos and the Santacruzes, in chorus.

El Mozambique lumbered towards José to finish him off, but the Mandinga kicked him in the belly making the giant double over briefly. José made the most of this to pick up the machete he had dropped. He swung viciously, attempting to cut off his rival's head, but El Mozambique ducked and slammed him against the table which immediately collapsed, sending the Mandinga crashing to the floor and driving into his back a long iron nail from one of countless *santería* cauldrons lying around. José started to bleed. 'Come on, José, don't toy with me,' roared El Mozambique. 'Get up and stop being such a pussy.' This silenced the cheering of those on the far side of the fence.

At that moment, Melecio arrived.

'Son of a bitch!' he cried, and ran to help José. El Mozambique blocked his path, smashing an elbow into Malecio's face that knocked him unconscious. Then he grabbed one of his machetes, the one he used to cut the throats of horses, and stepped towards José who was howling with pain and bleeding like a stuck pig. El Mozambique lifted him off the floor, looked him in the eye and gave a twisted smile.

'Now do you understand what life is, José? Who would have thought that these very hands would be the ones to end yours? Nothing is written. There is no justice, none at all. Everything is a lie.'

'That's what you say,' said José. 'But I'm sure your death will be much worse.'

El Mozambique's smile faded. For a moment, everything was stilled: the roar of the villagers, the wails of the women, the barking of the dogs. There was only the quiet buzz of flies and the echo of an agonising silence that sent a shudder rippling through everyone. In that moment, El Mozambique swung his machete, aiming to cleave José's head from his body. He did not succeed: his arm was blocked, something held him back, a strength greater than his own. When he turned, he found himself face to face with Grandpa Benicio.

'What . . . What are you doing? Let go the machete, Benicio.'

'No. Your journey ends here.' This was all Grandfather said. Lifting El Mozambique by the throat, he slammed him with all his strength against the floor. The giant hit his head and passed out. Then everything happened quickly. In a split second, the thirty people who had witnessed what was happening rushed into the garden, some smashed windows the better to see, others peered through cracks between the timbers waiting for the fatal blow that would satisfy once and for all their thirst for blood.

'Kill him, Benicio! Kill him now!'

Grandpa Benicio pinned El Mozambique to the ground. Reaching down, he picked up the giant's machete and held it aloft. 'Kill him, damn it! Kill him now, Benicio!' He looked first at José who lay sprawled on the floor nodding his head in agreement. Then he looked round for Melecio, but his brother still lay unconscious on the ground. Scanning the faces outside he saw Betina and she, too, nodded. Lastly, he looked for Gertrudis who was standing in the midst of the mob, tears in her eyes, her hand over her mouth. Then he brought down the machete and embedded it in the floor next to El Mozambique's head.

'This ends here,' he roared.

'What do you mean, it ends here?' roared the crowd. 'Kill that son of a bitch!' Benicio did not listen. He got up off the floor and ordered everyone to go home, saying that though

El Mozambique might be a monster, that was no reason for anyone else to become one. 'This ends here,' he repeated.

For a while, the crowd went on protesting, waving their arms, shouting, cursing the Blessed Virgin and all the saints. Then gradually the flame inside them guttered out and slowly they began to trudge home.

Benicio picked up José and sat him on one of the chairs that was still in one piece. Betina and Gertrudis kneeled next to Melecio, who had come round. Grandfather brought water from the kitchen for the wounded.

'Water is not going to help me,' said José. Then they noticed that the nail, a long spike used to secure railway sleepers, was deeply embedded in his back. There was little anyone could do. Still, Benicio refused to admit defeat. 'It's all over now, Papá José,' he said. 'Let's go home.' Everyone, including José, turned to Benicio in surprise. His eyes were different, filled with tears and remorse. Benicio explained that he had arrived back from the river famished to find a cake sitting on the table. He ate a slice of the exquisite delicacy and then found Ester on her bed sobbing uncontrollably and Juanita trying to comfort her. The *santera* told him what had happened and the news was like a body blow. The cake had a curious effect on him: suddenly his head was filled with all the terrible things he had done, with how he had torn his family apart. In his mind he saw the face of everyone he had ever hit, among them the twisted rictus on José's face; he wept to think about how heartless he had been to Melecio, to Betina, and especially to Gertrudis. Juanita shook him hard and told him this was no time to cry, that José was in danger, that saving him would be his own salvation.

'But there is nothing to be done now, my son,' said José. Betina, Melecio and Gertrudis watched as Benicio began to weep. José asked him why he had not killed El Mozambique. He dried his eyes and turned to look at his family, then turned and looked at José as though he did not understand the question. 'He is my blood father, Papá José. Besides, if I had killed him, I would have become a murderer like him.'

Melecio finished his glass of water and said that Benicio had done the right thing and that El Mozambique could not have been other than he was. 'What can you expect of a man who has never known a friend, a mother, a father; who has never known the love of a woman? Can you imagine the hatred he must feel? Knowing only hatred, anyone might become a killer.'

'How many times do I have to tell you,' came a booming voice. 'Hatred is not so bad.'

Betina was the first to scream, then everyone turned to face the fearsome figure of El Mozambique who was now standing, laughing, brushing dirt and blood from his hands.

'What did you think? That a little knock on the head would kill me? Did you really think it would be so easy? And you . . .' He pointed at Benicio. 'Expect no mercy from me, do you hear? You will pay dearly for what you've done.'

El Mozambique launched himself at Benicio and grabbed him by the throat. The villagers reappeared and once again took up their posts, peering through windows and cracks in the boards, hurling insults and obscenities as though watching gladiators in the arena. José sat in his chair, unable to do anything.

'Get ready to join that bastard Oscar!' roared El

Mozambique. He began to throttle Grandfather with both hands. 'The monster,' yelled the crowd, 'he's going to kill the boy!'

Grandfather was on the point of being strangled when the back door of the shack was thrown open and, like a thunderbolt, Ester suddenly appeared in the room. 'Let him go, Mangaleno!' screamed Ester.

'You? You fucking whore, what are you doing here? Get out and go home, you wh—'

Ester did not allow him to finish. From the folds of her skirts, she took an axe and with a single blow sliced Mangaleno's head clean from his shoulders. The hulking body crumpled. The head rolled out of the door, past the neighbours. Epifanio Vilo picked it up and spat at it several times. Someone else punched it. They were about to toss it into the swamp when Melecio came outside and reminded them of Benicio's words earlier: they were not brute beasts but human beings.

Melecio and Ester rushed back to where José was sitting. Benicio was already by his father's side. The moment his real father had been felled, he had not wasted a second. Betina ran, Gertrudis ran and lastly Juanita the wise-woman who had just arrived. Through the shattered windows and the cracks in the boards, the neighbours stared at the bloody body of the Mandinga. There was so much blood, seeping through his clothes, pooling on the floor, that it seemed hardly possible he could have any left.

'Do you know what your first word was?' said José, squeezing Benicio's hand. 'Tell him, Betina.'

'Papá,' said Betina, drying her tears.

'One day you just looked me right in the eye and said "Papá",' José went on, squeezing Benicio's hand, struggling to breathe. 'I wanted to cover you in kisses.'

'Forgive me, Papá,' said Benicio.

'There is nothing to forgive. I am the one who should be asking for forgiveness, son. Now I realise that Juanita was right when she told me you were different. And you are, Benicio. You are different for the simple reason that you are better. We all wanted blood, and what did you do? You stood up for something none of us cared about. Loyalty, Benicio. That is something truly important. To be loyal to those who gave you life, to your sons, to your family, however bad they may be. It was something I did not think about when I threw you out. That's why, for all your faults, you are a better man than I.'

Benicio squirmed at every word, unable to accept this obvious truth. José told him there was no reason to cry, that he had lived a long life and a good one and that his last wish had just been granted: he had been reconciled with his son before he died. 'I'm dying in peace,' he said and kissed Benicio on the cheek. He looked at Melecio. Then at Gertrudis. Lastly he gave Betina a long look and whispered: 'I love you, *mi amor*.'

He was buried in a dark hole next to Malena and his inseparable friend Oscar. The day after the funeral, Grandpa Benicio and Grandma Gertrudis said their goodbyes to everyone; they could not go on living in Pata de Puerco because the memories were too painful. Betina and Melecio and all the other villagers watched sadly as they moved off down the Callejón de la Rosa, heading nowhere. This was how they came to live in Havana, to settle in a *barrio* called Lawton. The death of José and the departure of my grandparents Benicio and Gertrudis closed for ever an important chapter in the history of that long-forgotten village.

Part Two

To the Roots

The Road to Lawton

All the stuff I've just told you makes me terribly sad, and that's the honest truth. That's why I never talk about it to anyone. Commissioner Clemente, with his bald head and his moustache like some Mexican *bandido*, forced me to tell him the whole story and then the son of a bitch refused to believe me. He looked at me like everything I'd said was gibberish, like I was insane. All he wants to know is how I came to be here and why I smashed in the face of that rat whose name I hope I never have to mention. This was the real reason for the hours of cross-examination when he wormed his way inside my brain. So that's how things stand now, me with the blues, reliving the story of my grandparents and the chrome-dome commissioner with that look that says 'like I give a fuck'. You don't have to worry: I'm going to tell you what Clemente really wanted to know about – all that murky business about the Nicotinas. But before I get to that part, let me get a glass of water because my throat's parched from all this yammering.

Aaaaah, lovely. Just what I needed. I have to say right now what I'd really love is a sticky guava *masa real*, or a traditional

Cuban cake. What I'm saying is this is the hunger hour, though in this part of the world hunger has no hour, it's as contagious and as commonplace as madness. These days anyone who's starving is labelled mad – not that I give a shit. The important thing for me is to cure my weakness, it's just that I'm not used to going hungry. In 1995, what with the 'special economic period', everyone is used to running on empty, as though we're all sleepwalkers wandering through a dream that seems as though it might never end. I call it a madhouse. But, well, madness is a different story, it has nothing to do with the one I'm telling. Or does it?

This is exactly what my grandparents Benicio and Gertrudis discovered when they arrived in Havana: a madhouse. It was the capital in the 1920s, the capital of noise, of chaos, but also of progress. A vast metropolis full of automobiles roaring up and down the streets at all hours. Full of streetcars, of hawkers selling fruit, of well-dressed gentlemen, of ladies mimicking the latest American fashions, with their hair crimped and straightened like Bette Davis. Full of men wearing straw hats and white linen suits. Full of flower shops and shoe shops. A powerful city with a thriving commerce and billboards in American.

All this, my grandparents saw in the moment they stepped out of the train station; it was as though they had been transported to another galaxy. Naturally, curiosity got the better of them and they strolled around, studying this landscape peopled by alien life forms, by individuals from a different species, trying to work out whether this new world were innocuous.

As you probably know, El Capitolio – The National

Capitol Building – started out as a patch of swampland, a rubbish tip dotted with slaves' huts, then a botanical garden was planted there before they built the Villanueva Railway Station which in turn was torn down so they could build El Capitolio. My grandparents watched carts and trucks transporting sand and blocks, cement and steel raising clouds of dust that blotted out the sun and impregnated everyone's clothes. There were trees here and there, struggling up between the rows of buildings and more trees in the Parque Central and the Manzana de Gómez. Benicio and Gertrudis walked on, carefully studying every detail. They passed the Teatro Nacional and the Hotel Inglaterra and walked slowly down the Paseo del Prado to the sea. On the Prado there were more trees, more well-dressed people, more hawkers. They did not stop but carried on walking as though hypnotised by the sea. 'I swear the waves were calling to us,' Grandma Gertrudis would tell me years later as she remembered her first encounter with the ocean and her first frightening, thrilling glimpse of Havana. According to her, the waves were shrieking at them, screams that were more enthralling than the monumental buildings or the automobiles and the trams they were seeing for the first time.

They carried on walking, ignoring everything, until they stepped into the crystal-clear waters of the sea. Only then did they feel at peace. For a moment, they forgot the recent events in Pata de Puerco, the death of José, the regret they felt at leaving their mother and their brother and their arrival in the unfamiliar world of the capital. They stood in the waters off the Malecón, arms around each other, for a long time. They were in no hurry since they had nowhere to go and at that moment the ocean offered everything they needed to allay their exhaustion and their fear. Eventually a policeman appeared, asked what they were doing and pointed out that Negroes were not allowed to bathe on this section of the beach. Immediately, they collected their belongings and left.

They walked for miles, taking the first direction that occurred to them. After a few hours, Grandma Gertrudis was so exhausted she could not carry on. Their feet were swollen and tinged with purple. Grandpa Benicio asked a mule driver with a cart to take them as far as possible from the centre of the city, somewhere there would be no automobiles, no infernal tramways, somewhere they might be close to the soil and animals.

Were it not for the fact that by now Grandma Gertrudis could barely walk, Benicio would never have dared to speak to a stranger. He was a white man, but he was dressed in rags like a backwoodsman, a white shirt stained with mud, a pair of filthy green trousers and a hat woven from *yarey*. Despite his being white, he seemed to my grandparents to be the only man with whom they might have something in common in this strange modern world.

'Somewhere outside the city?' said the stranger, doffing his hat. 'You're in luck then, that's exactly where I'm headed.' He had dark hair, though this was barely noticeable since his high forehead extended beyond the hairline to the middle of his head. His face was deeply lined but genial, his eyes as keen and wise as those of a cat. Everything about him seemed friendly.

'Pilar, go on, budge up and make room back there,' he said.

'Excuse me, señor, but my señora's name is Gertrudis,' said Benicio.

'No, no, I was talking to my nephew.'

My grandparents stared at the child with the mane of black hair who seemed both wary and intrigued. Benicio and Gertrudis glanced at each other and then looked at the child again, still puzzled by what the man had said.

'Don't worry, most people have the same reaction,' said the man. 'I've said it to my brother a thousand times. With all the names there are in the world, what possessed you to give the boy a girl's name? My name is Augusto, what about you?'

'I'm Benicio and this is Gertrudis. We've just arrived from Pata de Puerco.'

'Pata de Puerco? And where might that be?' asked the man, scratching his head.

'Near Santiago,' said Benicio, though he was not very sure.

'Santiago? Now that's strange, I've been down that way many times and I've never heard mention of it. Is the old church at El Cobre still standing?'

'Yes. It's still there.'

'It's a beautiful building. Well now, you two make yourselves comfortable, it's a long ride. And, Pilar, you mind your manners.'

My grandparents settled themselves on the cart next to the boy named Pilar with the jet-black hair and the awestruck expression. Gertrudis offered him one of the sweets that Betina had given them for the journey while Benicio massaged her tired feet. Pilar ate the sweet without so much as a thank you. Gertrudis smiled, but the boy did not return her smile.

'If you're from Santiago, I assume you don't know anything about Havana,' said Augusto. My grandparents nodded. 'In that case I have no choice but to offer my services as your guide,' said the man and turned round to signal to them. '*Bueno*, first off let me explain that this road is the Calzada de Jesús del Monte. Until the eighteenth century, it was known as the "Santiago road" since it leads to Santiago de las Vegas and Bejucal which are a few miles straight ahead. This used to be the only road leading out of the city into the countryside, and a dozen tobacco growers were hanged from the trees that lined this road for protesting against the Spanish Government's monopoly of the tobacco trade. Obviously, a lot has changed since then and, as you can see, there's not a single tree left standing.'

Augusto removed his hat and with a sweeping gesture indicated the utter lack of vegetation.

'The Camino de Santiago became the Calzada de Jesús del Monte sometime around 1800. Then, after 1918, it was renamed the Calzada del Diez de Octubre, though no one really calls it that. I assume you know the story of Pepe Antonio?'

My grandparents shook their heads.

'Pepe Antonio was the mayor of Guanabacoa, a little town over that way,' the man pointed to the north.

'In 1762, when Havana was captured by the English, Guanabacoa was known as Pepe Antonio's villa, because according to the stories he was a brave man indeed. I'm sure you know that Havana belonged to the English for a year before they traded it with the Spanish for Florida.'

'We don't even know how to read and write,' said Grandpa

Benicio, and Grandma Gertrudis glared at him as if to say 'speak for yourself', since she had learned to read and write fluently at Melecio's classes.

'Ah, I understand,' said the man. 'Well, anyway, Pepe Antonio was the man who led the resistance against the English. Even so, it came to nothing because one of his men ousted him and then rolled over for the enemy. Pepe Antonio died at home, his house is still there in Guanabacoa. After that, the English gave Havana to the Spanish in exchange for Florida, and the way things are going with the new president, it looks like he'll hand it on a silver platter to the Americans.'

'And who is the new president, if you don't mind me asking?' my grandfather said.

'Of course you can ask. His name is Gerardo Machado y Morales and everyone in Havana has high hopes of him, especially my brother Itamar who is in the army. He says Machado will do wonders for this island, but I have to say personally the guy gives me the creeps. I'm from the old school, like Maceo and Martí, I believe Cuba should belong to the people. But my brother maintains that an island the size of a sardine can't govern itself, that one way or another it is dependent on the whale in order to thrive. Are you interested in politics?'

'To tell the truth, I don't really know what it means,' said Benicio.

'Well, well, Benicio,' said Augusto, taking off his hat again and turning to look at my grandparents. 'You might not be able to read or write, but that's the most intelligent thing I've heard a Christian say in a long time. And the honest truth is *nobody* knows what it means. Some people claim it's the art of words and lies, but I think it's a weapon used to control the people for personal advantage because all politicians follow the same pattern: they say what people want to hear and once they're on the horse they make sure no one can unseat them. That's how it is with the new president. Now he's elected he's scheming to try and change the constitution so he can govern for another six years. Can you imagine? A president ruling for eight years? That's a long time. But nobody will say anything, people will keep their mouths shut and the exploitation will carry on.'

'Who is being exploited?' asked Benicio.

'The Cuban people, who else? You and I are being exploited. That's why I'm on the side of Alfredo López's Confederation of Cuban Workers; they're the only people who seem to be fighting against waste and inequality. But it'll cost them dearly, because our new president doesn't tolerate opposition. He's quick to get rid of anyone who opposes his policies. Not long ago Julito Mella and his troops – actually Mella lives just down there,' Augusto pointed. 'Anyway, they organised a peaceful demonstration at the university, demanding freedom and improvements for the people, and the army waded in and arrested twenty of them. All this just for saying they didn't agree with some policy or other. So you should probably be careful while you're here, because things in Havana are pretty tense. I don't know what it's like in Pata de Puerco, but round here, every day you go out in the street could be your last.'

Gertrudis clutched her chest and looked at Benicio, petrified. Little Pilar reached out his hand towards her. Gertrudis smiled and dug out some more sweets which the little boy wolfed down as though he had not eaten in days.

They continued their journey along the Calzada del Diez de Octubre, my grandparents drinking in every detail. They watched as the asphalt roads gradually petered out to become lanes which in turn became dirt tracks that stretched away into the distance. In this part of Havana, horse-drawn carts were more common than automobiles, but progress was such that the glamour of the city extended even to the remote suburbs. My grandmother Gertrudis pointed out a man herding a flock of goats as though it was impossible to believe such a thing could exist in this part of Cuba. All around there were still majestic houses and lavish cars, but for the most part the inhabitants seemed to be working class.

'You see those African tulip trees in the distance near the big white house with the roses? Enriquito Diaz lives there; he was the first man in Havana to make a silent movie like the ones Charlie Chaplin makes. Some say he was the first filmmaker in Cuba even though most people didn't like the film. They said it was boring. I thought it was good. Maybe because the main character is called Manuel García and I was excited because he had the same surname as me. Though there's no shortage of people called García here in Cuba. What's your surname, if you don't mind me asking?'

'Mandinga,' said Benicio.

'And the señorita?'

'She's Mandinga too,' said Benicio.

'Are you sure there's no one named García in your family? That's strange. I have to say, though, I'm obviously not quick on the uptake, because I would have thought you two were too young to be married.'

'You're right, we're not married,' said Grandfather.

'Then how come you share the same name?'

'Because we're brother and sister.'

'Really? Well, well. I must be going deaf because I was sure that when you introduced me to the young woman, you called her your señora.'

'It's true, I am his señora,' said Grandma Gertrudis, 'but that's a long story.'

'Ah . . . I understand,' said Augusto and then fell silent.

They carried on along the Calzada del Diez de Octubre until they came to the junction with the Calzada Dolores. Here, Augusto stopped the cart and pointed out the neighbourhoods: to the north Regla, to the east San Miguel del Padrón and to the south a district known as Arroyo Naranjo. They had left El Cerro behind, he said; once you turned the corner and headed down the Calzada Dolores, you came to Barrio Lawton, which was where he lived.

My grandparents thanked Augusto and said goodbye to little Pilar, then quietly stepped down from the cart. They stood there waving, but still Augusto's cart did not move. The *habanero* lit up his pipe and stared out at the horizon like a man in no hurry to be somewhere. Ten minutes passed. Fifteen. Twenty minutes later, Augusto was still in the same spot.

'Tell me, Señor Augusto, you wouldn't know where we might find work and perhaps a place to stay?' asked Gertrudis shyly.

The man turned and smiled at my grandmother. 'Of

course I would. Why do you think I have been sitting here waiting for you to ask? I have a perfect solution. As long as you like laundry, of course. And boxing, obviously.'

My grandparents glanced at each other.

'Well, there is no problem as far as laundry is concerned,' said Grandpa Benicio, 'but I don't know about boxing . . .'

'We love it, we love boxing,' said Gertrudis, pinching my grandfather.

'Well, that settles it then. Welcome to my house,' said Augusto enthusiastically, and my grandparents clambered into the back of the cart once more.

Augusto turned the corner and headed down Calzada Dolores, passed a small park filled with trees and drove through narrow streets and markets. From time to time, they passed city blocks with just a single mansion perched on a hill and, a hundred metres further on, a serried row of tumble-down shacks where Negroes lived. Some of the blocks had ordinary houses, many of them ruined, while other blocks were rows and rows of shacks. What most struck my grand-parents was the number of black people everywhere – in colonial times, the whole area had been used to house slaves, later there had been *cabildos* or African guilds, eventually they became tobacco plantations – some people walked around dressed in finery, but very few, most were in rags; they were bootblacks, newspaper sellers and street traders or hawkers as they were called back then. Others sold straw hats or bunches of flowers.

Augusto set down Pilar García outside one of the grand mansions. The boy's parents looked my parents up and down. They asked Augusto whether he had taken leave of

211

his senses. 'It's my life, Itamar,' said Augusto. 'You mind your own business.' Then he set off again through the streets and finally pulled up next to a short driveway that led to a small stone house which, to my grandparents, looked like a palace. Augusto lived all alone in this house which had two large bedrooms, a living room, a dining room, a kitchen, a bathroom and a courtyard planted with fruit trees.

'We can stay out here in the courtyard under the avocado tree,' said my grandfather, 'or wherever we won't be any bother.'

'I won't hear of it, young man. I have considered you my friends since the moment I gave you a ride and don't go asking me why, because I don't understand it myself. Let's just say that I might not have grey hair, that's only because I've got no hair at all, but I have a lot of experience sizing people up, and you seem like decent folk. Besides, I've always got along better with country folk because they tend to be more honourable, and they have dignity. In this city, it's a long time since anyone has had any dignity. Every last one of them would trample over their own mother for money.'

'At least let us pay you for the journey,' said Grandma Gertrudis.

'Don't worry, señora, you've more than paid your fare simply by listening to me. You've no idea how long it's been since I got to tell the story of Pepe Antonio and all that stuff back there. Living alone has its compensations, but you get used to not talking and little by little you start to forget everything. Let's get you settled into your room.'

Augusto helped them with their luggage, then showed them the bathroom and the kitchen. Then he excused himself, explaining that he would be right back but first he had to deal with the cart, and he headed outside, whistling a little tune.

'I can't believe our luck,' said Grandma Gertrudis as she stared at a real bathroom for the first time in her life, a genuine bathroom with tiles and a shower, with a mirror and a privy. It was a little early to be celebrating, Grandfather said, because from what they had seen and from the stories Augusto had told them, Havana was a hellhole. By now, night was drawing in. The mango and the avocado trees cast dark shadows over the house, shadows whose tentacles slithered into the rooms. When they were finally tired of exploring, they lay down in their room and made love.

When they woke the following morning, my grandparents found a mouthwatering breakfast waiting on the table: boiled eggs, buttered toast, tropical fruits, orange juice and coffee, all carefully set out on a red tablecloth. In the middle of the table was a jug filled with brilliant flowers. They were so hungry they could have devoured everything in a single mouthful, but instead they called out to Augusto to ask whether he was expecting guests or whether the breakfast was intended for them. Their host was nowhere to be found. So they decided to stroll through the courtyard filled with fruit trees, to wander through the kitchen and the bathroom to check that what they had seen the day before had not simply been a dream. Grandma Gertrudis reached out to touch the bathroom tiles one by one. Then they went back to their bedroom.

Two hours later Augusto arrived back with another man and found the table exactly as he had left it.

'What . . . what happened . . . ?' he said, knocking at the door of my grandparents' room.

'It's just . . . we weren't sure who the food was for,' said Grandma Gertrudis.

'For God's sake, Gertrudis, I don't want you fading away while you're living in my house. Now go eat the breakfast before it spoils.'

My grandparents went into the living room and saw Augusto's friend, who immediately doffed his Bolshevik hat and introduced himself as El Judío – the Jew. He was as pale and bald as Augusto, but shorter than their host and had a large aquiline nose which permanently propped up a pair of spectacles; he had a curious manner of walking on tiptoe, his heels hardly touching the ground, which made it seem as though he moved on springs. He was about forty years old, the same age as his friend.

El Judío shook Grandmother's hand, bowing deeply and complimenting her appearance which he described as beautiful. Grandmother smiled shyly. Then he shook Grandfather's hands and carefully studied them as though they were bedecked with jewels.

'You see what I mean?' said Augusto, clapping his friend on the back.

Grandfather asked if there was something wrong with his hands and El Judío replied that they were magnificent and that, at first glance, they signalled a great future. Benicio looked at Gertrudis. Then he said that he had something he needed to confess; Augusto had been more than generous to them, he said, and he felt they could not lie or keep secrets from him. The truth, he admitted, was that these supposedly magnificent hands had never touched a bar of soap; his hands had never laundered so much as a pair of underpants.

Augusto and El Judío burst out laughing.

'Nor have mine,' said Augusto, and once again he bid them go and eat the food, he told them to take their time but that he would be waiting for them outside with the cart so that they could all go to the laundry which was only a few blocks from here. My grandparents waited until Augusto had stepped out into the hallway, and El Judío had bounded after him, then they fell upon the food like animals. They did not leave so much as a crumb of bread behind.

They drove down the Calle Armas. The day was sunny and the gentle breeze cooled their skin, a blissful relief from the sweltering heat. Along the way, my grandparents noticed that the throngs of people were even more numerous than they had been the night before. Morning is when one can really see people go about their business in Barrio Lawton. Hundreds and hundreds of people walking up and down the street, stopping off at baker's and butcher's, children heading to school, hawkers dragging carts behind them, men weaving straw hats. The neighbourhood teemed with life and my grandparents could see little difference between Barrio Lawton and the centre of Havana other than that there were fewer imposing buildings and fewer people dressed in finery passing in expensive cars.

Something else they noticed was the level of deference and respect, as though, in spite of the obvious divisions between social classes, everyone was keenly aware of the position of everyone else. Respect was something my grandparents were always talking about, lamenting the fact that all the magic words and the courteous phrases of yesteryear had long since disappeared. They were very critical of the modern world. For example, they used to tell me that in the old days, in spite of their poverty, paupers would say 'good day' and 'thank you' and use words like 'please' and phrases like 'if you would be so kind', and they doffed their hats to women. There was a pleasing harmony about things, though this was superficial since the reality, as I'm sure you know, is that back then the effects of slavery, and all the suffering it caused, were still keenly felt. Even so, a certain respect prevailed between people. My grandparents were quietly drinking in all these new sights when suddenly they heard something surprising.

'Did you know that the first European to set foot on Cuban soil was a Jew?' asked El Judío, turning in his seat to look at my grandparents.

'Oh, no,' said Augusto, raising his eyes to heaven. 'Here we go again.'

'There's no "Here we go again" about it, Augusto. They need to know these things. It is part of every Cuban's education,' said the man and lit a fat cigar.

My grandparents looked at him, puzzled. A cloud of smoke billowed towards them. They did their best to waft it away, but the little man went on puffing and blowing smoke as though he had not noticed.

'This is the story. The first person to set foot on Cuban soil was a man named Luis de Torres, a converted Jew, what are commonly called *Marranos*. Luis de Torres was sent as an interpreter to accompany Christopher Columbus. He spoke four languages including Spanish which is why Columbus asked him to go ashore when he was exploring, looking for the Cuban king. Obviously, what they found were Indians. They also found something else. Can you guess what it was?'

'Come now, that's enough. Leave them alone, I'm sure Benicio and Gertrudis don't even know what a Jew is.'

El Judío's face took on a look of shock as though he had just seen a green cat jump on to the cart, as though the sky had suddenly fallen in.

'You don't know what a Jew is?'

'Of course they don't know,' said Augusto. 'No one in Cuba knows.'

'What are you saying, Augusto? This is sacrilege. There are more than eight thousand Jews in Cuba, we have synagogues and even our own cemetery. A Cuban who does not know the meaning of the word Jew is a heretic.' As he said this, El Judío blessed himself three times.

'And what exactly is a Jew, señor?' asked Gertrudis, frowning. 'We thought Judío was your name.'

'It is my name. Judío Alemán is my name – it means German Jew. And it so happens I am a German Jew.'

'What you are is a German-Jewish pain in the ass,' roared Augusto and my grandparents laughed.

'That's not funny, Augusto. Every Cuban should know the history of the Jews, especially you since you are my friend. It's not just the story of Luis de Torres; through history many Jews have contributed to the wealth of our country.'

'Explain it to us, then,' and he jerked the horse's reins, bringing the cart to a juddering halt.

'Explain what?'

'What exactly is a Jew?'

My grandparents looked at the short, hook-nosed man curiously.

'Very well,' said El Judío. He adjusted his spectacles and cracked his knuckles as though about to undertake a task that required great strength. 'Well, in the first place, a Jew is a person, or rather it refers to a group of people; well actually they are a nation from far away on a different continent where they don't have buttered toast for breakfast, instead they have *shakshouka* which is eggs poached in lots of spicy tomato sauce. Jews don't care much for exploitation because they have been exploited throughout history. The Jew is an honest and intelligent man who likes to pray, but he does not pray to Changó or to Jesus Christ or to any of the gods people believe in here in Cuba, but to a different god, and above all, Jews like success . . .'

Judío Alemán concluded his explanation and inhaled a deep puff of smoke, smiling all the while, satisfied with his line of reasoning. Grandma Gertrudis knitted her brows again and Grandpa Benicio glanced at Augusto, who, he realised, had also not understood a word of this explanation.

'Is that it? Is that what Jew means?'

'That's what it means,' said his friend.

Augusto exclaimed that this was the most preposterous twaddle he had heard in all his life. Everyone prayed, everyone liked success and no one liked exploitation, which, by his friend's description, would mean that the whole world was Jewish. He pulled a face and explained to my grandparents that his friend liked to play the fine gentleman in front of guests when in fact at home he had an Eleguá altar with a dead chicken and believed in Changó and all the African gods that real Jews deny. His friend was angered by these comments and brusquely stubbed out his cigar.

The first thing they saw when they got to the laundry was a large sign with the words '*El Buen Vivir*' – The Good Life in red and green letters above a large metal shutter which protected the premises at night against thieves. Augusto took a key from his pocket and opened the padlock, then gave a sharp tug and the metal shutter coiled up inside the top shell as though it were a snail.

Inside, there was a wooden counter set against a black wall which Grandma Gertrudis thought looked very depressing. On the wall hung a blackboard on which was written: 'The Good Life begins and ends here. It can be yours for just a few *reales*.'

Grandfather helped to unload the soap powder and the various chemicals used for washing, and stepped into the back of the shop only to realise it was a dingy little room measuring barely eighteen feet by twenty full of sacks of laundry, sacks of coal, blocks of wood and, right in the middle, a huge machine that looked like a concrete mixer you see everywhere these days. The room gave on to a courtyard where a dozen ropes and wires suspended at different heights were simply washing lines on which to dry the clothes.

After they had inspected the brown-tiled floor and yellow-stained walls and after they had brought in all the laundry, my grandparents asked Augusto where the wash trough was. It was right in front of them, he said, pointing to the concrete mixer in the middle of the room. The rickety appliance consisted of a cylindrical steel drum mounted on a rectangular frame, also made of steel, which was set over a pit in which was a water heater: a coal fire. The drum had a window through which one pushed the clothes and once this was closed you only had to crank the handle in order to turn the drum.

It was very simple, the *habanero* explained. All they had to do was light the fire which heated the water, feed the clothes into the drum, add some soap powder and turn the handle.

'This also was invented by a Jew, this machine,' said El Judío, but nobody paid him any heed. Augusto continued to explain: after half an hour, the laundry had to be taken out and rinsed in one of the drums out in the courtyard and then hung out to dry.

'And people pay to have their clothes washed?' asked Grandma Gertrudis.

'Of course, we almost always get a full sack every day,' said Augusto, pointing to the laundry sacks on the floor. And not only did they wash clothes, he added, they ironed them using five-pound flatirons that needed to be placed in the fire until they were red hot. The laundry business was still new and needed time before it took off, but in general, the customers always left satisfied and invariably returned with more bags of dirty clothes.

'To address Benicio's earlier concern,' said Augusto, 'as you can see for yourselves, thanks to this machine neither of us have ever had our hands in a wash trough.' And with that he clapped twice and everyone got to work.

Grandpa Benicio turned the handle, my grandmother dried the laundry in the courtyard and ironed it while

Augusto manned the counter, dealing with customers, and El Judío ran the cart, fetching and carrying laundry supplies. This was how The Good Life was run.

They started early every morning and finished at nightfall, making it exhausting work. In his first week there, Grandpa Benicio realised why no one had ever lasted working in the laundry. It required almost superhuman strength to spend all day turning the heavy handle. And the pay was meagre. Even so my grandparents were profoundly grateful to Augusto, the white man who had offered work and lodging to two black people from the country he had only just met. Not everyone is so generous and so they never protested. They never complained but welcomed this new life with the same enthusiasm they welcomed this new city. Within a few short weeks, Augusto, El Judío and my grandparents were like a family.

How People Marry

One day, some weeks after my grandparents' arrival in Havana, El Judío took advantage of a moment when Grandma was hanging out laundry in the courtyard to ask my grandfather whether he could smell something.

'Smell what?' said Grandfather, still turning the drum filled with washing.

'Sweaty tits.'

Benicio burst out laughing. El Judío adjusted his spectacles and kept a straight face.

'The smell is coming from that sack there. Could you pass it over to me?'

Grandfather walked over and brought the sack to El Judío who rummaged through the clothes until he found a huge orange bra. He pressed his nose into the cups of the brassière and began to inhale. As he did this, he rolled his eyes back until they were white. These were the tits of Marta the Jew, he explained, and the smell of them drove him wild.

'Damn it, Judío, you're such a pervert,' said Augusto, clipping him round the head. 'Now get your hands off the customers' clothes and stop messing around.'

'What was the other thing Luis de Torres discovered when he arrived in Cuba?' asked Grandpa and watched as the man's face lit up. The little Jew flung his arms around Grandfather's waist exclaiming that he knew all was not lost. He rummaged in his pocket, fished out a cigar butt and cried: 'This!'

According to El Judío, this man named Luis de Torres had been much impressed when he saw the native Cubans smoking; he was responsible for bringing tobacco to Europe and for the first agricultural plantations on American soil. El Judío lit the cigar butt and Grandpa waved the billowing clouds of smoke from his face. The little man looked at his hands, mesmerised. 'Tell me, Benicio, have you never been bitten by the boxing bug? Because with your build and those hands you could fight the great heavyweight Jack Johnson.'

Grandpa replied that, having had a violent past he did not care to think about, he had sworn never again to punch anyone, unless the man deserved it.

'That's what you say now. Let's see what you think when you see the tough guy from El Cerro who's recently come on the scene,' said Augusto, fishing four tickets from his pocket.

They quickly despatched the washing and the ironing for the day and at five p.m. they closed the laundry. Benicio told Gertrudis that it would be better for her to stay at the house, that women were not accepted at boxing matches, but Grandma said that she would not miss it for the world.

The boxing ring was on the Explanada de la Punta near the Malecón. When they arrived, Augusto asked for someone named Pincho Gutiérrez. Ten minutes later, a man who introduced himself as Jesús Losada appeared and led them down a narrow corridor to the ring where the boxers were sparring and warming up. Pincho Gutiérrez came over to them, looking worried.

'What's going on?' asked Augusto.

'Our sparring partner hasn't shown up,' said Pincho Gutiérrez. 'The Kid has got no one to warm up with.'

Augusto introduced the man to his friends. Gutiérrez bowed to Gertrudis, shook hands with El Judío and lastly with my grandfather. He stood staring for a moment at Grandpa, then glanced back at Augusto.

'I know what you're thinking but no, Benicio is not interested in boxing,' said Augusto and handed him an immaculately ironed white linen suit. It was on the house, he said. Gutiérrez was still staring at Grandfather.

'*Oye*, Augusto, don't take this the wrong way but could you persuade Benicio here to take a few punches?'

Augusto shrugged. Benicio looked at Gertrudis. El Judío kept punching Benicio on the arm and nodding.

'I'm sure that someone would have some use for ten pesos,' added Gutiérrez.

'Ten pesos!' cried Gertrudis.

Ten minutes later, Grandpa Benicio was in the boxing ring kitted out in blue shorts and black boxing gloves. There were a few people gathered around the ring who clapped as a black boy of about five foot six climbed over the ropes. His arrival was greeted by wild cheers and my grandfather realised that this was no ordinary boxer. The boy had slicked his hair back with so much brilliantine it was blinding; he had the sleek, silky skin of a horse and a face that betrayed not a hint of violence. He looked to be about seventeen.

'Listen, Kid, my friend Benicio here is going to be your sparring partner today. He's never boxed in his life, so go easy on him, OK? And you, Benicio, you don't need to do anything, just roll with the punches, all right?' Pincho Gutiérrez climbed out of the ring. The two boxers were formally announced. The Kid told my grandfather he was happy to take a few punches, but to only throw a punch when he was asked. They touched gloves and the sparring match began.

The Kid started laying into Benicio from all directions like he was a punchbag.

'The little bastard hit me hard,' Grandpa would tell me years later. He had the speed of a panther and a jab that could inflict serious damage. My grandfather did as he had been asked; he took the punches and tried to make sure they did as little damage as possible.

At some point his opponent said, 'Now punch me.'

'You want me to punch you?'

'Yeah, punch me.'

Benicio hit out, landing a harmless punch to the Kid's chest.

'Harder!' said the Kid, throwing a jab at my grandfather's face.

Benicio threw a left hook, putting a little more force behind it this time.

'Harder!' yelled the Kid.

So Grandpa did as he was asked, lashing out with his right fist and landing a punch on Kid Chocolate that sent him sprawling, unconscious, to the mat.

The audience leapt to their feet, hands above their heads.

Pincho Gutiérrez, looking horrified and open-mouthed, rushed to the ringside with Augusto and El Judío.

'Hell, Benicio, you KO'd him!' roared Pincho Gutiérrez, signalling to someone to fetch a bucket of water which he threw over the unconscious boy.

'I'm fine, I'm fine,' mumbled the Kid a few seconds later. He shook the water from his hair like a wet dog then scrabbled to his feet. The audience clapped and cheered.

'It's my fault. I told him to hit me. But, Benicio, I told you to punch me, not fire a cannonball at me!' the Kid said, smiling. Pincho Gutiérrez relaxed. 'Guess I'm ready for the fight now,' said Kid Chocolate. My grandfather apologised again. He took off his gloves and his boxing shorts and sat down next to Gertrudis who kissed him and told him she was proud that her man was a real man.

It goes without saying that the champion won the fight that night, defeating Pablito Blanco with a KO in the seventh round. But to tell the truth it was like Augusto and El Judío didn't even see the fight. They spent the drive home talking about the miraculous right hook by my grandpa Benicio that had knocked out Kid Chocolate, a boxer who not only never lost a fight but one on whom few fighters managed to land a blow, or even muss up his hair. The next day the champion went to visit Grandfather to ask him how he did it. Grandpa said it was easy, that all he had to do was follow the left jab with a right hook. And showed him. 'You see, it's easy. Try it.'

The champion took Grandpa's advice; he did a quick one-two, followed by a right hook.

'That's the way, Choco! Cross and hook! Cross and hook,

Choco!' Benicio cheered him on, but when he suggested they practise it together, Kid Chocolate said better not, it was getting late and he had to go. 'But I'll see you around,' said the champion and, having thanked Grandpa again, he sauntered down the street, punching the air and chanting, 'Cross and hook, Choco! Cross and hook, Choco!'

Much was said later about Kid Chocolate's boxing style, about how he had learned his moves watching movie footage of Joe Gans and all that. But anyone who really knows the story knows: Kid Chocolate learned to box from my grandpa Benicio.

These were the years when Machado was president, the years which, according to my grandparents, brought terrible misery to Cuba. That's what they used to say. It's also what it says in the history books because obviously I wasn't alive back then and I'm guessing you weren't either. All I can think about is how things are these days, about the hundreds of *balseros* jumping into the sea with rafts or inner tubes or anything that floats desperate to get away from this country, about the power cuts and the shortages and, the way I see it, things are just as fucked up these days. Still, my grandparents insisted that things were even more fucked up back then, that Machado was a son of a bitch just like Commissioner Clemente.

I agree with what Bacardí said, that no one is absolutely good or absolutely evil, we're all a combination of both, a whole that is flawed and sometimes stinking, and that we should be proud of the fact because it is inasmuch as we are imperfect that we achieve perfection, if you take into account the fact that we expect human beings to be imperfect. I'm telling you this because I'm the most cynical, selfish guy on the planet, the sort of guy who sticks his nose into other people's lives; I'm filthy, I'm pedantic, I'd even say I'm a yob. But there's one thing in my favour: I can say 'I was wrong'. Don't laugh, not everyone has the guts to be able to say 'I was wrong' and really mean it.

My grandparents also used to tell me that when Machado was president, he instituted a massive programme of public works, improving roads, building aqueducts, drainage systems, schools and hospitals. He built the vast stone staircase of the University of Havana and the stadium, the Capitol, the Parque de la Fraternidad and the Carretera Central. Of course the guy stole loads of cash while he was at it. But as you know, stealing is nothing new, particularly not now.

Someone who works in a paint factory survives on the paint he steals every day. The same is true of someone who works in a tobacco plant, or as a builder. Engineers have no choice but to work as taxi drivers; doctors don't steal, but they prioritise patients who can give them presents – a bottle of perfume or a crate of beer; even young people are abandoning their studies because they suspect their careers will not provide for them financially in the future. That's why so many of them are becoming whores and rent boys because it's the only way they'll ever know what a disco is, or visit Varadero, and so it goes on, it all becomes a never-ending chain. Everyone steals. I stole a pile of fruit from my neighbours, I even stole a watch.

Now the Romans, for example, they gave the world

architectural wonders like the Coliseum using stolen money. The Vatican was built with stolen money. The Medicis in ancient Florence built their kingdoms on stolen money. The Taj Mahal, the Great Wall of China, Big Ben, all of these wonders were made possible by money stolen from the people. With the sweat and toil of the oppressed. A friend of mine says that what's important is not work, but what you become through work, because at the end of the day all men die, but their work lives on in spite of the suffering and the sacrifice. Just tell me, who in Cuba doesn't admire the majestic Capitolio? What's really sad is when, as years go by, a government's legacy is barely noticed.

Obviously this doesn't change the fact that Machado was a bare-faced thief and Augusto was right when he said the man gave him the creeps. He already sensed something was amiss, but he had no idea how bad things would get.

One day, in 1929, Augusto showed up with a face like a slapped arse and a copy of the newspaper. My grandparents asked what was wrong, but Augusto didn't say anything. El Judío took the paper from him and read aloud that Julio Antonio Mella had been assassinated in Mexico. Alfredo López, leader of the Confederation of Cuban Workers, had also been murdered.

'And who's he?' asked El Judío.

'Julito was from round here. We should mourn him.'

They watched as Augusto walked out the door. That day on strict orders of the management, the laundry, did not open. Augusto did not go back to bed; he went off somewhere, into some dark corner, to pay his respects to the memory of his friend Julito.

The 1930s began with a significant event, the general strike which was joined by more than 200,000 workers all over the island. The strike, which was a great success, had been coordinated by Rubén Martínez Villena who was immediately sentenced to death and had to flee to the United States. But according to my grandparents, 1931 gave them reason to celebrate. Kid Chocolate, who had left in 1928 to continue his career as a boxer in the United States, became world champion for the first time, becoming the first world boxing champion in the history of Cuba.

On the day of his victory, my grandparents helped hang signs painted by El Judío above the laundry. 'That's our Kid Chocolate, *Viva El Kid!*' read one of them. Another read simply 'Kid Chocolate: World Champion'. Augusto insisted they take down the third sign which said 'Kid Chocolate is Jewish', something that deeply upset Judío Alemán.

At two o'clock in the afternoon, they closed the laundry and Augusto invited his friends to take a stroll through the centre of town. There were signs everywhere celebrating the Kid's victory; they hung from the windows of the houses, they were pasted in shop windows, everyone in Cuba was proud. Many people dressed in white and threw their hats in the air while the whoops of joy that echoed through the streets, joined by the blare of horns from a fleet of omnibuses, were a heartfelt addition to the jubilation. The Kid piled up the titles, junior lightweight, lightweight, featherweight, he fought a total of 152 matches, winning 136 – fifty of them by KO – losing only ten and drawing six which led him to be considered among the ten greatest featherweights of all time.

My grandparents were very impressed by the Capitolio, built in a record time of three years, its interiors adorned with fifty-eight different types of marble and precious woods like mahogany. To my grandparents it seemed like only yesterday they had arrived in Havana when there was nothing on this site but piles of sand, stone blocks and steel and now here was the monolithic building. It was a blue and breezeless day, boundless was the bustle of business in the city, the spark of hope to be seen in every face, all brought about by the Kid's boxing triumph. My grandparents used to describe Havana as sheer organised chaos. I figure it must have been a lot more organised than the chaos we have today.

'Look, Benicio, it's Melecio's building,' Geru commented as they passed the Bacardí Building.

'It's not called the Melecio Building, it's called the Bacardí Building. The people who own it are Jewish.'

'Enough already, Judío,' said Augusto, spurring on the carthorse. 'Sometimes you really are insufferable.'

My grandparents said nothing.

Back at the house, Augusto took advantage of Gertrudis being in the bathroom to take Benicio out into the courtyard.

'I noticed that Gertrudis doesn't wear a wedding band,' he said.

'Why are you telling me this?'

'Because it's high time you made an honest woman of her, don't you think?'

'An honest woman?'

'You should marry her, lad. And don't hang about too

long. I can tell you, by the time you get to sixty, you stop living.'

'You stop living at sixty?' Grandpa Benicio did not understand.

Augusto replied that this was one of life's great truths: after the age of sixty, you no longer lived, you *survived*.

'Before you reach sixty, you get pleasure from love, from the temptation to seduce women, from putting on a new suit of clothes, making an effort so that you can swank and later conquer them. But after sixty, love becomes just a commodity. The time for seduction is over, because you can't get it up any more, because the body's defects can no longer be hidden by clothes, however new, however fashionable. The truth is you've become an old man and no one now can save you. You simply survive, Benicio. Vicariously through your children, for example. For those who have them, that is.'

Augusto looked down. 'To put it simply, you feed on memories. I don't know about you but, to me, that's not living, that's surviving.'

'And why did you never marry?' asked Grandfather.

'I did marry. I married an angel, the most wonderful woman in all the world. Olga, her name was. We met at university in the glorious days of our youth. I thought she was too good for me, because, well, I was a depraved young man. There I was going from brothel to brothel while Olga was the purest creature I had ever met. She clearly deserved a better man than I. It was she who changed me the day I gave her a gift of a basket full of bread rolls from the bakery on the Esquina de Toyo. She tossed the basket on the ground and said that if I wanted her to go out with me, I should stop

232

buying bread rolls and start to change my ways. So I changed. I gave up the whores, the gambling, all of my vices, and I devoted myself completely and entirely to her. Never in my life have I met a woman who completed me as she did, with that mane of blonde hair tumbling to her waist, those eyes green as the ocean, that statuesque figure. I knew from the moment I first kissed her that, for me, Olga was the beginning and the end. And so I wasted no time. We were engaged within a month of our first date, and a month after that we were married. I spent every penny I had so that the wedding would be worthy of her – though to find something worthy of Olga was simply impossible. I proposed to her in the Gato Tuerto and then whisked her off to the Cabaret Nacional. It was the most wonderful day of my life. Two years later, Olga died of tuberculosis in my arms. She was only twenty-five. Since then, I have never loved another woman. And I never will.'

This gave Grandpa Benicio pause for thought. This was the first time in the three years since he had met Augusto that he had heard the man speak in such a manner, head bowed, tears in his eyes.

'That's how life is. When it decides to fuck you over, it fucks you good and proper. At least I came through it. El Judío, now he really suffered. You see him all the time joking and laughing, anyone would think he's the happiest man in the world, but it's all an act to hide his grief. First his parents abandoned him. They came here from Europe intending to go to the United States, but when El Judío stood firm and refused to leave Cuba, they left him. Then he found himself a paramour, but before long she cheated on him with another man. Eventually he met the love of his life, the woman he married, the woman who divorced him and took what little he possessed, including his house. It was a disaster. Once he started bragging to me about how he didn't need money because he had friends. I'm rich in friends, he told me. I laughed in his face and told him straight out that no one in the world has more than two or three real friends and that if he wanted proof, he had only to come to my house at three a.m. that night.

'El Judío knocked on my door in the early hours. I took him to a little farm I used to own down Cotorro way. I took hold of one of my pigs, I slit its throat and I smeared him with blood from head to foot. He glared at me, his eyes like a dinosaur, roaring at me asking what the hell I thought I was doing, but I went on smearing his clothes until he was nothing but a mess of pig's blood. "Who did you say your friends were?" I asked him. He said he had lots of friends, that he didn't know where to start. "Give me one name." "Esteban the cobbler," he said and without wasting a minute we went to Esteban's house near Cuatro Caminos. "I was in a fight and killed some guy. The cops are looking for me. Can I hide out in your place?" said El Judío with a look of terror on his face. His great friend Esteban made the sign of the cross three times and said no way, don't come bringing your troubles to my door. So we went and we knocked on the doors of all the supposed friends of our friend the beak. They all said the same: get the hell out of here, sort out your own problems. Only Julio, who looked like a starving wretch and whose clothes were falling off him, had the decency to offer his friendship in time of need. As soon as he opened the door and saw El Judío covered in blood, the first thing he did was ask what he could do, how he could help. You need to come with me to Cotorro, said El Judío, and without a thought the guy pulled some clothes on and came with us. When we got to my farm, we told him it had all been a lie, that we had been trying to find out Judío's true friends. And this decent, loyal man was the only one of Judío's friends who ate the pig I killed that night.

'It was then that El Judío realised that when you laugh the whole world laughs with you; cry, and you cry alone. That's why he's my friend, because we are bound by the memories of the miserable lives we've had to live. So when you see him tomorrow morning, drink a shot of rum in his honour, because his life is well and truly fucked up.'

After Augusto had finished his confession, the two men stood in silence for a long time. Grandpa Benicio felt he had to change the subject, so he went back to talking about marriage, explaining that he knew without a doubt that Gertrudis was the love of his life, it was simply that back in Pata de Puerco people were not in the habit of getting married.

'What do I do after I buy the ring?' asked Grandfather.

'I'll tell you. We all go to a church, you get married and we throw a big party.'

'Marry in a church? We don't believe in God, Gertrudis and me.'

'Neither do I, *chico*,' said Augusto, 'but that's just how it's done.'

That same day, Grandfather began saving money so that he could buy my grandmother a ring. In the laundry, El Judío, who heard about what he was planning from Augusto, constantly teased him, falling on his knees, his Bolshevik hat clutched to his chest, simpering, 'Of course I'll marry you, sweetie-pie.' One time my grandma nearly walked in on them. El Judío, acting the fool, started pretending to play the guitar and my grandmother looked at him suspiciously. 'He does it to hide his grief,' thought Grandpa Benicio. In that moment he realised that Judío's pain was truly terrible since he was constantly play-acting, and Benicio stood looking at him sadly.

Something else I just realised about my grandparents: they were incurable romantics. Not like me, I'm a cynic about most things in life, though even I have my Mr Darcy moments. The love between my grandparents was one of those glorious lovey-dovey relationships with flowers and fine words and great respect. I never heard them say a harsh word to each other, or even heard them argue the way couples usually do, because there are times when you just want to tell your other half to fuck off. Like I did one day with Elena. She was really lovely, she was funny and all that, but sometimes she'd just push my buttons and I'd wind up exploding. Once she started on at me about how I never held her hand and never kissed her in public, about how a bunch of her girlfriends had said I was boorish, that I had no romance.

'Tell your girlfriends to go fuck themselves and stop messing with my head, Elena, unless you want a kick up the arse,' I said. I regretted it afterwards. Truth is, I really loved the bitch.

Anyway, to get back to my grandparents, now they were as sweet as a slab of sticky toffee. That's why I was surprised when Grandpa Benicio told me all the stuff he told me, all that stuff about Pata de Puerco, about saying that Gertrudis was ridiculous, that she was punishing herself. Grandpa wasn't like that. In Lawton, everyone knew him as someone who was polite to dogs, even the vicious mutts. So I wasn't surprised when Grandpa Benicio told me how he proposed to Grandma Gertrudis.

Augusto had suggested that he hide the ring in one of the sweet buns they sold at the bakery on the Esquina de Toyo, wrap it up in a box and present it to her at El Floridita.

'But what if she swallows it?' said Grandfather. Then they thought it might be simpler and more sensible to tie the ring to the leg of one of Judío's carrier pigeons, for example, and release it while Benicio and his future wife were out walking near the Lawton parish church. The dove would come and land on Gertrudis's shoulder and she would immediately notice the ring attached to the bird's foot.

El Judío, for his part, thought this a barbaric idea; if Benicio planned to propose to Gertrudis, he should do so like a Jewish gentleman, save up his money little by little until he had enough to pay José Matamoros and his Band to come and play at the laundry. 'Pack it in, Judío,' said Augusto, 'this is no time for jokes.'

They considered the idea of a drive into the city to the Bodeguita del Medio so that Benicio could propose either on the Malecón as they walked along the seafront, or on the majestic steps leading up to the University of Habana. Eventually, Grandfather told them not to worry about it, he would think of something.

A year later, Grandpa had finally saved enough money to buy an eighteen-carat gold ring for my grandmother. That

August of 1933, Havana was in the grip of a sweltering heat-wave, the sun beat down on the flagstones and by mid-morning clothes were sodden from the humidity. Grandfather asked Augusto if he might have the day off and his friend hugged him hard and wished him luck. 'Cross and hook, Choco!' called Judío and my grandfather watched as they left the house and headed for the laundry.

Gertrudis and Benicio walked along the Calzada Dolores and then turned and headed down the Calzada del Diez de Octubre, stopping to stare in the shop windows. Every time Grandma pointed out something, Grandpa dashed into the shop to buy it for her. 'You're going to bankrupt us, *mi amor*,' said Gertrudis anxiously, but Benicio simply said it was only for today. After that, Grandma stopped pointing out toys and clothes in the shop windows.

They ate *spaghetti à la Napolitana* at a pizzeria near the Esquina de Toyo. Then, since it was Tuesday, the day when women were admitted free to cinemas in Havana, Grandfather took her to the Cine Valentino on the Esquina de Tejas which was showing *One Good Turn* with Laurel and Hardy. They enjoyed the film. At around five p.m., they began to stroll back up the Calzada del Diez de Octubre.

Stopping at a florist, Grandfather bought her a beautiful bouquet of flowers and Gertrudis told him they were beautiful and covered him with kisses. Someone in a passing car shouted, '*Vaya Negro fino!*' while passers-by stopped and applauded, saying, 'Well done. That's the way to do it!' Benicio slipped an arm around Gertrudis's shoulders and they walked on up the hill. They turned and headed to the Lawton church which was just off the main street.

'Where are you taking me, Benicio?' In front of the church was a glorious, towering flame tree. 'I'm taking you to the only flame tree I could find. The only one in the *barrio*.' Gertrudis rushed over, hugged the tree and sighed. 'It's beautiful. Just like the flame tree in Pata de Puerco, remember? I wonder how everyone is back home? I wonder if . . . ?'

'Forget all that, Gertrudis,' said Grandfather. They stood in silence. Grandma Gertrudis asked what was going on. Grandpa sat down on a bench next to the flame tree and buried his head in his hands, as though he were tired or feeling ill. An old woman coming out of the confessional stopped and stared at the two strangers as a younger woman went in to confess her sins.

'Are you feeling all right, Benicio?'

'Listen, Gertrudis,' my grandfather was trembling, 'I brought you here to say that I can't compose poetry like Melecio. I don't know how to read or write. But there is one thing I do know, something I knew from the day I first opened my eyes: that you are the love of my life, Gertrudis. I would like to marry you. Would you do me that honour?'

Grandmother was pale. Grandfather slipped a hand into his pocket, went down on one knee and, still staring at the ground, he held up the ring. Gertrudis lunged for it and the ring flew into the air, then rolled down the street. They raced after it, finally catching up just as it was about to fall down a drain. Grandma gave a little laugh and then slipped the ring on to her finger.

'Why are you shaking?' said Gertrudis. 'Your hands are all sweaty. Don't tell me you were nervous.'

'I was scared,' said Grandfather.

'You're such a fool, Benicio. Were you really afraid I would say no?'

'No. I was afraid that having blown all my savings, the cursed ring was going to roll down the drain.'

They laughed again. Then they kissed beneath the flame tree that brought back so many happy memories. The faint glow of the gathering dusk illuminated them. Suddenly, a soft breeze blew up and they felt a wave of joy surge through them. And that was all. No carrier pigeons, no sweet buns, no Matamoros and his Band. Not everyone realises that magic lies in simplicity. It's something I have come to know only too well.

A moment later, they heard the celebrations. People came pouring into the streets with passionate excitement, singing, screaming, turning their music up full blast. From where my grandparents stood, they heard something like the sound of a baseball bat hitting a column. It could easily be somebody's spinal column, my grandparents thought, or the six-foot column of a house. And then more screams. When they asked people in the street what the celebrations were about, they were told Machado had been toppled. He had fled the country for Nassau.

The festivities continued with their friends back at the laundry until the small hours. My grandparents' engagement and the fall of Machado, two good reasons to celebrate. My grandparents were married a month later at Lawton church in the presence of their loyal friends Augusto García and Judío Alemán. The laundry didn't close that night either.

The Homecoming

Time, as it does, went on passing. By now Machado was dead and the Jackal of Oriente had hanged the forty-four peasants in Santiago. The Pentarchy of 1933 had been dissolved, Batista had mounted the coup d'état that overthrew Grau San Martín and construction of the art deco López Serrano Building had been completed. The Hotel Riviera had crowned itself the first hotel in the world with centralised air conditioning and work had begun on the FOCSA Building which, for a time, would be the tallest reinforced-concrete building in the world.

I know I've just leapfrogged the rest of the 1930s, the whole of the 1940s and landed slap bang in the middle of the 1950s, but to be honest nothing that happened during that period is relevant to the story. Besides, I'm the narrator and I don't feel like talking about it, and anyone who doesn't like it can fuck off. Fuck 1940 and its 'progressive constitution'. I don't want to argue about whether *chicharrones* are meat or espadrilles are shoes. I'm sorry? Did you say something? I already told you, I don't want to talk about Carlos Mendieta, Miguel Mariano and that bunch of old duffers, so stop being such a drag or I'll kick your ass out of here too.

Bueno, we've just skipped from the part where Ernesto Lecuona was nominated for an Oscar, to Pérez Prado's song 'Patricia' topping the American hit parade for fifteen consecutive weeks, a record unmatched even by Elvis Presley or The Beatles. All that stuff had happened when my grandparents decided to go see a doctor to find out why Grandma Gertrudis couldn't get pregnant. They had been trying for a baby for a while by then. They tried during fertile periods when Grandma was ovulating, they tried at the full moon, but nothing worked. There came a moment when Benicio began to think it was his fault.

'My milk is no good,' he said sadly.

The blood that flowed through his veins, the blood of his father, was a curse, he said. My grandma said that if anyone was to blame it was her, that every time after they had sex, she would go to the bathroom to pee to stop Benicio's sperm getting any farther. Benicio said she was crazy, insisting that he was to blame. Grandma insisted that she was. So they concluded there was only one way to find out.

The doctor first examined Benicio. He told him to masturbate and ejaculate into a little cup. Then he examined Gertrudis, touching and palpating her, something that infuriated Benicio who waved his arms, demanding to know what the hell he was doing; Gertrudis was his wife.

'And I am her doctor, so if you could stand aside and let me do my job.'

Gertrudis begged Benicio to calm down and stop being so jealous.

Two weeks later, my grandparents received the sad news: they could never have children. Grandma Gertrudis had an obstruction in her Fallopian tubes, there was nothing to be done. This was followed by long weeks of grief and tears when Grandma locked herself in the bathroom and would not open the door, not even to God Himself. Benicio talked to his friends about his wife's condition, about how worried he was. He asked their advice.

'Love and affection,' Augusto recommended. 'Be loving and affectionate towards her, Benicio.'

But all his love, all his affection, were not enough to comfort my grandmother. Gertrudis felt that it was not worth carrying on. Her reason for living had died the moment the doctor gave his diagnosis. Her appetite and her sex drive dwindled. She forgot how to eat and how to fuck. For my grandparents, food and sex became something else, something unattainable, ineffable, something beyond action, beyond words. Simply undressing to put on fresh clothes was like flaying my grandmother alive. Grandma Gertrudis was really ill.

In the morning, she would refuse to go to work at the laundry. She would drink her coffee then lock herself in the bathroom. Benicio had run out of ideas. Then El Judío said, 'Leave it to me,' and he too disappeared from the laundry for several weeks. Augusto and Benicio now began to worry about the Jew as well. Nobody had heard from him. Nobody had seen him leave his apartment. One day, my grandfather went to his house. He lived in a rented apartment on the Calle Armas, in a dilapidated, ramshackle building. Grandfather peered through a chink in the blinds. El Judío was performing some sort of ritual. It was not exactly *santería*, though in the middle of the room there was an Elegúa altar on which lay the bloody carcass of a chicken; strewn on the floor and in the shrine were candles and sweets. There was also a large, thick tome lying in a corner of the room with the inscription תּוֹרָה embossed in gilt on the cover. El Judío, dressed in black and white, was holding a candelabra.

He did not look like El Judío, but like some demon.

'The devil has taken possession of El Judío,' thought Grandpa and ran to tell Augusto. El Judío never meddled in such things, Augusto said; in all the years they had known each other, this was the first time he had performed a Jodío–Cubano ritual.

'Jodío–Cubano?' asked Benicio.

This, Augusto explained, was the correct term for a freakish fucked-up cod-Jewish part-Cuban ritual but asked Benicio not to use the phrase since it would only anger El Judío.

'He is doing it because he loves you both. Even though we all know that a dead chicken and a few prayers from some old book will not change anything.'

Grandfather stared at the ground. Augusto came over and patted him on the shoulder.

'Chin up,' he said, and offered the sage opinion that life is shit. Then he turned back to his work.

A month later El Judío reappeared at the laundry. Grandpa Benicio and Augusto hugged him and told him he looked terrible. He had lost a lot of weight, his sleepless nights had left him with dark circles around his eyes which were further magnified by his spectacles. El Judío said that he had done all he could and that there was nothing to do now but wait.

'Wait for what?' asked Benicio.

'For a sign,' said El Judío.

A month passed.

'Is Gertrudis pregnant yet?' asked El Judío.

'No,' said my grandfather.

A second month passed.

'Still nothing, Benicio?'

'Nothing.'

'That's strange,' said El Judío.

The truth was that neither my grandfather nor Augusto took El Judío seriously, and they were certainly not waiting for a sign or indeed anything to come as a result of his cunning ritual.

And yet, in the third month, something did happen. For years my grandparents had been sending letters to Pata de Puerco telling Betina about their new life. They had never had a reply. Nor did they expect one. And so they were extremely surprised when one morning a telegram arrived.

'Come quickly,' was Betina's message. 'I don't have much time.' My grandparents packed up a few things and caught the first train heading for Santiago.

When they arrived in Pata de Puerco, the village was exactly as they had left it, with the same communal well, the same flame tree, the same cemetery – though this last had increased in size to cope with the small thicket of wooden crosses planted in the earth. Having lived so long in the greyness of Lawton, the green of the trees seemed deeper, more intense. More than ever, the sun seemed to hurl its golden daggers. The sky was a dazzling, almost metallic blue, but for the most part little had changed since they left, except that now there was not a single familiar face.

To my grandparents' surprise, people came out to greet them as though meeting with a living legend. At first no one recognised them. The villagers assumed they were travellers who had lost their way. Then someone shouted, 'It's Benicio – Benicio and Gertrudis!' and suddenly children and adults began to pour from the houses and the shacks that still smelled of coal and kerosene. The villagers hugged them warmly, as though they were long-lost friends. Some were so moved, they had tears in their eyes.

'Where is Ester the midwife?' asked Benicio.

'She died years ago,' they told him.

'And Juanita?'

'Dead too.'

The Santacruzes, the Aquelarres, Señor and Señora Jabao, Eustaquio the *machetero*. They had all been cured of life and now rested in peace, lying face up in the cemetery.

They stepped inside the little shack where they had spent their childhood years. Memories were everywhere: in the wooden table bleached by time, in the bedrooms with no doors, in the chinks and holes in the walls through which my grandparents had peered as children. Benicio rushed to kneel by Betina's bed.

'What's the matter, Mami?' he said, taking her hand.

'Nothing, *hijo*. I'm dying, that's all.' Betina hugged her children. Then she told them that before Juanita died, she consulted her cauldron and told Betina that she would die on February the fifth.

'Why do you say that?' Betina had asked.

'Because you are going to die,' said the *santera* and explained that Betina needed to make plans so that her children could be with her. Betina had asked how she would die and Juanita told her that first her heart would receive a terrible shock, something Juanita felt it better not to reveal to her in advance. Then, in the early hours of February the fifth, she would die of nothing specific, that eventually the hour comes for all of us, and this would be Betina's hour.

Having said this, the wise-woman stepped outside to gaze one last time at the collection of beautiful African orchids planted in her garden.

'Say my goodbyes to the village. Thank them for sharing with me the good times and the bad times of old age and tell them I will wait for them on the other side.'

The following morning, the body of Juanita was laid to rest beneath one of the forest of crosses in the cemetery.

Juanita had made a mistake, Benicio cried frantically, everyone was wrong; Betina was coming back with them to Lawton. Betina replied that the wise-woman had always had a talent for predictions and she had never been wrong before.

'Where's Melecio?' asked Gertrudis.

'Ah, now that's another story. Go warm up the coffee, Geru, and pull up a chair, because the tale I have to tell is a long one so it's better that you make yourself comfortable.'

Gertrudis warmed the dark brew and took a seat as her mother had asked.

'You both know that Melecio is not like other people, it's hardly a secret here in the village,' said Betina, sipping the coffee. 'Well, after José died and you left Pata de Puerco,

Melecio got it into his head to turn the village into a town with paved streets and schools and hospitals. Your brother always was a dreamer, as you know. So he picked out a small group of promising pupils – Anastasia Aquelarre, Ignacio and Juan Carlos el Jabao – in order to teach them what they would need to know. It would be a difficult task, he explained, but a necessary one, and if they should fail it didn't matter because he knew that in the future others would carry on their work.

'After a while Melecio's pupils became experts in law and politics, even in architecture, and learned to express themselves like attorneys.

'"It's time," Melecio told them, and signalled to Ignacio el Jabao to follow him.

'Oh, I forgot . . . remember María, Melecio's girlfriend, the beautiful black girl he used to mention in his letters? Well, she was pregnant and she came here to live with him in a house they built down by the river. She always encouraged him to dream, he had come into this world to do great things, she told him, and I saw for myself how much she loved and respected him. And so Melecio and Ignacio went to El Cobre to see Emilito Bacardí, the son of Don Emilio, who had passed away by then.

'They explained everything to the nobleman, showed him meticulously detailed plans of the new city, with drains and aqueducts and the famous streetlamps that José used to dream about. Emilito loved the idea and promised to present it to all the politicians and the lawmakers who had the power to make the plans a reality.

'These powerful men could not believe that there was a village in Cuba so remote that it did not have so much as a sewerage system. They pledged to fix the problem, insisting that everyone in Cuba – or at least in the district of Santiago – should have electric light. But days and weeks and months went by and no one did anything. Melecio realised that he had wasted his time, that it had all been false promises and white lies.

'So your brother decided that if he could not do this by fair means, he would do it by foul. Slowly he began to bring together all the farmers and the labourers in the area who lived in similar conditions to ours and explained the situation to them. Over time, there were more and more of them, and one day they demonstrated in front of the presidential palace, carrying placards, chanting slogans and demanding improvements. Obviously no one dared to lay a finger on them. Everyone knew Melecio was the adopted son of the Bacardí family.

'It was then that Ignacio el Jabao showed his claws; he turned against the protestors, saying that this was no way to behave. Ignacio had ulterior motives, and besides he had always been jealous of Melecio, whose fame had now spread far beyond Santiago. Everyone was talking about the new messiah, about the madman who had dared to champion the plight of the poor. The politicians did everything they could to get rid of him. They tried to reason with him, but Melecio simply replied that there was nothing to talk about and went on dragging his people through every street of the city.

'Some of the politicians saw Ignacio as the solution to their problem. They called him up one day and promised him mansions and castles, promised he could be a councillor, a congressman, on one condition: "All you have to do is get rid of Melecio."

'No one knows for certain what Ignacio said. His brother Juan Carlos swears that Ignacio had nothing to do with what happened, that he did not betray Melecio. All we do know is that one day, some months after Melecio and María's son was born, Ignacio showed up to present an invitation to dinner at the house of Governor X during which the future of the new city was to be resolved.

'"In that case, we'll go," said Melecio and he and María left for Santiago early the next morning. Ignacio went with them. This we know because Ignacio himself told us that on the way back to the village, a group of armed men in suits and hats stopped them and forced them into a ditch. It was there that they shot Melecio and María.

'It was Ignacio who brought the bodies back here the following day. El Jabao swore he did not know why he had simply been knocked unconscious. Everyone in the village watched as he stood there, sobbing and writhing in agony. A week later, Ignacio el Jabao was mysteriously summoned to take up a position as councillor in the Chamber of Representatives in Santiago, which is where he lives now.

'That's what happened and, just as Juanita predicted, my heart was split in two. I ordered that the bodies be buried next to Oscar and Malena among the ruins of the old sugar plantation and I told them while they were there to dig a grave for me next to José since, as you know, tomorrow is the fifth of February, the day I am destined to die.'

Benicio and Gertrudis listened to all this, eyes filled with tears. Grandfather had been pacing up and down the room. 'I'm going to find that bastard Ignacio,' he roared, but Betina and Geru stopped him and told him it was not worth it, that revenge would solve nothing. The most important thing, said Betina, was to take the poor child sleeping in the next room as far from Pata de Puerco as possible, to a place where he might have a better future, a place where he would never know such misery.

'That will be difficult, Mami,' said Benicio. 'There are not streets enough in this country to escape from misery.' In Havana, he explained, there was poverty greater than this.

Gertrudis ran into her old bedroom. The little boy was sleeping in a wooden cot. Betina called for her to bring the baby in so they might all sit around her bed. When at last she could see their three faces, Betina let out a heavy sigh.

'Do you remember, Benicio, that day you came home cursing and swearing, using words you'd learned from Ignacio?' said Betina.

My grandparents laughed.

'And the day Melecio recited that poem in El Cobre?'

My grandparents laughed again.

'Remember the day Melecio cooked the chicken, Mami? Remember the beating Papá José gave him?'

Since neither Betina nor Gertrudis remembered this incident, Benicio told them what had happened and everyone laughed again.

'Remember . . . ? Remember . . . ?' And so the children and their mother went on remembering happier days that brought great comfort to their spirits. Betina told them about the first time she had met José down by the river. She remembered her sister Malena, her brother-in-law Oscar, recounted stories about each of her three children. Each flickering memory in her mind transported her back to distant days when the world was young, as young as she. Those far-off days were lost now in time, but still they existed, their bright, vivid colours stored in memory. Happiness filled her as it had not done in years.

'To remember is to live. Now I understand,' she said, her voice a faint whisper.

And still she and her children continued to wander the labyrinthine pathways of the past until, by midnight, all of them had fallen asleep.

After they buried Betina, my grandparents came back to Lawton with Melecio and María's son – with me. This is where my story begins. I don't know whether I already introduced myself, but in case I didn't, shake my hand. Pleased to meet you. My name is Oscar. I shouldn't need to tell you my surname, you're clever enough to work it out for yourself. But I'll tell you anyway, it's Mandinga. Oscar Mandinga. That's my name.

Gunned Down

So now you know. Oscar Mandinga, at your service. Like I said at the start, I don't remember any of this stuff. And I can hardly blame my grandparents for not asking Betina before she died about the precise date and time I was born, which means of course that I don't know. The poor things had enough to deal with, going back to Pata de Puerco after all those years only to find my great-grandmother dying. About me, Betina told my grandparents only one thing.

'Whenever little Oscar plays up, just put him in a basin of mud. It's the only way to calm him down.'

'What do you mean?' asked my grandparents, and Betina told them the story of how I was born in muck and mire in accordance with the ancient traditions and beliefs of my mother María's family. Imagine it. I slid down the thighs of the mother I never knew and into the mud like a slug and as soon as my mother plucked me up out of the muck, I started bawling like I'd been stuck with a fistful of needles. Only when she set me in the mud again did I calm down. So my grandparents always kept a basinful of mud in the bathroom beside the glass that held Grandpa

Benicio's teeth during that phase of my life they called the 'mud period'.

They told me about a little bald man with a hooked nose called Judío and another man who owned the laundry called Augusto. They told me that when I was four I hung around with them all the time and called them Uncle. El Judío even put one of the little round caps Jews wear on me which made everyone laugh. My grandparents tell me they were magical years, but I of course have no memory of Judío or of Augusto.

By the 1950s, Lawton had changed a lot. The laundry business was booming with the introduction of new electric washing machines from America. Financially everything was fine until Batista mounted the military coup in 1952 which led to terrible unemployment. The mafia started to take over, though it has to be said that as far back as the 1930s Meyer Lanski and Lucky Luciano had been wandering round the streets of Havana dreaming of creating a casino paradise where the mafia would control not just the country's finances but its future leaders. I don't know if you've seen *The Godfather, Part II*, the scene re-creating the meeting at the Hotel Nacional in 1946 that attracted every mob boss in organised crime from Albertos Anastasia to Santos Trafficante. The top two floors of the hotel were closed to the public, and this is where Meyer Lanski revealed his long-held dream of converting the island into the Monte Carlo of the Americas, a vast metropolis of hotels, casinos and private air-ports even bigger than Las Vegas. With Batista back in power, anything was possible. Once they had him in their pocket, they began building the Hotel Riviera, the Duville, the

Capri, the Comodoro, and the Havana Hilton – what we now call the Habana Libre.

Cash began to flood into the country, and there was a lot of conspicuous wealth; meanwhile on the flipside of the coin only a third of the population had running water, and the salary of the average family was barely six pesos a week, which resulted in starvation and destitution. Pretty quickly, the people started to rebel which only made Batista adopt a trigger-happy policy meaning that anyone caught up in any form of sedition was dead meat.

Augusto and Judío joined the underground resistance. They really hated Batista. The government was illegitimate they maintained and therefore unconstitutional, that elections could not be cancelled, that the people had a right to choose their own future, their own president.

'That bastard Batista is sullying the reputation of Lawton,' Augusto would complain. When my grandparents asked why he said this, he explained that he knew Batista who had lived for some time above the Cuchillo Café near Toyo and that whenever he went to the bakery, he used to meet him queuing to buy bread. Judío said this was why he preferred people to be either black or white, because mulattoes like Batista, if they don't fuck up in the beginning, they'll fuck up in the end. In spite of everything, my grandparents still lived a relatively peaceful existence, though overnight the laundry's clientele began to dwindle because everyone was being frugal, carefully guarding what little money they had. But Cubans like to dress well, and given that the middle classes were least affected by the slump and many of them lived in Lawton, money kept coming in.

A thousand times Benicio and Gertrudis told Augusto and Judío not to go mixing with revolutionaries, that they were too old for such shady business, but their friends went on distributing posters for 'M-26-7' – the 26th of July Movement – and storing them in the laundry. They took part in strikes, marched in public demonstrations, saying they were tired of all the lies. Grandma Gertrudis asked Judío what he had to do with any of this, given that he was a Jew and came from Europe. 'I'm a Cuban Jew. That's something very different,' said Judío Alemán and went on conspiring against Batista.

That morning, the tension on the streets was palpable. José Antonio Echeverría had been murdered a few days earlier. 'Manzanita', as Echeverría was known, had already taken many beatings, but he had gone on fighting and in 1957, after leading students storming the Presidential Palace and the headquarters of Radio Reloj, he was cornered by a patrol near the University of Havana and gunned down. Things were spiralling out of control, people started to shut themselves up in their houses, they were afraid to go out. Some stooge had grassed up the M-26-7 sympathisers in Lawton and the cops were out looking for them with orders to shoot to kill. They searched print shops, bodegas, grocery stores and shoe shops, investigating, poking around, putting pressure on people to find out where the meetings were being held, where the posters were being printed. And that's how it happened that seven men in plain clothes, sporting the sort of hats worn by mobsters in movies about Al Capone, turned up at the laundry. By chance, my grandparents had stayed at the house, leaving me in the care of Judío and Augusto.

'Judío, grab little Oscar,' Augusto said to his friend when

he saw the cars draw up outside. El Judío popped his head above the counter and then took me out the back.

'How can I help you?' said Augusto. The men pushed past him and started rummaging through everything, tossing things on the floor. It didn't take them long to find the posters in an empty washing powder drum.

'Found them,' said one guy.

Four starving dogs appeared from nowhere. One of the men who had stayed outside drew his gun, flicked the safety catch and fired. Judío and Augusto jumped. One of the scampering dogs fell dead, its body skidding across the pavement; the other three bolted as Augusto watched helplessly.

The man who had fired walked over to the dead dog and kicked it. He was a tall, blond guy with a moustache that made him look like Errol Flynn, and he was smoking. He ducked as he stepped into the laundry, like he was afraid of hitting his head on the doorframe, then smiled as though he had just pulled a prank.

'Hey, Augusto, you know what this means, don't you?' said the guy, obviously in charge. El Judío, meanwhile, was trying to sneak out the back door with me in his arms.

'Hey, hey, where d'you think you're going? Get the fuck back in here, I've got business with you too,' said the boss and his men pushed Judío back into the laundry. The man turned back to Augusto. 'Now listen up, don't think we don't know what you've been up to. We didn't arrest you before now because you're Colonel García's uncle, but this is serious. This time we have no choice but to use force.'

'The reason of force cannot prevail against the force of

reason,' said Augusto and the man looked at him as though he were ill, or had got the wrong person.

'Fucking hell. I didn't know you were a philosopher. Shame, actually, because I love philosophy. Got any other words of wisdom before I put a bullet in you?'

At that moment, Judío opened his eyes wide and set me down on the ground.

'Yes,' said Augusto, 'tell Pilar, that thug of a nephew of mine, that his time will come. Tell him that. Now do what you have to do and get it over with.'

Hearing this, the man tossed his cigar butt on the floor.

'OK, in that case . . . You heard the philosopher, boys. When you're done, I'll be waiting for you at Pío Pío in Santa Catalina. Oh, and bring me the little black brat.'

The boss climbed back into his car and disappeared. His men began loading up boxes of pamphlets. They ripped the washing machines out, leaving the walls bare. A bunch of them headed out, but three of the men stayed behind.

'Don't let the kid see this,' shouted Augusto.

'Walk over to the wall,' the men ordered.

'Wait a minute,' said Judío. 'Oscarito, come over here.' I tottered over and gave Judío a kiss, and one to Augusto. The men grabbed me roughly by the arm and dragged me away. Then, without wasting a second, they gunned down my grandparents' friends, riddling them with bullets. The sound of the shots could be heard all over Lawton. They killed them right before my eyes. Someone ran to tell my grandparents what had happened. My grandmother started wailing.

'Stay here, Gertrudis, and try to calm down,' said Benicio and set off running down the Calzada Dolores.

Arriving at the laundry, a grey pall of steam from the boiling clothes slowly rose to the ceiling where it formed a dense, dark-yellowish cloud that obscured everything. He groped his way around, and heard a moan like a child trying not to vomit. He came upon the bodies, drenched in blood and soapy water. He shook Augusto and Judío, but they could no longer speak, could no longer moan. He stumbled out on to the street again and saw the dead dog on the pavement. He screamed my name. 'They took him, Benicio,' people told him, 'they took him down towards Santa Catalina.'

He ran on down the Calzada del Diez de Octubre. He almost upset a flower cart that appeared from nowhere. He dodged the cars, the streetcars, the motorbikes, and when he finally arrived at the Avenida Santa Catalina he looked around. There was no sign of me. He looked in the cinema and searched the lobby then came out again and wandered up and down Santa Catalina and then along Soledad through a little square that locals used as a car park, then he carried on down Santa Catalina and as he came to Avenida Mayía Rodríguez he saw a line of cars parked on the avenue outside Pío Pío. The sound of celebrations reached him on the breeze. The sound of people having fun. Some men were forcing two small boys to fight. One of the boys was me. I had blood around my mouth and tears in my eyes. Grandpa waded into the crowd, elbowing his way through the circle of men and was just about to pick me up when one of them grabbed him by the shoulders. It was the same man who, minutes earlier, had given the order to kill Augusto and El Judío. Grandfather turned and instinctively threw a left hook that hit him square on the jaw, knocking him unconscious.

The other men pulled their guns. Some ran to help their boss Rolando Masferrer who lay sprawled in the road. The others simply aimed their pistols at my grandfather's face.

'Don't touch him. Leave him to me,' said a uniformed man of average height with the sort of pot belly that comes from too much beer. He asked my grandfather to walk with him to his car. The other men went on trying to revive Masferrer, but he was not coming round. We got into the swanky car and the man floored the accelerator.

For a while we all sat in silence. My grandfather hugged me to him as though afraid that the car would hit a pothole and I would go flying through the windscreen. The driver was smoking panatella cigars. He was staring straight ahead as though he did not know what to say.

'If there's one thing about me, it's that I never forget a face,' he said finally.

'I don't know what you're talking about,' said my grandfather.

'I'm talking about thirty years ago. You and your wife had just arrived in Havana. My uncle gave you a lift in his cart. I'm Pilar, the kid who was sitting next to you. Remember?'

'Of course I remember. Just as I won't forget that you had your uncle murdered.'

The man took a deep breath and tossed the cigar out the window.

'Yes. I know,' he said. 'It seems nobody forgets anything. I'll never forget the beatings my uncle gave me, or the sweets your wife gave me. You'll never forget that I ordered men to kill your friends. And Masferrer will never forget you knocked him out with a single punch.'

When Grandma Gertrudis saw us arrive back in the car, she rushed over and hugged me.

'Thank you, señor. Thank you for bringing them back safe and sound,' said Grandma, sobbing. From his pocket the man took another panatella and lit it. Then he turned to Grandpa Benicio. 'Now that no one owes anyone anything, I'd advise you to get out of here.'

'Is that what a man has to do to live in peace? Go somewhere else?' said my grandfather, still cradling me in his arms.

'I don't know,' said Colonel Pilar García. 'You could try. Go somewhere else, go back to the country, go back to Oriente. Hide in a cave if you have to. But don't trust to hope. There's no hope left in this country.'

Having said this, Pilar García climbed back into his car and took off with a squeal of tyres down the Calzada Dolores.

We buried Augusto and the Jew in Colón cemetery. They were solitary men, with no family, no friends, and so the only people at the wake were my grandparents, Gertrudis and Benicio, and me. We went on living in Augusto's house since we had nowhere else to go and no heir came to claim it. Batista fled Cuba in the early hours of 31 December 1958 after a farewell cocktail party as the revolutionaries were marching into Havana. Gradually, American businesses were nationalised and eventually private property was abolished. The Bacardís moved their rum business to Puerto Rico. Masferrer was blown up by a bomb placed in his car in Miami in 1975. Pilar García died of cirrhosis of the liver.

I remember none of this. The psychologists diagnosed me with elective amnesia, a defence mechanism used by people to forget traumatic events. I don't remember Augusto or El Judío or the day they were riddled with bullets before my eyes. All I remember is that time when I strangled the fucking cat. That I remember only too well.

The Biggest Maggot in the World

This is where I begin . . . but before we get to my part of the tale, you need to know that it's difficult to tell a story and be objective when you're locked up in a dark room. What I mean is it's not the same as telling the story lying on a sandy beach with a mojito in your hand. It's difficult not to talk about depressing things when you're strapped to a bed in a bare cell and have whiteshirts – who, like I told you earlier, are really members of the Cuban Ku Klux Klan – come by every two days and split your skull in two. Commissioner Clemente says that not only did I make all this stuff up, but he even insists that I don't exist. Imagine if someone told you that you are not who you think you are, that your grandparents, your neighbourhood and everything you've ever known is a fiction, that you're a ghost, a head case, a fabulist who goes through life spouting fairy tales and bullshit. The bastard has tried to convince me that I'm mad and that's what really pisses me off. It's enough to make you want to kill somebody.

But that's what that damn fool Clemente said to me when he interrogated me. I'm not going to bore you with all that shit though, or with stuff about when I took my first steps or what my first word was. The story about the cat is simple, there's nothing else to add to it except that the cat ate my lunch: fried chicken, vegetables, rice, black beans and guava jelly. The bastard cat only left the guava jelly. 'I'll get you,' I thought. I went back into class and after the last lesson, at about six o'clock, I came across the cat, rummaging though a garbage bin. I went over and held out a piece of bread. The cat came over to me. It started eating the bread and I stroked its back. When I got it to trust me, I grabbed it by the neck and strangled it. All the way home, I gripped it tightly. People were staring at me and shouting, 'Leave that poor cat alone.' But I ignored them. I kept on walking. Grandma jumped when she saw me appear in the doorway. I told her what had happened and she yelled at me, told me that was no reason to strangle a helpless creature. I tossed the cat on the ground, the head came off the body and rolled across the pavement. Then I slammed my fist into the front door so hard I broke my wrist. And that was that for the quadruped.

My grandparents said that they used to have to take me by the hand and lead me to school because otherwise I'd head for any river or marsh or swampland along the way. Can you imagine? You have to remember that I took the stories Grandpa Benicio told me very seriously. He used to tell me stories before I fell asleep. One day he told me about the brave feats of Martí and Antonio Maceo, the same tales his father had told him when he was a boy. The next day, I came home with a face covered in bruises, two black eyes and my nose bent out of shape.

'Oscarito!' said Grandpa Benicio. 'What on earth happened to you?'

Well, what had happened was during the game of marbles we played every day in La Loma del Burro park in Lawton, this boy named Enrique – everyone called him 'the Terror of Lawton' – took some other boy's marbles. None of the other kids had the guts to stand up to him because Enrique wasn't called the Terror of Lawton for nothing. But the story my grandpa had told me convinced me that I too had been put on the earth to free mankind.

'If you don't give Congo his marbles back, I'm going to kill you with my stone axe,' I told the Terror of Lawton. When he heard this, fifteen-year-old Enrique drew himself up to his full height and launched himself at me. Then he blacked both my eyes, covered my face in bruises and broke my nose.

Grandpa Benicio angrily asked me who I thought I was to go round saving people.

'José Martí would have done the same thing,' I said.

'Martí didn't go round killing people with a stone axe,' said my grandfather, then burst out laughing. I can remember that like it was yesterday. The reason I remember it so well is that the next day Elena enrolled in my school, in my class, and soon we were inseparable.

The first time I took Elena to bed, she warned me that it was nothing serious, that she didn't want me getting the wrong idea. I liked Elena a lot, so didn't tell her that she was the one who had to be careful because I was the most cynical guy she would ever meet. I just told her that I would let her decide the boundaries of our relationship and that I would

265

respect her decisions. I knew she'd been with other guys, I'd even met some of them because she always introduced me to them and I introduced her to my ex-girlfriends like it was some sort of competition, like the Grand Prix for who had fucked more people. All the same, I was taken by surprise when Elena referred to our first sexual encounter as 'satisfactory'. I knew that 'satisfactory' was way short of the mark after the eight-hour non-stop rollercoaster of sex I'd given her. We met up again a couple of weeks later and it was even better, but this time Elena didn't say anything, she just kissed me on the cheek and left.

Sometimes I would call her, usually in the afternoon when she was involved in Party meetings and all that political bullshit, and we'd chat for five or ten minutes about what had happened that day. It was only when she called me that we would arrange to meet up, always at her place, an apartment in a cooperatively built *micro-brigada* block on the Calle Jesús María where doctors and lawyers lived, several dentists and a couple of university professors. Our encounters always followed the same pattern. I would go up the stairs, knock twice on her door, she would open it and we would greet each other with a kiss, but without touching each other. In Act Two we'd sit down and drink rum, stare out at the neighbouring buildings, dark hulks in the faint evening light, made darker by the grimy glass of the window, and we'd talk about the Revolution, about the new edition of *Sputnik* and about school stuff. We'd watch the movies on *Veinticuatro por Segundo* or *La comedia silente* with Armando Calderón. Then, without any preamble, we'd go into her bedroom and fuck for hours. When we were finished, she'd put on a cream-coloured cotton bathrobe and go for a shower. By the time she came out, I'd already be dressed and sitting in the living room staring out – not at the buildings, but at the bicycle on her balcony. The silence was absolute. Sometimes there would be a party in one of the neighbouring buildings; we would stare at the lights and at the people down below walking past or going up and down as though guided simply by the smell of the food or the music spilling out from somewhere. Elena would say nothing and sometimes I would have to suppress the urge to ask her questions. Or tell her things about my life that I'd never told anyone, things like that fact that I'd never known my real parents. Then she would remind me that it was time for me to leave, that her father would be home soon – he was the only member of her family still in Cuba, all the others had left for Miami. I'd leave without giving her a kiss and a couple of weeks later we would meet up again and everything would be exactly the same. Obviously, there weren't always parties in the neighbouring buildings, and sometimes we didn't or couldn't drink rum, but the faint flickering lights were the same, she always took her shower, and the gathering dusk that enveloped the buildings all around never changed.

The truth is that I'd never wanted a woman the way I wanted Elena. I fucked her endlessly in every position that exists or ever will exist, I yanked her hair, I spat on her, I spanked her arse because she liked her sex down and dirty. But Elena was insatiable. Sex with her was like running a marathon. Sometimes I was surprised by her capacity to screw. She fucked like it was a matter of life and death. On more than one occasion I almost said she didn't need to make so much effort, that a five-hour fuck would be just as good, but when it came to sex Elena was practical and efficient. She'd suck from me my last drop of semen, my soul, what little life I believed I had left in those moments of pleasure.

Sometimes, when I hadn't seen her for several days, I would get to thinking about how different we were. She liked art; she could watch a ballet or look at a painting and recognise the painter or the choreographer. She read books I'd never heard of and although I liked the music she listened to, after a while it made me want to close my eyes and sleep. I tried to fit in with her, or rather to fit in my new situation with her, and sometimes I'd listen to Mozart or Beethoven. But I'd always wind up falling asleep and I'd have to put on NG La Banda to wake me up again because, unlike Elena, that was the music I'd always preferred.

Back then, Elena, like everyone else, was involved in the revolutionary process. She went from patrol leader in the Young Pioneers to head of the Student Collective at school and she was one of the first kids at school to get a membership card for the UJC – the Young Communist League – and as you know, back then being a member was the greatest thing in the world. It was every student's greatest wish . . . The Revolution was young, changes that kept everyone busy were taking place every day. The programme of agrarian reform had been enacted and land confiscated from private owners now belonged to the government who in turn transferred it to farmers so they could work the land. Illiteracy had all but been abolished and infant mortality had declined; more importantly, everyone now had the right to study whatever they wanted, and get treated in hospitals and clinics for free. Basically Cuba had already become what it is today. Well, not what it is today, because these days it is something else. Let's say it had become a beacon of hope, an example to Latin America and the world: a tiny island that had stood firm against the arrogance and barbarism of Yankee imperialism, as people put it.

Truth is, even an anti-Communist maggot like me has to admit that a whole bunch of good things were done back then that brought with them a whole bunch of illusions. I remember when I used to take Elena out for a stroll, back when – I'm sure you remember – back when the Cuban peso was actually worth something. A pizza cost $1.20, something even the poorest people in my *barrio* could afford, and the spaghetti at Vita Nuovo too. Elena always liked the ice cream at Coppelia which only cost $1.50 and I was always happy to attend to her whims.

Elena was a beautiful mulatto girl tending towards white, with thick lips that were wet as though constantly moist with dew, crowned with a beauty spot as coal-black as her piercing eyes. The most beautiful thing about her was her eyes, humble eyes that knew how to persuade. I loved to see her laugh, and I did everything I could to please her without asking for anything in return since I never believed in love – that's the truth – though I have to admit that Elena made my life as a cynic impossible.

Sometimes, in the evening, we would stroll down the Calzada Dolores to the little park just before the Diez de Octubre. I would hold her hand and we would silently immerse ourselves in the spectacle of Lawton which, back then, was nothing special, being one more outlying district of Havana with few houses and a vast number of ruined buildings and ramshackle hovels. It smelled of bread and guava cakes, of basil and rosemary. I would take her to the park and sometimes, during carnival season, even early in the evening, we would run into a line of drunks or some transvestites heading down Dolores to catch a bus to the Malecón. Thinking about it, I can say in all honesty that I was happy back then. Not always. Only when I was with that infuriating woman named Elena.

But anyway, like I said, it was a different time. A time when you could go to the beaches at Varadero and see hardly a single tourist. Sometimes, we'd check into the Hotel Nacional and pay in *pesos cubanos*, something no one would be allowed to do these days because, as you know, these days, Cubans are forbidden from going into hotels. I remember when we were back in primary, the school used to take us to Tarará. I don't know if there was something like that in Santiago. But anyway, it had never occurred to anyone to fill a campsite, which was really more of a holiday resort, with thousands and thousands of kids. Elena and I had great fun on the fairground rides in the amusement park, in the freshwater pools and at the concerts every night, and the food was, well, it was amazing, with flavoured yoghurt for breakfast, chicken, pork and all sorts of salads for lunch and dinner and, lastly, the best thing about the place was it was completely free. Excuse me for banging on about the food, it's just that I'm absolutely starving . . . And those fucking whiteshirts won't give me so much as a dry cracker.

So anyway, everyone left Tarará thinking the Revolution was the coolest thing, and, in a way, it was. Years later, when everything went to hell in a handcart, Elena and I would remember those years as the most magical of our childhood. No one knows exactly when things started to go wrong. I don't know what you think. Elena was convinced that it started with the fall of the Berlin Wall and the collapse of the Council for Mutual Economic Assistance in '89. According to her, that's what triggered the 'special economic period' that led to people eating cats and turkey vultures and steaks made out of dishrags, pizzas made with melted condoms instead of cheese, and micro chickens, which never grew, that you could get in stores, there were power cuts twenty hours a day and I don't know what all. Nitsa Billapol's recipe for grapefruit steak became a delicacy in our house. Every day we'd sit around the dinner table and force down this experiment in silence, I felt like screaming my frustration from the rooftops but at the same time I didn't want to hurt the feelings of my grandparents who, to the bitter end, maintained their dignity and their undying faith in the Revolution.

But my generation was different, something I tried to tell my grandparents a million times. We didn't know anything about the olden days; our only frame of reference was the terrible years we had to live through. To be honest, I think things started to fuck up a long time before the Russians turned their backs on us. I say that, because even back in the eighties I was already what they call a *gusano* – a maggot, a fully fledged anti-Communist Cuban – even then I had no illusions. Obviously, I did my best to bite my tongue so as not to ruin the illusions of my grandparents who were always telling me about all the injustices before the Revolution we've already talked about, but the minute I stepped out the front door, I went right on being disillusioned and I thought shit, things today are even more of a clusterfuck. This was my story, it was the story of Elena, of my whole generation.

My disillusionment started with the whole business with UMAP – the military units set up to eliminate bourgeois and counter-revolutionary values. I was still in primary school when they were going round arresting every kid with long hair. They'd pile them into the back of a truck and take them God knows where. They took Ricardito, my neighbour. Besides having long hair, he listened to The Beatles and The Rolling Stones and any other rock band he could find. Sometimes, in secret, he played them for me on his battered RCA Victrola. I thought they were horrendous.

'Cool, right?' he'd say, smoking shave grass and pretending it was marijuana. 'It's really cool, man.' He was a quiet kid, and good-looking too, the bastard. They snatched him off the street, shaved off his hair, tossed him in the back of a truck and took him God knows where. Big mistake. And still no one said anything, because Tarará was still open, education was better than ever, healthcare was free, the streets were safe, there were hundreds of things to be proud of, something my grandparents never tired of reminding me.

Ricardito showed up again a year later. A lot of his friends tried to get him to talk, to tell people what had happened. But tell who? Who was the guilty party, who was he supposed to tell, and what was the point? No one ever apologised to him, no one ever said, 'Fuck, Ricardito, I made a mistake.'

I mean nobody's perfect, everyone makes mistakes, so I don't understand why people won't just stand up and say 'I made a mistake'. I don't know about you, but I think they're afraid. Afraid of losing everything, that's why their instinctive reaction is to keep their mouths shut. I mean here I am telling you all this stuff and honestly I'm shitting myself. For all I know you could be with the Security Service, in which case I'm truly fucked.

But it's the same for people who make mistakes. They're scared too, and it's only logical for them to wonder what price they might have to pay for their mistake if they ever admit it to the public. 'They'll bury me in the shit,' they probably think. This is where our animal instincts take over: if it's a choice between me and you, I'd rather you got fucked over. But it makes me sad, to tell you the truth. Because a society that lives in fear is a dead society, and therefore it can't move forward. Nobody should be afraid to say 'I don't like that' or to admit that they've made a mistake. Don't you think?

I talked to Elena a lot about Ricardito's case and we always agreed, but whenever I talked about it to Grandpa Benicio, he ducked the question.

'What do you know about what life was like before the Revolution, Oscarito?' my grandfather said to me once.

'Nothing. But I can tell you what life is like now: no one is in favour of shortages and power cuts.'

'You're an ungrateful little brat,' said Grandpa and then he and Grandma Gertrudis gave Elena and me a lecture about how Machado and Batista used to have people gunned down in the street, and did whatever they had to do to cling to power. And that bitch Elena looked at them with her noble eyes, like a cat's eyes, as though these stories were a complete surprise.

'And I won't even bother to tell you what life was like in Pata de Puerco, a place no one cares about, a place where no one could read or write.'

'I don't know the first thing about Pata de Puerco. But you can't deny that our leaders now have completely forgotten the people. Things are serious, Grandpa. Just ask Elena. Go on, Elena, tell him, and don't go playing the little saint, because you're as much of a *gusana* as me.'

'A *gusana*? Me?' said Elena with a look on her face like a scalded cat. 'What are you talking about, Oscar? I completely agree with your grandparents, apart from one or two small points.'

'One or two small points?' I said furiously. 'You're a bare-faced liar, you don't agree with any of it. Don't be a hypocrite. You're just like your father.'

'Leave my father out of this.'

'But it's true. And speaking of fathers,' I turned back to my grandparents, 'when exactly are you going to tell me about my real parents?'

And that was the end of the discussion. My grandparents sent us to my room and that was that. Elena didn't even want to fuck. I went outside with her, watched as she walked away with that sexy sway of her hips that gave me goose-bumps. I was right when I said she was a hypocrite. That's what she was. But God I loved that bitch.

On another occasion, when my grandparents were calmer, they told me for the first time that my parents had died long ago. That their names were María and Melecio. That's all they said. They didn't like to talk about the past, so they only told me as much as they had to. Like that time when I came back to the house in tears because I'd never had any brothers and sisters, never had a mother or a father, just grandparents, and Grandpa Benicio told me he had never known his mother and barely knew his father. This all happened in the late 1980s. My grandparents were really old by then; they were fragile, with papery skin, while I had just turned twenty-eight and was still getting it on with Elena who by now was my steady girlfriend. By then all the stuff with the writers had happened, the Padilla Affair and all that, and books by Reinaldo Arenas, Cabrera Infante and Virgilio Piñera were banned in Cuba.

'So you're just like me,' I said to Grandpa. 'Parents are shit. When they don't get themselves killed, they dump you at someone else's house and let them bring you up. If it weren't for the fact that grandparents are always prepared to take responsibility for their kids' mistakes . . . I suppose you could say we're united by the same misfortune?'

Grandfather took a deep breath, as though a great weight had been lifted from him. He asked me to fetch him a glass of water.

'Actually, bring me a litre of milk.'

'A glass of milk?'

'No. Bring the whole bottle.'

I ran into the kitchen and came back with the milk. Grandpa poured himself a big white glass and drained it in a second. Then he told me that when he was young, there was no such thing as glass, there were no litres, no milk, no cows.

Only rich landowners had cattle, and a few Chinese people who traded in contraband.

I told him that, thinking about it, we were united by more than one misfortune, since even now no one could buy a cow, still less eat it. Grandfather tilted his head to one side. Gertrudis was still sitting on the sofa in the living room, listening to our conversation. 'And as for glass,' I said, 'sure, people these days know what it is, but who wants a litre of empty glass? If Antonio the milkman didn't sell it to us on the sly at an exorbitant price, you wouldn't even have that glass of milk.'

The old man stared at me with his big, bewildered owlish eyes. He wondered if I was comparing the times I lived in with his own. I told him I wasn't, but that he couldn't deny that we didn't have milk these days.

'Maybe you don't have milk these days. But you have paved roads, you have electricity. Imagine living in a place with no electricity, no television, no radio, completely cut off from the world.'

'What's the difference today, Grandpa? Cuba is completely cut off from the world. And ever since the Russians turned their backs on us and the "special economic period" started we don't have electricity, or radios or television. The streetlights outside are just decoration, they're there just to make the place look ugly. We were lucky this morning the electricity came on early, but you'll see, they'll cut it off in a minute. I don't know if you've noticed, but the fridge is broken. I asked Elena to ask Colonel Heriberto on the corner if he'll store our meat and fish in his fridge so it doesn't go off. I'm just worried that everyone else in the neighbourhood will have got in before us, since he's the only one round here with electricity. That's just how things are. A hundred years later and the only thing different is that at least we have lampposts.'

My grandfather said I didn't know what I was talking about, that for all its faults Cuba was much better today than it had been, that young people these days knew nothing about history and spent their lives complaining, not realising how much worse things used to be.

'Fine, Grandpa, have it your way,' I said, wiping his forehead. That was the last time Grandpa and I talked about politics. I'll never forget what happened next. Grandma Gertrudis, who had been sitting in deathly silence, suddenly started to laugh.

'What have you got to laugh about, Gertrudis?' asked Grandfather. The laugh began as a trickle but slowly caught like tongues of flame until it became a thunderous belly-laugh that startled Grandpa and me. 'Gertrudis, what's got into you? What on earth are you laughing at?' Grandma went on laughing uproariously, tears in her eyes, spraying spittle everywhere. I tried to calm her, I fanned her with the ration book, brought her a glass of water, but her laugh was contagious and I caught it. I ended up laughing like her, doubled over and clutching my belly. Only Grandfather remained solemn, probably because he knew what would happen next. He barely had time to take her hands in his before Grandma Gertrudis's heart burst as she suffered a heart attack.

Grandfather tried to pick her up in his thin, feeble arms, to lift her from the bed and run. I stopped him and said this was

277

madness. I took Grandma's pulse, checking for any sign of life, but her spirit was already somewhere else.

'There's nothing to be done, Grandfather,' I said.

Then he began to sob like a little boy. It was the saddest thing I had ever seen in my life. Elena arrived a little while later and together we tried in vain to comfort him.

The neighbours helped us to dress Grandma in her favourite dress. Elena did her make-up, using her lipstick and blusher, and she tucked a pink rose behind her ear. She looked like a sleeping Madonna. There was not a hint of pain on her face, as though she had not suffered. Later we called the Funeraría Mauline on the Calle Diez de Octubre near Santa Amalia, the most respectable undertakers in the area, and they sent a hearse. With a few of the neighbours, I helped lift her on to the gurney. Then we all headed to the funeral home where we held a vigil until dawn, then we cremated her. Grandma had always been one for staying at home, and recently she had barely left the house so there were only three neighbours at the vigil. Afterwards, they tossed a flower into the coffin and left, terrified by the eerie smile on her face. Grandma was laughing still.

Alone

Grandpa Benicio ceased to be the cheerful man everyone knew. That's what people said in the neighbourhood. He walked around with his head bowed, his arms hanging by his sides, he no longer talked to anyone when he went to get bread at the store, no longer went for a drink at the bar on the corner. 'Cheer up, Benicio,' the neighbours would say, 'why don't you come and play a game of dominoes.' But he simply ignored them and went on his way, looking like grief incarnate. Everyone said my grandmother's death had put years on him, but I think it was Facundo's death that really finished him off.

A week after Grandma died, Facundo, our dog, suddenly became ill. We went to fetch the local vet, who, after examining him, wrung his hands, saying he realised it was a bad time to give bad news, especially since we were mourning Señora Gertrudis, but there was nothing he could do to save Facundo.

'I hate to give bad news to people like you. Especially you, Benicio, you being the only man who ever knocked out that son of a bitch Masferrer, but Facundo will die four days from now.'

We had had Facundo for fourteen years. He was a black and white English pointer and my grandparents adored him, especially Grandpa Benicio who always said that, after Gertrudis, he loved Facundo more than anyone.

'All of my friends are shits,' I'd heard him say at times. 'Facundo, now he is a true friend.'

Facundo's liver and spleen were enlarged and, given his age, there was little that could be done for him. On the fourth day, just as the vet had predicted, his body lay beneath a mound of black earth, having been buried at the foot of the mango tree in the garden.

After that, Grandpa Benicio never put in his false teeth again. He stopped eating, stopped washing and more than once we found him sitting in the middle of the Calzada Dolores. Elena and I were worried about him, we tried to get him to talk, but he preferred the shade of the mango tree, the hammock, silence. He felt strange sleeping in his bed. Most nights he did not sleep. Soon he started to talk to himself; in the cracked mirror in the bathroom he would see a young man who gradually transformed himself into the balding ninety-year-old man who stared back at him sadly.

Then came Grandma Gertrudis's will: two letters. Nothing more. One for Grandfather, and one for me which I was not to open until Grandpa Benicio died. Grandfather's letter read: 'The greatest happiness I have had in life was to have you as my husband. I will be waiting for you by our flame tree, but before that, tell Oscar everything. Everything. It's time that he knew who he is.'

I read it to my grandfather and he listened carefully, without so much as blinking. Then he asked me to fetch him a glass of milk. I brought it to him and then took a shower while Elena cooked something. A few minutes later, when I came out of the bathroom, I found Grandpa lying on the living-room floor.

Elena and I carried his six-foot frame to the vast marriage bed where for the past two months he had been sleeping alone. His frail body looked like a wild flower in a meadow, fragile and defenceless.

'I'll be right back,' said Elena and went out into the streets of Lawton, half naked, wearing the floral top and checked cotton trousers she used as pyjamas. I saw her run past the window that served as a headboard for my grandparents' bed, watched her vanish into the narrow streets, into the crowds.

Grandpa Benicio regained consciousness just after Elena left. For a moment he stared at me like he did not recognise this boy sitting by his bed. He looked at me curiously, as though he had seen me somewhere before but could not remember where. His mouth suddenly opened. He said that if there was one thing I should learn, it was that events never begin in the moment that they happen. As he said this, he set the pillow up against the window so he could lean back and get a better look at me.

'Don't talk, Grandpa. Just lie there and rest, Elena has gone to fetch a doctor. What's happened has happened, and there's nothing to be done about it now.'

'Ah, that's just the problem. If you think it was the deaths of your dear grandmother and poor old Facundo that caused my heart attack, then you don't understand anything. This heart attack began a long time ago. Now get me some coffee and listen to what I have to tell you.'

I went into the kitchen. I picked up the coffee pot and poured a little of yesterday's coffee into a plastic mug, then ran back to my grandfather's room.

'Now listen to me and try not to interrupt, because we don't have much time. The time has come for you to know who you are.'

I told him I knew exactly who I was and rather curtly told him to get some rest.

'Don't speak to me in that tone, I've not been fitted for a wooden suit just yet, which means I'm still your grand-father . . . You think you know who you are, yes? Well, tell me then, how can anyone who does not know their history truly know who they are? Now, listen to me carefully, and don't interrupt.'

All I could think about was that Elena was not back yet as I stared at the wrinkled, careworn eyelids of that toothless old man who had given me everything. These were his last moments on earth so I had no choice but to do as he wished and say nothing. And then he told me that in the 1800s, Pata de Puerco was just a sweeping plain with a few scattered shacks between the Sierra Maestra of Santiago de Cuba and the copper mines of El Cobre. That the earth was so red and so green that it looked as though this was the last place God made. About the Santistebans, about José and Oscar; he told me everything I've told you here.

'I know how you must feel right now, Oscarito. I'm sure you're wondering why I'm telling you all this now just as the last of your relatives is about to die,' said Grandpa Benicio when he had finished. 'At this stage, I'd rather not fill your head with problems that can't be solved, but I have to fulfil your grandmother's last wish. All I can think to say to you right now is that the best time to plant a tree is always twenty years ago. If, for some reason, you did not plant it then, the next best time to plant a tree is now. I hope that helps you.'

I hugged him hard and looked into his eyes for the last time; he said he hoped I would have lots of children with Elena and, more importantly, that I would come to understand the value and the meaning of things so that I might finally find peace. Before I could say anything, there was a power cut and at that moment Elena burst through the door with the doctors who, despite the darkness, evaluated my grandfather's condition. Elena wept inconsolably. As she did so, I realised for the first time that my grandparents were in fact my uncle and aunt, though really they were my parents.

'We're sorry for your loss,' the doctors said, adding that I shouldn't hesitate to call them if I needed tranquillisers. Elena and I walked them to the door and, after they left, Elena put her arms around my neck, a gesture that turned my trickle of tears into a never-ending flood.

We sat vigil for Grandpa Benicio at the Funeraría Mauline as we had two months earlier for Grandma Gertrudis. He had had more friends in the neighbourhood and so more people came to pay their respects. Towards dawn, just before the body was taken to be cremated, a little black man appeared with prominent cheekbones and thinning, grey hair meticulously slicked back. He wore a black suit and shuffled slowly through the crowd, dragging his feet. He stood for a long time staring into the coffin and Elena asked me who he was. I shrugged. Then we saw him throw a red rose into the coffin and whisper, 'Cross and hook, Choco!' A moment later we watched as Kid Chocolate disappeared into the crowd, not knowing that the famous champion would die a few weeks later.

We brought Grandpa's ashes back to the house and placed them next to the urn that held Gertrudis's ashes. Their absence was a heavy cloud that crushed us and there were times when I forgot what had happened and found myself about to call to Grandma to make me some coffee. But there was no one in the house now but me, Elena, the mosquitoes and the power cut. I didn't know whether it was a different blackout or the same one that, only hours before, had carried off Grandpa Benicio's soul. Elena and I lay down, our bodies sweaty. Memories flooded back, the good and the bad, but mostly memories of those times when for some reason or other I had shouted at Grandma Gertrudis and made her cry, the times I had argued with Grandpa Benicio about politics, the times he had been angry at my insolence. It was too late now to apologise, too late to hug them one last time. My grandparents were gone and I was left with so many things unsaid.

I hugged Elena to me until the heat of her body fused with mine. I didn't dream that night, but I woke up with my eyes red and swollen. It was Elena who woke me to tell me she'd had a nightmare: she'd dreamed the mop and the floor cloth had been chasing her and trying to eat her. The mop had lifeless black eyes and could only move up and down to signal to the floor cloth to go after Elena.

'Jesus, Elena, what goes on inside that head of yours?' I said as I made breakfast. She told me it was the most surreal dream she'd ever had in her life. Usually, she had the classic nightmare of falling from a skyscraper and waking up just as she hit the ground. She had even had dreams about being buried alive, in which she felt herself suffocating, felt the maggots eating away at her. This thing with the mop and the floor cloth was a completely new addition to her collection of nightmares.

And yet Elena's dream made sense, since in the past two months we had barely left the house except to go to the funeral home, and I knew that the deaths of my grandparents had affected her as much as they had me because she thought of them as family. And then, not everyone is as lucky as I am: I never dream about anything, ever, or at least I never remember my dreams. Elena remembered her dreams in astonishing detail and every morning she would tell me about them, talking about the colours of the clothes, the things she could smell around her, the vividness of the scenery, as though they were movies she had recently watched.

What was most worrying was that, even five months after my grandfather died, Elena was still having horrifying nightmares: the avocado trees in the garden were trying to devour her. The neighbour in the Committee for the Defence of the Revolution who lived in her apartment block wanted to devour her. Everyone was trying to eat her. She would talk about these dreams to me and some-times to her girlfriends, one of whom suggested she should go and see a *babalao*. Elena didn't believe in *babalaos* or *santería* or any of that shit but even so she went to see Babalao Alfredo, a famous Ifá priest in Lawton.

'You have a dark aura. That is why you feel you are being

persecuted,' said the extraordinarily tall black man people called Babalawo Alfredo. He walked us to the door and then, squeezing Elena's hands, he told her she had to leave here immediately.

'Leave here? And go where?'

'To America,' said the *babalao*, 'to Miami. Is that not where your family live? Then you must go there for no good awaits you here.'

Elena thanked the man and we headed back to my house.

'Don't listen to that guy, Elena,' I said, 'he doesn't know what he's talking about.' But when I looked into her eyes I saw they were shining and I realised that something inside her had changed, that Alfredo's words had brought back all the dormant hopes she thought she would never feel again.

That night, I undressed her slowly, with a tenderness I rarely demonstrated. I covered her beautiful body with oil and massaged her every muscle to relieve the tension that for months now had been causing her nightmares. Then I gave her everything I had saved up, my whole erection, every inch of the slippery cock just dying to slide between her legs. That night I didn't tug her hair, I didn't spank her arse, I didn't spit on her like I usually did. Thinking about it, it was the only time we didn't fuck. We made love, as it's more elegantly put, and I can tell you now, it was good for me. I wanted to repeat that night of massages, of trembling skin, of whimpers produced not by violence but by the compassion of two souls shielding one another, two bodies sheltering one another, trying to protect each other from the pain caused by the emptiness of the everyday, the inability to understand the young, by everything we are daily confronted by when we open the door. It was good for me, but it was not good for Elena. Her eyes stared at a fixed point, at the huge spider's web hanging from the ceiling. Her mind was already in Miami. Her body followed a week later. She got in touch with old student friends and they encouraged her to come with them and leave from the Playa Santa Fe. She asked me to go with her. I told her it was all the same: Miami, Havana, London, Paris, it's all the same, I said. She thought about this but in the end she couldn't accept that it was all the same, though it saddened her to contradict me, so she said nothing.

In the early hours of the morning, I went with her to the slipway with a wariness that verged on paranoia, glancing around looking for any suspicious characters who might be from the Security Service. Back then, the borders had not been opened and it was illegal to try to leave the country. The raft was little more than a platform made with tractor tyres and some oars. They had no compass, no idea of what the weather would be like, nothing. It looked like a storm might break at any moment.

'This is madness, Elena. Better a known evil than an unknown good.'

'I'm sorry, Oscar, I can't stay here another day. I have to try to be happy somewhere else.'

It was then I realised that my hopes had been castles in the air, illusions which in that moment crumbled to dust. I begged her again to stay, but Elena had made her decision. She kissed me on the lips and I watched her melt into the darkness that instantly swallowed them all.

I went back home feeling more depressed than ever, dragging with me a loneliness that seemed never-ending. All I could do was think about Elena and remember the last words my grandfather had said to me before he died, about the tree that I should plant, about his hope that Elena would bear me lots of children. I wondered if I had made a mistake in not going with her to Miami. But two days later I heard that they had hit a storm while at sea and everyone, including Elena, had been drowned. My heart skipped a beat. For a moment I thought I was having an asthma attack because I couldn't breathe. I collapsed on the living-room sofa and for a long time I sat there trying to make sense of things. I thought maybe Elena's nightmares about everyone wanting to eat her had been a signal for her not to leave, that it wasn't the avocado trees or her neighbour in the CDR who would devour her, but the sharks. Who knows?

All I know is that it would be impossible for me to describe what I felt in the days that followed, when the stars came out and I realised that I was alone in this vastness; those moments when the events of my life flickered past inside me as though fading, as if some mysterious virus were coursing through my veins. It is true that man is born to suffering, but I would never have guessed that in the end I would wind up making do with the pockmarked moon that every day shines down from the heavens. All I know is that within the space of five months I found myself utterly alone. Alone in a house that hurtled on towards privation rather than plenty. Alone in my own cell. Alone, alone. In a country where I served no purpose.

To the Roots

As I said when I began this story, it's impossible to imagine the man you'll become when you find yourself alone. I had several options: I could go on breathing, ignore everything that was happening around me, or I could go whoring – because the market for whores was well established by then, and for a few pesos I could find beautiful young women all along Quinta Avenida or on Calle Monte. But I couldn't get Elena out of my head. I didn't feel like fucking a whore or waking up alone again.

On the other hand, for a while now Lawton had become a madhouse. Neighbours poked their noses into everyone else's business, followed each other around like they were spying. Caridad, a member of the CDR, gave me an earful when I built a pigeon loft on the flat roof, then some inspector came and told me to take it down. I tried to bribe the guy, offered him a pile of cash, but he was ruthlessly incorruptible and completely inflexible and in the end the son of a bitch ordered me to rip it down right away and warned me that if I got mixed up in anything else, he'd have me banged up. He was like some retired colonel because he talked like he owned you.

Then there's the double standards everyone has these days. They think one thing and they say something different, hiding behind words to make their lives easier. I was tired of everything; all I wanted was to know how to deal with the situation I was in. Then one morning, everything was clear to me; suddenly I knew what I had to do.

I found a rope, tied it to the mango tree, but the first time I tried to hang myself, the branch snapped and I was left with a bruise around my neck. I refused to give up. At eight o'clock in the morning, when the traffic on Calzada Dolores was heaving, I sat in the middle of the road and waited. I didn't get run over by a car but I did manage to get myself thrown in jail. The next day they let me go. I walked into the centre of Havana and climbed to the roof of the FOCSA Building. I thought about the air rushing past my face, imagined the moment when I hit the ground, and I realised I didn't have the balls to jump. So I took the easy way out: I managed to get hold of twenty haloperidol tablets; I gulped them down and sat on a kerb with my face to the sun. My belly growled like a dog and promptly threw up everything, I coughed a couple of times and just then some woman came over with a glass of water and saved my life. I had no temperature, no bellyache and no luck killing myself.

That was the fourth night I didn't sleep. I couldn't get used to this empty, funereal house. I spent most of the time sitting on my bed, staring at the ceiling and thinking, until I realised that too much thinking was the problem. I got up and on the dresser I saw the letter that my grandma had left me in her will. I read what it said on the envelope: 'to be opened only at the right time'. I tore it open and found a note inside that read: 'Don't let our deaths stop you. Follow the cobweb in the bedroom.'

My eyes focused on the long spider's web strung between the window and the wardrobe door in my grandparents' room. Without knowing why, I went to the wardrobe and took everything out: two of my grandmother's dresses, her high heels, my grandfather's suit, his two white shirts, his tie and his boots, but I found nothing out of the ordinary. Then I looked at the cobweb again and followed another strand that was connected to the toilet bowl. I didn't need to investigate the contents, since I could see them. There was a thread connected to the ceiling, another to a plant and a third to a shoe: I carefully checked every thread leading from the web and found nothing special about any of them. The last strand was attached to the drawer of the dressing table. I opened the drawer and found a pig's foot which turned out to be some sort of necklace, and a note in my grandmother's handwriting that read: 'Your happiness is in the amulet. Follow the pig's foot.'

I looked at the pendant in disgust. The pig's foot was not dried and shrivelled, in fact seemed to be alive; the veins pulsed, the flesh was red and bled constantly. I fetched a damp cloth to wipe up the blood inside the drawer and on the floor then ran back into the kitchen and threw the gruesome amulet in the bin. I went back to bed after drinking a glass of water with sugar but spent the rest of the night sitting thinking, unable to get to sleep.

At eight o'clock I instinctively rolled over to hug Elena. It was a beautiful day, with the sun bringing out the vivid colours of everything, but all I could think about was some new way to be reunited in death with the rest of my family. As I wandered into the kitchen, I found the bin knocked over and the pig's foot lying bleeding on the floor.

'What the fuck is this!' I said aloud. I grabbed the amulet and held it up at eye level. I got a cloth and mopped up the blood on the floor and took a damp rag and wiped the pig's foot. Then I took the plunge and fastened the amulet around my neck. Mysteriously, it immediately stopped bleeding and I no longer felt the urge to kill myself. A powerful feeling of adventure overcame me and I felt a strange sensation, as though something were telling me I had to leave Havana for ever, not for Miami, but for Oriente. I tossed some clothes into a backpack, went to the main railway station and caught the first train for Santiago.

As soon as I arrived in Oriente, I headed for El Cobre. I passed a dozen parks, neighbourhoods of little shacks with terracotta pots outside and finally I arrived at a little village near the famous church where Bacardí had met my father Melecio almost a century ago. I had no idea who to ask, but this looked nothing like the place my grandfather had described.

On the corner of a little square, I found a pharmacy where I asked: 'Could you tell me the way to Pata de Puerco?' The fat, very black woman on the other side of the counter looked up and shrugged. She had never heard of such a place. 'Pedrito Blanco is that way, down this way is El Polvorín, and that road leads to Santiago. Over in that direction is Cabeza de Carnero, but that's a very different beast.'

I thanked the woman and headed for the various places she had mentioned. I combed every one of them, but no one had heard of Pata de Puerco, nor of anyone called José or Oscar or Melecio. 'The only place round here named after an animal is Ram's Head,' everyone told me. 'Cabeza de Carnero.' So I caught a streetcar that dropped me off at a station in the middle of nowhere, then I covered several kilometres on foot, hitched a ride on the back of an oxcart and another on the back of a horse-drawn cart until finally I arrived in a little town set in a valley of red earth but it had paved roads and stone houses. It was a simple place like any country town, and yet everywhere there were signs of civilisation that immediately confirmed to me that this village had nothing to do with the godforsaken place Grandpa Benicio told me about, with its communal well, its wooden shacks and no electricity. Here there were schools, clinics, hospitals, sports centres, even a nightclub.

'I don't suppose you've ever heard of someone named José Mandinga?' I asked a well-dressed, rather professional-looking man of about fifty.

'José Mandinga with a dick like a finger?'

'No, I'm serious. What about Oscar Kortico?'

'Oscar Kortico, with a prick like a yo-yo?'

This idiot who thought he was a comedian was busting my balls, so I had to walk away.

I approached an elegant woman with a long face and a little wispy moustache who was walking along the road and asked if she had heard of José Mandinga.

'The only Mandinga I've ever heard of is Melecio Mandinga, the architect who designed Cabeza de Carnero. Have a look at that plaque over there.' The woman pointed to a wall on which was a rectangular plaque sculpted in high-relief depicting a man with short hair and a noble face; he was smiling.

As I walked over, I felt a shudder run quickly along my spine, up my neck and into my brain. For a split-second, I felt as though I were looking into a mirror. I couldn't have known that I was the spitting image of my father Melecio, no one had ever told me. The plaque read: '*Melecio Mandinga, architect of Cabeza de Carnero, did not live to see his dream become a reality, but his work lives on for ever in our hearts.*'

After reading this, I walked around for a long time, a little lost, a little gloomy, mostly exhausted by my geographic and genetic disorientation. I came upon a bus stop and had a daydream, or rather with my eyes open I dreamed that a man with gold teeth and an Armani suit driving a limousine was reaching out to shake my hand, introducing himself as Bacardí. 'My name is Emilio Bacardí,' he said and invited me to climb into the plush car, where my father Melecio was already ensconced. I saw myself roaming the interior of the limousine, a network of corridors that were actually the hallways of a prison; I could see the bug-eyed prisoners, as I walked determinedly through this labyrinth of muttering voices and nightmares, alert to what was happening in each cell. From time to time my father Melecio would wink at me or Don Emilio would wave me onward and I walked on until I came to the brink of an abyss, since in my dream the prison was like a castle built on the edge of a cliff. There, unable to turn back, I lifted up my arms to glorify the heavens; I tried to speak but I realised, or at least I had the fleeting impression, that someone had sewn my lips together. And yet inside my mouth, I could feel something that was not my tongue or my teeth, but a piece of meat that I tried to swallow as with one hand I fumbled to rip the stitches from my lips. Blood ran down my chin. My gums were numb. When at last I could open my mouth, I spat out the piece of flesh and then groped for it in the darkness. Having found it, and turned it over carefully in my fingers, I realised it was the nose and moustache of Commissioner Clemente.

The scene shifted into another dream in which once again I was strangling the damned cat. I watched the head roll away. I kicked the remains of the body into the bin and then the head suddenly opened its eyes and said: 'Careful of the consequences, Oscar.' I woke up with a start. A few kids were playing in the street. They were laughing and playing. From time to time a horse-drawn cart drove by, like the one that had brought me here. I couldn't stay a moment longer. Night would soon be drawing in.

In the distance I could see the mountains of the Sierra Maestra. I walked in that direction. I walked for miles, until suddenly the paved roads petered out leaving only dirt tracks, which gradually disappeared into a tangle of trees and brambles where the heat was suffocating. I walked without stopping, heading nowhere in particular, but as far as possible from mankind, from the misery of the city, from the memories of those I loved now dead. Night fell, the darkness was eerie, the mountain gradually grew steeper. A dense thicket of sicklebush blocked my path. There was no way forward. I thought about going back to my old life, but that only made me walk on doggedly, ignoring the thorns long as bayonets ripping at my clothes, burying themselves in my flesh, oblivious to the blood and the pain. On the far side of the sicklebush grove, when I realised that I had left the bustle of the city behind, I lay down on the ground, aching and exhausted. And fell asleep.

Atanasio's Story

The first thing I noticed was that the pig's-foot amulet was no longer around my neck. Then I realised that I was lying in a circular clearing the size of an empty football pitch ringed by tall sicklebush like the walls of a fortress, keeping it beyond the reach of men, preserving its mystery. In the middle of the circle it looked as though it had just rained. Clouds were gathered just above the clearing and a fine mist hung in the air, which gave the place a pleasing temperature while beyond the walls of sicklebush the sun still split the stones, the earth was cracked and parched.

The grey sky did not seem to be lit by the sun's rays, as though day was about to dawn or night about to draw in. At first I thought a tropical storm was brewing but, looking more carefully, I realised that there was something ghostly about this place that had nothing to do with the weather.

'I must be dreaming,' I thought as I stared at the throng of animals gathered in the centre of the clearing: wild boar, hutias, deer, crocodiles, all happily sharing the thick black mud rising to cover trees and plants and creepers. Mud coated everything, every animal and tree – the only flash of green came from the feathers of birds as they flitted from branch to branch like lights.

The animals were not startled by my sudden appearance. The crocodiles watched, jaws wide, still as statues; the deer carried on wallowing in the mud as though I were not a man but simply another animal come to shelter from the heat. A pall of thick black smoke hung in the air as if by magic. Looking closely, I saw it came from a shack built of timber and royal palm with a roof of thatched palm leaves, invisible against the mud. On the porch of the house were four stools and a table carefully laid with a chicken stockpot, bread and two bottles of homemade rum, though there was not a soul in sight.

'Anyone there?' I shouted at the top of my voice. The cry reverberated among the trees, sending back an echo of my voice. 'Anyone there?' I called again, and was about to knock on the door when an elderly man no more than four feet tall threw it open and introduced himself as Atanasio Kortico. Around his throat I saw an amulet similar to mine, with a shrivelled pig's foot.

'At last!' he said. His skin was a black so intense it was bluish, the deep wrinkles around his eyes fanned out across his face like a river's tributaries. His hands were large, entirely disproportionate to the size of his small body. His hair and beard were completely white, and his eyes, half-grey, half-yellow, seemed to divine my thoughts. He hugged me with the same enthusiasm he might a long-lost relative which led me to think that no one had visited this part of the world for a long time.

'Your amulet looks a lot like mine,' I said, staring at the old man's chest.

'Ah, your amulet. We'll talk about that in a moment. Lucumí! Palmito! Our guest has arrived. Take a seat, señor.' The old man clapped twice and instantly two men appeared, no taller than him and with the same blue-black complexion. The men looked about fifty, and both wore pig's-foot amulets. They hugged me with the same effusiveness as Atanasio and we all sat down at the table.

'As you can see, we all have pig's feet. This is your necklet.' The little man gave me back my collar which I immediately fastened around my throat. 'You brought the missing pig's foot, something precious and much coveted in these parts, which is why we took it and put it in our house for safekeeping; we wouldn't want . . . well, I'm sorry, but the pig's feet must be protected. After all they are our salvation.'

I did not feel like discussing how a pig's foot could offer salvation; instead I apologised for my appearance, explaining that the mud and the sicklebush had done their work. Atanasio Kortico told me not to worry; mud, he said, was not as bad as people thought. I looked at the three little men warily, but I was too hungry to ask about this muddy kingdom, about the animals, the four amulets, the desolation of this lifeless place.

I glanced down worriedly at the crocodiles crawling around the table.

'They've only come over to say hello,' the old man explained. 'They want to be a part of this momentous occasion. Just eat up.'

'Occasion? What occasion?'

'Your arrival in our village,' said the three men in concert.

'You call a place with three inhabitants a village?'

The three men looked bewildered and began to whisper among themselves: 'You mean he can only see us? You mean he can't hear the bells from the Casa de la Letra?' 'Exactly. You have to remember his mind is still filled with the sounds and voices of the city.'

I went on eating. What was this talk of bells; were they the only ones who could see them? I looked around, but all I could see were doves fluttering against the grey sky; no houses, no rooftops, no children playing, the place was utterly lifeless.

'Tell me, señor,' the old man said, 'are you a believer?'

'You mean do I believe in God?'

'Not necessarily, but let us start there.'

'Absolutely not.'

'And why not, if I may ask?'

'Because if there were a God, my life – or at least my death – would have been a lot easier.'

'Would you credit it . . . ? That's exactly what I said to the reverend years ago. All this business about God and virgins and saints just confuses things. As if we didn't have problems enough in the real world. So, as far as you are concerned, there is no God?'

'No. Or if there is, he obviously doesn't like me much.'

Atanasio winked his yellow-grey eye, and his brothers got to their feet, cleared the table and disappeared into the house.

'Tell me – and I apologise for prying – but do you believe in anything?' enquired the old man.

'Yes. I believe that I am sitting here with you. I believe in the plate of chicken I've just eaten.'

'Perfect!' said Atanasio. 'And what if I were to tell you that our meeting was predestined?'

'I'd say it corresponds to the doctrine that everything is willed by God, meaning that human beings have no control over their actions, that what happens depends on outside forces.'

'Then . . . you are a man of science.'

'No, I wouldn't say that.'

'So you believe in chance and coincidence, which means you are an atheist in the broadest sense of the word.'

'Exactly, I'm an atheist.'

The brothers came back with coffee, handed me a small tin cup and another to the old man and sat down again. I thanked them and said: 'If you'll excuse me, I have to go.'

'Go where?' chorused the three men, leaping to their feet.

I said I didn't know, that I had felt a sudden impulse to come to Santiago but now that I was here I didn't know what to do or where to go. I picked up my backpack. As I was about to leave, the old man caught my arm.

'I'm sorry, but since it seems likely we won't see each other again, I'd like to ask you one last question.'

'Sure, go ahead. Ask away.'

'Let's say . . .' the old man began, 'let's say that for no particular reason your grandmother had a laughing fit and her heart inexplicably burst. That your dog died unexpectedly and a little later your grandfather had a heart attack. Let's say your girlfriend takes off for another country, leaving you completely alone. Like anyone in such a position, you try to commit suicide, but in this you fail because even death carefully chooses its quarry and decides your time had not yet come. Let's say that one day you open your eyes and find yourself sitting opposite an old man in a strange place. Do you really believe all this is the result of coincidence?'

I started back and bumped into the table.

'How do you know all this?'

'Know what?' said Atanasio, pretending to be puzzled.

'Everything. About my grandfather, my dog. Are you with the police? What is this place?'

My body was rigid; I felt a sudden, violent urge to be sick. I stumbled over the animals lying around the table, doubled up like an accordion and fell to my knees in the mud. The old man helped me to my feet and led me to the centre of the clearing where the mud was thickest. Palmito, Lucumí and the animals followed, keeping their distance.

'There, between the mangroves . . .' said Atanasio, pointing. 'Can you see?'

'You mean the mud trees?'

'Try to see beyond what the eye can see.'

Try as I might all I could see was an empty expanse ringed by trees and the high wall of sicklebush and the blanket of clouds above sheltering us from the sun.

'I don't understand what you're talking about.'

'That's precisely what I mean. You cannot see anything. The good news is that can be fixed.'

Still feeling slightly queasy, I stared into the old man's yellow-grey eyes and asked him what exactly was this place.

'It's a long story, and one I barely have the strength to tell, but if you agree to stay for a little while, I will tell it to you. I promise that by the time I am done, you will see everything more clearly. Is it a deal?'

Atanasio held out his hand and I stared at it for a long

time. I glanced around at the placid animals, the green plumage of the birds in the trees, the sicklebush, the mud. I had nothing to lose: no one would miss me, no one would weep for me. I shook Atanasio's huge hand and he smiled and with uncontrollable excitement said: 'Welcome to Pata de Puerco.'

We sat down again and Atanasio told me a curious tale similar to the one my grandfather had told me. He talked about the founding of Santiago in 1515 by Diego Velázquez, about the first shipments of Korticos that arrived in Cuba in 1700 when this place was known simply as 'the great forest'. Then all three men stood up, dropped their trousers and showed me how their dicks dangled down into the mud. 'It is known as Elephant's Trunk Syndrome, and it is just one of our many curses,' said Atanasio as the men pulled up their trousers.

Atanasio talked about his ancestors who were despised even by the other Negroes, who had been slaves among slaves until the birth of Yusi.

'Yusi the Warrior? I thought that was a legend,' I said. It was no legend, Atanasio insisted, Yusi the Warrior had actually existed.

'In those days, people said that Pata de Puerco was the lair of the devil himself,' Atanasio went on, 'when in fact it was the most beautiful place in Oriente. There was no mud, no grey, it was an earthly paradise, but such magical places are not destined to survive. The calamity began with the killing of the magic pig.'

'The magic pig?'

'Yusi's closest friend. A creature of extraordinary powers

which, besides being able to speak, could divine the fates of men. It was this creature who gave to this place the name by which it came to be known, Pata de Puerco.'

I leapt to my feet, my voice rising to a scream as I said this was all lies. The old man replied that all he could offer was *his* truth. There were many truths, he said; I had to open my mind to the possibilities.

'You're telling me I should believe in this invisible village and this talking pig? Next you'll be telling me there are men made of nicotine . . .'

'You are beginning to see,' said the old man.

'See what?' I said, angry now.

The old man ignored my question.

'In 1811, Yusi and the other slaves on his plantation rose up,' he said. 'It was the first slave uprising in Cuba, one that would serve as an inspiration for the massive rebellion led by José Antonio Aponte in 1812, and it was upon the ruins of that plantation that the Santistebans would later build their house. Yusi met and married Mariana, a beautiful Mandinga woman, despite the warnings of the magical pig that such a union would have grave consequences, that the blood of a Kortico and a Mandinga should never be commingled. But by then, Mariana was already pregnant and there was nothing to be done.

'Drawn by the legend of the magic pig, the Nicotinas began to arrive. Some claim they are the last descendants of the indigenous Guanahatabey from Baracoa, wiped out centuries before by Hernán Cortés. Others claim they are the spawn of Satan himself – a theory I personally favour.

'The pig knew it was his destiny to die at the hands of the

Nicotinas, and pleaded with Yusi not to fight. The Nicotinas seized the animal, slaughtered and devoured it, thereby acquiring the power to manipulate the minds of people and rule the country for ever. Foolishly, they threw away the feet and Yusi ended up in possession of the most important gift: the four pig's feet, which would once and for all ensure an end to the misery Cubans had suffered. For it is said that when the pig's feet are united everyone in Cuba would prosper.

'The Nicotinas, logically, had to gain possession of the four feet since, otherwise, their chances of ruling the country for ever would disappear. So it was that Pata de Puerco was divided between two clans, the Nicotinas and the Korticos, and in that moment darkness descended, mud covered the trees and clouds blocked out the sun.

'For a time, the pig's feet were all in one place and the country prospered. Mariana bore twins. One, my great-great-grandmother who gave birth to a daughter, my great-grandmother Macuta Uno, who in turn had two children: Macuta Dos, mother of Oscar, and Esteban, my grandfather, who was sold into slavery as a boy. And so the tainted blood went on coursing through veins until it reached me.

'The four pig's feet were dispersed and Cuba's fortunes began to slide. Macuta Dos, Oscar's mamá, inherited one of the amulets and much of the tainted blood, which accounts for Mangaleno's terrible wickedness, for Oscar's temperament and for the violent past of your grandfather Benicio. The descendants of the Nicotinas also multiplied and with them the ancient hatred which has long blighted these lands of mud.

'The struggle between the Korticos and the Nicotinas continued while we waited for the heir to the missing pig's foot to finally arrive. So you see, Oscar, our meeting is not the result of chance and coincidence. It was written in my destiny that I should meet you on the day I died and you would carry on my work here in Pata de Puerco. But before my hour comes, let me tell you one last thing.'

The old man led me back into the centre of this wasteland, where the mud was thickest, and, his voice quavering, he said, 'When you arrived, everything here seemed dead to you because you were dead inside. But I would like to think that in the course of my tale some hope was kindled in your heart, for in such evil times as these only hope can lead to salvation. I leave you to the care of my brothers Palmito and Lucumí, knowing that one day you will heal the divisions in this land of mud and that the sun will once more shine on Pata de Puerco. I take this hope with me to my grave.'

With these words, Atanasio's body crumpled.

'Señor! Atanasio!' I shouted, trying to revive him, but the old man's lips were sealed for ever. 'Quick, we have to get help,' I cried frantically. No one listened.

'This is his destiny,' said Palmito and Lucumí. In silence the two men walked over and kneeled by the body of Atanasio, they embraced him and said their goodbyes. Gradually, the animals gathered around the corpse. I stood and watched this ritual of men and animals who, incredibly, accepted death without grief. I thought about my grandparents, about Elena, and I felt my heart tighten. Then gradually I heard a rising murmur which I recognised as the animated sounds of a village, and when I looked up I saw a long street lined with houses and, in the distance, the majestic wooden belfry of the Casa de la Letra. I could just make out the chalk line that divided the rival factions and the distinctive stone well. I saw children, shopkeepers, street hawkers, farmers, craftsmen and labourers: all cloaked in the caramel colour of the mud.

'I don't believe it,' I said, staring at this world that had suddenly appeared before my eyes. 'There are houses, people, an entire village.'

'Yes, yes, I know. But we have to hurry, the Nicotinas will be here soon,' said Palmito and asked me to help him lift Atanasio's body. Lucumí interrupted to say that I should be allowed to savour this moment of revelation since the Nicotinas could not cross the chalk line into Kortico territory without suffering the wrath of Commissioner Clemente. 'Though to be honest,' Lucumí added, 'I'd like to see Clemente give those sons of bitches a good beating.'

I asked who this Commissioner Clemente was.

'The Imperial Wizard of the Ku Klux Klan in Cuba, the most powerful man in this area, the man who maintains order in Pata de Puerco.'

'Really?' I asked.

'Really. Those he takes away rarely return,' said Palmito and explained that this was the war of the mute, of those without a voice.

'The war of the mute?' I said.

'The war of the oppressed,' said Palmito. 'The Nicotinas oppress the Korticos and the Ku Klux Klan oppresses everyone.'

'But no Cuban has ever belonged to the Ku Klux Klan,' I said. 'Nothing like that has ever existed in Cuba.'

'That's what they want us to believe,' said Palmito. 'In fact, the Klan is everywhere. In Oriente, in Havana, in Pinar del Río. Artemisa is full of Klan leaders.'

'Who?' I asked.

Palmito named three officials in the Politburo, and two directors of Televisión Cubana.

'You're telling me the head of Cuban television is a member of the KKK?'

'Of course. Have you ever seen a black person on television?'

'Not many.'

'And the few black people you do see are only on TV because racism and segregation are supposedly banned in Cuba,' said Palmito.

Looking down at Atanasio's body I asked if it was true that Korticos could foretell the future. Palmito explained that they could not see their destinies, but knew only the day when they would die. It appeared to them in a dream, he explained, hazy at first and shrouded in mist, but over time it took on colour and form like a photograph and they understood that they were seeing their own death.

'What does it feel like, to know when you're going to die?'

'Wonderful,' said Lucumí. 'You have a better life, you're not afraid of lightning or diseases.'

'What will you do with his body?' I said, looking at Lucumí who told me they would hold a wake and then burn the body according to Atanasio's wishes. In the meantime, Palmito said, people he called the Allies were coming to meet me.

'To meet me, or to pay their respects?'

'Both. But mostly to meet you,' said Palmito. 'We all knew that our brother would die today, so we have long been preparing for this moment.'

I told him I found it strange they did not grieve for their brother, that his death did not make them sad. Of course he would miss Atanasio, Lucumí said, especially his terrible farts. And then he laughed. I don't know why, but he reminded me of Judío Alemán.

'Don't pay my brother any mind, he's not as insensitive as he likes to make out,' said Palmito. 'The thing is when you have lived your whole life embracing the prospect of death, you learn to accept its nature, and in time you feel no fear.'

I thought about the time I had climbed to the top of the FOCSA Building and not had the guts to jump. I had accepted the idea of death, but I had never been able to rid myself of the fear.

The three of us carried Atanasio's body into the house, into a narrow living room furnished with smooth rocks in place of chairs and a beer crate for a table. On the walls were animal figures cut from sackcloth and two crossed machetes. The only light came from lanterns filled with fireflies. The dank smell of mud crept across the wooden floor and mingled with the smell of mould. Surprisingly, the house was clean, but it was a spartan cleanliness that lacked the feminine touch, a sterility that evoked a monk's cell.

We wiped the mud from our feet, washed the dead man's body, dressed him in a white cotton shirt and beige trousers and brought him out on to the porch. People were beginning to arrive. First came a couple and their little girl, all dressed in sackcloth decorated with flowers, who introduced themselves as the Buenaventura family. They kneeled when they saw me and I begged them to get up. The little girl stood and handed me a parcel wrapped in banana leaves which contained sackcloth clothing like theirs. 'My grand-father's suit,' she explained. 'It is our greatest treasure.'

I thanked them as another couple arrived, looking for all the world like European royalty. The pale-skinned man, wearing a tuxedo, a waistcoat and a silk cravat, introduced himself as Monsieur Julián. 'Thees is a *graaate* moment for our cause. Ze rebel Nicotinas will get what zey deserve,' he said. '*Ah, j'ai oublié . . .* This is Madame Mirriam. *Allez, dépêche-toi, Mirriam.*' The woman stepped forward, pale-skinned as her husband, wearing a light-blue colonial-era dress with a cinched waist and an alarming bustle. She wore a large hat and clutched a white silk kerchief.

I said that I did not realise there were foreigners in Pata de Puerco and Mirriam explained that her husband was from Guanabacoa and she from Regla; like me, they both came from Havana. Julián was tetchily interrupting, claiming they hailed from Paris, when Lucumí stepped forward to intro-duce a blonde woman of about forty with gentle eyes, silken lips, perfect teeth and a slim curvaceous body wearing a green dress, her hair swept back with a red rose pinned to one side.

'Allow me to present Matilda,' said Lucumí, 'the sweetest woman in these parts.'

I took the lady's hand; Matilda curtsied and then shyly withdrew. Lucumí winked at me and punched the air. I laughed, which had Monsieur Julián and his wife laughing too, the Buenaventuras hooted, their daughter stamped her feet and sniggered, Matilda giggled and threw up her hands. The hysterical laughter rose to become a symphony of treble and bass notes, of spittle and tears.

Only the Korticos retained any semblance of solemnity.

'There, Lucumí, behind the palm tree,' said Palmito, pointing towards the tangle of undergrowth. Lucumí raced into the house, grabbed a machete from the wall and ran to where his brother had pointed.

'Shut your mouth, you little bastard, or I'll slice you in two,' he roared, dragging a man who was shorter and blacker than himself, with bulging eyes like a frog, into the middle of the muddy circle.

I asked what was happening and Palmito explained that it was simply Wije Alberto up to his usual tricks. A *wije*'s laugh was contagious, he added, it could infect everyone around him. I thought of how Grandma Gertrudis died of a fit of laughing and wondered if perhaps a *wije* had snuck into our house and triggered the laugh that finally caused her heart to burst.

I asked whether Wije was his name or whether he was actually a spirit of *santería*.

'He is a true *wije*,' said Palmito.

'But surely such things don't exist,' I said.

'This is Pata de Puerco,' said the Kortico, 'a village where anything is possible.'

Next to arrive was Reverend Carlos, a white, freckle-faced man of about fifty who wore a cassock and carried a thick book. He seemed gentle and serene. He had spent his whole life waiting for my arrival, he told me, and now that I was here he did not know whether to laugh or cry. Last came a fat woman who looked Chinese and her twin boys. Her jet-black hair was tied into a long mane like a Shaolin monk and she and her sons wore ornate embroidered kimonos.

Taken as a group, I realised, the Allies represented the ethnic make-up of the Cuban people: black, white, Asian. All that was needed was a couple of native Cuban aborigines to complete the group. I felt as though I were in a fairy tale where reality and fantasy were woven together by some higher power. This curious place seemed to be the embodiment of someone's dream. Then something happened that shook me from my trance.

'Señores!' I shouted and everyone turned. 'The Nicotinas you mentioned . . . Do they look like Indians, with bronzed complexions and feathers in their hair?'

Everyone rushed to where I stood, their faces frozen in fear.

'The Nicotinas!' shouted Palmito. 'Hurry!'

Atanasio's body was carried back into the wooden house while I gazed at the group of Indians bearing down on us like a herd of buffalo. They stopped at the chalk line dividing the two factions. The leader of this group of seven men was immediately obvious. Pablo, as I discovered he was called, was the most physically powerful; his lips were curled into a rictus grin, his body was covered with scars and he had the arrogant, authoritarian air common to leaders. He wore leather breeches and sandals and about his throat were strings of crocodile teeth and antlers. He reminded me of a picture I'd once seen of a Taíno Cacique chief – Hatuey or perhaps

Guamá. The youngest of the group was called Iván; he had the same muscular physique, the same bronzed complexion and, like his chief, he wore his hair in a ponytail adorned with feathers. When he laughed, he brayed like a donkey. The other men wore similar outfits, but were leaner and did not seem to be related.

Pablo began by announcing that this was an auspicious day, since old Atanasio had finally kicked the bucket. His words were like a body blow to me: nothing could be more cruel than to mock a man who had just died. I felt it particularly, having recently lost my whole family.

Reverend Carlos looked up into the grey skies and asked whether Pablo and his troop were getting some sun or whether they had come to offer their condolences.

'Carlos, what a pleasure to see you,' said Pablo mockingly. 'I won't deny that marking the death of a Kortico is one of my favourite pastimes. Atanasio's death is terribly sad, though a little unexceptional since, to die, a man need do nothing but be alive.'

Palmito stepped towards the Nicotinas and said that it was sadder still that there were people who wanted to rule for ever.

'It's the most tedious thing in this world,' said Lucumí.

At that point, Iván, the youngest of the Indians, almost stepped across the chalk line.

'Some day soon all the Korticos will be dead,' he growled menacingly, 'the Nicotinas will inherit the four pig's feet and we shall see whether wielding power is tedious. But why should we wait – why don't we find out today?'

With these words Iván Nicotina drew his machete while

his comrades drew crowbars and baseball bats. The Kortico Allies moved into position, preparing for hand-to-hand combat. None of them were armed. Lucumí handed me a machete then dropped his trousers, grabbed his penis in both hands and roared defiantly that it would be interesting to see whether his prick or Iván's crowbar caused more pain.

'Listen, Pablo, we don't want any trouble,' said Palmito. 'You have crossed the chalk line into our territory but that we can forgive . . .'

'*Your* territory? This whole area, from the sicklebushes to the north to the sicklebushes to the south, was discovered by my grandfather, Alfonso Nicotina, the one true hunter of the magic pig, which means that this land belongs to his descendants. But I did not come to talk about that, nor about the death of Atanasio. I heard you have a new ally, a certain Oscar Mandinga. Is this true?'

'A new ally? And who told you that?' said Palmito.

'I may not be able to read destinies, but I have my spies.'

'Then tell your spies to check their sources. The only new ally we have is Napoleon, our newborn crocodile.'

Pablo's face became a mask of fury, the veins in his neck stood out, his eyes bulged as though he was about to explode.

'How dare you give such a distinguished name to such a lowly beast?'

And so the battle began. Pablo launched himself at Palmito, Iván swung out at Lucumí with his machete, Reverend Carlos engaged in fisticuffs with one of the Nicotinas while Monsieur Julián pinned another in the mud and Lucumí beat his opponents with his penis. The women fought just as viciously. I simply stood, frozen, and did nothing. I racked my brain, trying to think of some way I might help these people who believed I was the heir to the last pig's foot, the saviour destined to bring peace to this muddy world called Cuba. I was sick to death of all the Machados, all the Batistas, sick of the Communists, of Masferrer's Tigers, of the March of the Combatant People, the power cuts, the refugees throwing themselves into the sea, I was sick to death of history and the way it had of repeating itself.

Suddenly I realised there was only one way to resolve the situation: the leader of the Nicotinas had to be neutralised once and for all.

That's how I came to smash Pablo Nicotina's face in. I split his head in two, and let me tell you I don't regret doing it. That is what I told Commissioner Clemente when he and his whiteshirts came and dragged me off the battlefield.

And that's all there is to tell. Though you might not believe it and though it might not look like it, I am not a man of violence. But there are times when a man has to do what he has to do and take the consequences.

The Interrogation

So, tell me, Señor Ulises.'

'Ulises? My name is Oscar.' I spat the words at chrome-dome Clemente.

The first thing Commissioner Clemente did was to lock me in this miserable little cell, this termites' nest, this ramshackle hovel with snot-green paint daubed over the walls and on to the filthy floor. Commissioner Clemente and his three henchmen sat on one side of the dark wood table, I sat facing them. A wary cockroach scuttled up the wall behind the only whiteshirt not wearing sunglasses, a guy with piercing eyes like a Catholic inquisitor. A malevolent feeling hung in the air, swirling around me as though I were not the heir to Yusi the Warrior who had just freed my country, but a terrorist who had just colonised it.

The four men studied me for several minutes in silence, an impenetrable, endless silence made worse by those eyes as sharp as spears that drilled into my pupils. Then Clemente ordered his men to leave us alone and the whiteshirts got to their feet and left.

Clemente bombarded me with questions, wanting to know my name, where I was from, my age, the names of my parents, a whole shitload of stuff. I duly answered all his questions and I also told him *my* truth, the history of Pata de Puerco, just as I have told it to you. When I'd finished, I asked Clemente whether I might have some food and the commissioner got to his feet and yelled, 'Margarita! Margarita!', then sat down again.

'A fascinating story,' Clemente said. 'The most fascinating story I've heard in years. You tell it with such conviction, such passion, that I almost want to move to Pata de Puerco. I feel as though I know these characters personally: José, Betina, Oscar Kortico, Atanasio.'

It was not a story, I told him, the characters were people who really existed. The commissioner narrowed his eyes and jotted something down in his red notebook.

'I've no doubt that you believe it to be true,' he said. 'Such a tale requires considerable imagination, not to mention talent, though you should be careful to whom you tell it . . . some of your political comments are a little sensitive. Even so, I find it difficult to believe this place called Pata de Puerco, with pygmies called Korticos, a talking pig and *wijes*, ever existed.'

'Not existed, it *exists*,' I said, feeling blood rush to my face.

'All right, that such a place *exists* somewhere near Santiago,' said Clemente. 'Still, you must admit it is curious that your father Melecio supposedly knew Emilio Bacardí, that he supposedly invented the art-deco style, designing the Bacardí Building in Havana, that he supposedly drew up the plans for a town called Cabeza de Carnero – a place I've never heard of in my life.'

'Not "*supposedly* invented", Señor Clemente,' I interrupted him. 'He *did* invent the art-deco style, he *did* design the Bacardí Building and he *did* plan the town you just mentioned.'

'I've always believed that the architect of the Bacardí Building was Rafael Fernández Ruenes,' Clemente said.

'That's what the bastard wants everyone to believe,' I said. 'He stole the blueprints from my father Melecio and put his name on them.'

'So, tell me, Señor Ulises . . .'

'Why do you keep calling me that?' I snapped. 'My name is Oscar.'

'Tell me, Señor Oscar, where does this fixation with mud come from? I mean you were conceived in mud in a village of mud, you slid down your mother's legs into the mud, your namesake Oscar Kortico had sex with Malena in the mud, Melecio lost his virginity to María in the mud . . . I've never heard the like of it.'

'It's not a fixation, it's what happened to my ancestors,' I almost screamed.

'Don't upset yourself', Clemente said. 'I simply find it difficult to believe that as a child you had to be put in a basin of mud to calm you down, just as I find it hard to credit the idea that four pig's feet could determine the future of Cuba. Come now, even you have to admit that part is a little far-fetched.'

I said it was all true: all the stuff about the basin and the aforementioned pig's feet.

'Aforementioned . . . what a lovely word. What a man, what a way you have with words. Anyone might think you were a writer,' said Clemente. I ignored this remark and said nothing.

'Well, excuse me, Ulises – I mean Oscar – excuse me, but I have to be honest with you. Your story seems a little melo-dramatic. You are obviously an educated man, that much is obvious from your lucid account of Cuban history. Yet your story is full of contradictions, of inconsistencies that could only come from a disturbed mind. Take the murderer Pilar García, for example. It's interesting that you assume a mur-derer like that could forgive anyone.'

'A murderer is still a man, Señor Clemente. Are you tell-ing me that a murderer can never feel compassion?'

'That's not what concerns me,' said Clemente, adjusting his glasses. 'A murderer is still a man, in that you are abso-lutely right. What is abnormal is that someone should seek to vindicate a murderer, and I feel it explains much. The hatred in your story is palpable. And yet there are episodes of extraordinary tenderness. All that stuff about wanting to unite the country by bringing the four pig's feet together, Melecio's eagerness to build villages with paved roads and brick houses, is very pretty.'

'As pretty as the primrose way that leads to the everlasting bonfire?'

'Bravo! Another charming expression,' exclaimed Clemente. 'What poetry! What a man! Are you sure you're not a writer?'

Again, I said nothing.

'Tell me, Señor Mandinga, are you sure that your grandfather taught Kid Chocolate to box and KO'd Rolando Masferrer?'

'I'm sure.'

'But you surely realise that there are no direct descendants of Satan, that such a thing is impossible.'

'I believe what Atanasio said about the Nicotinas. There are many people in those parts with the devil's blood coursing through their veins. I think it is possible.'

At this point the bastard burst out laughing and said I was truly a fascinating specimen, the most fascinating he had encountered in his long career as a psychiatrist.

'Are you a doctor?' I asked.

'A psychiatric doctor, to be precise,' said Clemente.

When I told him I thought he was the leader of the Cuban branch of the Ku Klux Klan, his eyes narrowed again and he scribbled something in his little red notebook. I asked again about some food and he called for Margarita. A scream came echoing back down the corridors, the metallic shriek of an old man's voice. I opened my eyes questioningly and asked where I was, what this place was.

'This is the Santiago Psychiatric Hospital,' said Clemente. 'You have been brought here to determine whether you are cognisant of the fact that you murdered one of the hospital patients with a machete.'

At this, I leapt to my feet angrily and shouted that I hadn't murdered anyone.

'Don't upset yourself,' Clemente said again, never losing his composure. 'Your case is more intriguing than I first thought.'

'Intriguing in what way?' I said, not understanding what he meant.

'Let's say, for example, that I tell you I am not the leader of the Ku Klux Klan, but am actually the head of the Department of Psychiatry in this hospital, and that is the reason why my staff wear white coats. What would you say?'

'I'd say you were wasting your time because I don't need my head shrunk.'

'In that case,' said the commissioner, 'what might you think if I were to tell you that the place you describe as Pata de Puerco, the field with the chalk line where you arrived three days ago, is in fact a baseball pitch in the grounds of the hospital; that there is no one here called Atanasio, or Palmito, or Lucumí, and no one named Nicotina. What would you say if I were to tell you that Pablo, the man you killed with a machete, was an elderly patient who, far from being a muscular Indian warrior, was as weak and scrawny as Juan Primito, that the man you call Reverend Carlos is a paranoid schizophrenic and the boy you refer to as Iván Nicotina is actually called Iván Cortina who suffers from agoraphobia? If I were to tell you all this, what would you say?'

'I'd say you were accusing me of making the whole thing up . . . But it's true Pablo was one of the Nicotinas, and everyone agreed that he had to be stopped once and for all.'

'When you say "everyone",' said Clemente, 'you are referring to voices in your head. There were only three people on the baseball pitch you call Pata de Puerco. You, the dead man and me.'

'All the people I told you about were there: Reverend Carlos, Palmito, Lucumí, Alberto the *wije*, everyone. Stop trying to screw with my head, I'm getting out of here,' I screamed, unable to bear so much insolence.

'I'm sorry,' Clemente said, 'I really must ask you to calm down, otherwise I will have no choice but to resort to other measures. I have a different version of events, and I would be grateful if you would hear me out. It is a confession, if you like, one that I would like to tell to you and you alone.'

I stared at the peeling wall, spotting the cockroach I had noticed earlier, but I was so hungry now I could no longer tell what colour it was. And so I promised to stay very quiet while the man with the Pancho Villa moustache began . . .

The Crazy and the Sane

'First, let me start by saying that your real name is not Oscar Mandinga,' said Clemente. 'Your name is Ulises Correa Iglesias and you were born in a district called Pedrito Blanco in Santiago de Cuba. But you were right in thinking you are an only child. From an early age, you were responsible for looking after your mother Elena; you never knew your father, and had little contact with other members of your family. You have vague, fond memories of your uncle Emilio – not Emilio Bacardí, of course, but Emilio Correa Rivero who worked in a cardboard factory near El Cobre. He was the one who instilled in you a love of literature, the one who first encouraged you to write because he recognised you had a talent. You loved the countryside as a boy, and you had a happy childhood despite the fact that your family was poor. But you grew up to be a solitary child, reserved, an under-achiever. It took much coaxing on your uncle's part to bring you out of your shell . . .

'Emilio Correa Rivero never tired of telling you that, if there is something you don't know, the best remedy is to learn. He encouraged you to read whatever you could lay your hands on, to note down your thoughts and impressions of everything you read. You read magazines, my friend Ulises, you read newspapers and back issues of gazettes that the young men from garbage trucks tossed on to the local rubbish tip. You read the few books you could find at home: a battered Bible and a copy of José Martí's *Simple Verses*. Sometimes you read history and geography textbooks, sometimes horror stories – everything, in fact, that divine providence put within your reach. And you learned something from everything you read; sometimes very little, but something always remained with you, like a green leaf in a mountain of garbage or – to polish the metaphor – a book abandoned on a rubbish tip.

'All this I learned from Augusto, a neighbour who watched you grow up. He did not run a laundry like the Augusto in your story, he was an animal trader, goats mostly, though occasionally he would buy or sell cattle on the sly. Augusto told me you are a fine young man whose ill luck it was to inherit the misfortune of Elena – Elena, as I said, was your mother's name, and not the girlfriend you mentioned in your story. You also inherited the ambition of your uncle Emilio, a man who was as stubborn as one of Augusto's goats, and had a vicious temper. Your uncle would never take advice, nor listen to friends and neighbours who suggested that you should be out playing with other boys rather than having your nose constantly buried in a book.

'On one occasion, a friend of Augusto's, an old man known as El Mozambique who ran errands for neighbours for ten pesos and who was much loved in the area, suggested to Emilio that you were starved of affection and suggested he take you to the park to play with your little friends and soak up the human warmth you sorely lacked. Emilio lashed out and punched him, El Mozambique dragged him into the street where the brawl continued. As a result of the fight, both men spent a month in jail and you never spoke to El Mozambique again, so it's understandable that you should make him the villain of your story. It also explains the paternal relationship between Emilio Bacardí and Melecio, the character with whom you obviously identify.

'Augusto suggested I speak to Juanita, a neighbour who lived opposite your house. Juanita is not a *santera* or a wise-woman, though she does sell medicinal herbs – rosemary, rose periwinkle, mango bark extract and potions made from cassava and other roots. As a girl, she washed floors in a local polyclinic and physically she resembles your description, so I have no doubt that she was the inspiration for the wise-woman in your story, the neighbourhood healer. After all their professions are not so dissimilar.

'Juanita said that despite your falling out with El Mozambique, you were still the same gentle, intelligent boy you had always been. But all this changed after your trip to Havana. By this time your literary talent had been widely recognised, you had already won the Santiago Prize for Literature and later the even more prestigious Cucalambe Competition, which included writers from all the provinces in eastern Cuba.

'You went everywhere with a pencil and a notepad, setting down your observations, reciting magnificent poems which came to you with astonishing spontaneity. Very soon, your fame reached the loftiest intellectual circles in Oriente. The Natural Bohemian, they called you, for your ability to recite poems that occurred to you on the spur of the moment and so, gradually, your fame spread until the glory you had attained in your own province was not enough. It was then that you decided to participate in the National Prize for Literature, awarded by the Casa de las Américas in Havana, submitting your latest and most ambitious work – a novel in two parts that had taken you almost three years to write. A telegram arrived and, with trembling hands, you read it to discover that your novel had made the final shortlist. Two days later, you caught the first train you could and headed for Havana.

'"Something happened on that trip," Juanita told me as she pulled on her cigarette butt. Something that you would not talk about to anyone, not even your mother Elena. When people asked about the trip, you simply mentioned a neighbourhood called Lawton and claimed to be disappointed that you had come third in some literary competition.

'According to Juanita, Benicio and Gertrudis are not related to you, they are certainly not your real grandparents. They are an elderly couple – as old as the Sierra Maestra, as she put it – whom everyone in El Cobre refers to as "The Grandparents". Benicio and Gertrudis were always fond of you, and you regularly went to visit them, especially if you were very upset. When I asked Juanita whether I should speak to them, she told me not to bother, explaining they are both in San Juan de Dios nursing home now, having gone a little soft in the head after the death of their dog Facundo. The only person who might be able to tell me more, Juanita said, was Malena, the daughter of a local butcher, a short, bald, decent man known to everyone as El Judío.

'El Judío said that you and Malena had been friends since primary school, but had gone to different secondary schools. Even so, you remained close since you were both obsessed with books and both spent much of your time writing poems and stories. But like everyone else I spoke to, he knew no one named Mandinga or Kortico, and had never heard of a village called Pata de Puerco.

'Malena told me that you had confided in her that during your trip to Havana you had fallen in love with a young woman you met at the Casa de las Américas where the literary competition was being held. Her name was Ester – though obviously she was not a midwife. She was twenty-six with pale skin and dark eyes, she came from Camagüey and, like you, had never been to Havana before. You fell in love with her at first sight, but Ester thought of you only as a friend and a talented writer. You did everything you could to win her round, penning poems for her, yet still Ester insisted she had no time for love.

'In the end, however, your persistence paid off and you persuaded Ester to go to the cinema with you. The following Sunday, you took her to a shopping centre in downtown Havana where bands played. Later still you took her to your favourite place in Havana, the Plaza Roja on the Calzada del Diez de Octubre near Lawton where there was a flame tree like the one you used to sit under in your garden in Santiago; hence the central role Lawton plays in your story.

'In a derelict laundry on the Calle Linea you kissed Ester for the first time and it was in that same laundry you yourself described in your story that Ester eventually told you that she loved you. There was something in her voice that did not convince you, but when you opened your eyes and saw the real world, you managed to stop trembling and decided that it did not matter if things continued as they were.

'Two days later, the results of the literary prize were announced: Ignacio el Jabao won for his novel *Destarre*, Anastasia Aquelarre came second with her novel *Musica de Feria* and Ulises Correa Iglesias – you – came third for a novel entitled *Pata de Puerco*. You seemed entirely happy with the outcome, and during the celebrations that night you went looking for Ester to give her a new poem you had written. You could not find her. Someone told you they had seen her earlier heading down towards the Malecón. Ten minutes later, as you were walking back to your hostel, you saw Ester kissing Ignacio el Jabao in the dark doorway of the laundry where you had first learned to kiss. You stood frozen, contemplating the painful scene, and in that moment decided to kill them – not in a hail of bullets, as with Augusto and El Judío in your story, but with silence and undying hatred. I imagine this is why in your story you depict Ester as a grotesque, undesirable, obese character, why the characters Ester and Ignacio el Jabao represent the ugly face of betrayal, it also explains your connection to the laundry.

'Malena told me you came back from Havana a changed man, quieter and more reserved than ever. You took refuge in your books. You carried on writing. You hardly set foot outside the house, and barely spoke to anyone, even Malena – and when you did see her, she told me she found your attitude unbearable. You told her that women were spawn of the devil, that you would never fall in love again.

'Then, a few short weeks ago, your uncle Emilio Correa

Rivero died suddenly of a heart attack, and hardly had you grieved for him when, by a strange coincidence, your mother Elena also died. It was at this point that books became your only reality and the more you read, the more you obliterated reality from your mind. In a heartbeat, my friend Ulises, your whole world had fallen apart, as dreams fall apart when disillusion sets in.

'When you began your story, you told me that "it is impossible to imagine the man you will become when you find yourself alone" and you were right. At the tender age of twenty-three, you found yourself utterly alone. I know this to be true. Just as I know that you did once strangle a cat, that you twice attempted suicide after your first schizophrenic episode, first by hanging yourself and then by taking twenty haloperidol tablets. In the end, no one can escape death. No one. But it is possible in life to outwit death and, more importantly, to rescue those whose time has not yet come. You followed the course of your short, frustrated life until you came to the events that occurred a week ago when, sadly, you killed Pablo, a patient at the hospital, with a machete.

'You present as a paranoid schizophrenic, my friend Ulises Correa Iglesias. You suffer from psychosis, hallucinations, delusions, disorganised thinking. You need help now, before it's too late.' This was the diagnosis of Commissioner Clemente, told to me after he had subjected me to a tissue of lies that left me open-mouthed and gasping for breath.

When I could eventually speak I spewed a torrent of abuse and hurled myself at him. Everything happened in the blink of an eye. Clemente roared for help and two whiteshirts so huge they looked like gorillas immediately appeared, grabbed me by the arms and dragged me down the corridor past old men in tatters mumbling to themselves and people staring at the walls and laughing. They took me into a cell and there they strapped me to a gurney. I went on cursing and swearing and screaming for help as they stuck electrodes to my temples and stuffed a wad of cotton in my mouth. It was then that the lights went out and my head was split in two; it was then that Commissioner Clemente took away the sun for ever.

When I woke up, I once again saw the face of Clemente. He asked if I was feeling better, if I had had something to eat. I didn't know where I was, who I was, what day it was. I had a pounding headache and the room reeked of shit and vomit. 'Don't you remember me, Señor Mandinga?' said the bald man and I told him I didn't remember him and asked why he was calling me Mandinga.

'Because that's the name you gave me when you introduced yourself,' said Clemente. Then he said that it was normal that I couldn't remember anything and that I should be happy because that meant I had come back to reality. Then the questions started again: he wanted to know my age, my parents' names, where I had been born and whether there ever existed a place named Pata de Puerco.

'Of course there was a place called Pata de Puerco.'

'Ah, I see. Are you sure you're not referring to a novel that you wrote?'

'I'm sure.'

'And the name Ulises Correa means nothing to you?'

'Of course it means something to me.'

And this was the truth. From the moment I came round, I heard a cacophony of voices, shrieking voices that would not even let me think. Yet even in this world of confusion I recognised the voice of Ulises, just as I recognised the voices of Judío Alemán and Judío the butcher; I could clearly see the faces of Mozambique the murderer and Mozambique the old beggar in El Cobre; my real home, I knew, was in Lawton, though sometimes I was not even sure of this, because I saw faces I had never seen before, faces I might have seen once in a dream. The truth is, I no longer knew who I was.

'Let me tell you something, Commissioner Clemente. There is only one reality: the reality that makes sense inside our heads. In there, if you don't understand something, you ask questions and you keep an open mind since the answers often lead us to places we don't want to go. If your lack of experience means you cannot see that places like Pata de Puerco exist, that they're real, there's really no point in us continuing this conversation. If I am crazy, you are crazier still for dragging me back to this reality we live in, since the world we call real is the craziest of all. The sane are the real madmen, and the madmen are the sane, Señor Clemente.'

This I said to the Imperial Wizard of the Cuban branch of the Ku Klux Klan. Then I suggested he turn on the television so he could see whether what I had just said was true. Clemente stared at me with black eyes like bottomless wells and scrawled something in his red notebook. Only the howls of pain from who knows where reminded me where I was. A cracked voice rumbled inside me and then exploded like a grenade. It was the voice of Clemente ordering that I be given more electroshock. The gorillas stepped back into the room and reattached the electrodes. In the days that followed there were more shocks, more and more of them. Until one day I no longer even knew whether I existed or whether, as Clemente said, I was just another character, a figment of my own imagination.

Since then, I amuse myself in this dark cell telling stories to my faithful friends: the four walls, the roaches and the rats. What else is there to do? There are times when I feel certain that night has fallen, my mind stirs and I consider myself a prophet. But after a few seconds I fall back into this dark chasm of not knowing who I am. The images in my head are blurred and confused, as though with every hundred metres the world shifts and changes, and that's when the tremors start, the terrible earthquake that shakes the ground beneath my feet that will not let me live.

Sometimes, after the crisis has passed, I sit here quietly. I escape from my cell and soar high above everything, up to the peaks of the Sierra, from where I see dragonflies, the vast green expanse of the meadows and the rice fields. I am one of Evaristo's kites, floating in the sheltering blue sky. Down below everyone is gathered round the red flame tree waiting for me, ready to begin the festivities, to recite poems: Melecio with María, José and his friend Oscar and their wives Betina and Malena, Juanita the wise-woman with her Angolan orchids, El Judío, Kid Chocolate, the *wijes*, El Mozambique and Ester. In these brief moments, I am happy. Until I open my eyes again and find myself still strapped to this bed, in this darkness that smells of dog piss and death and despair. I hope that one day I will be able to find absolute silence, but the voices in my head never leave me, nor does the darkness.

You have to believe me when I say that it is not pessimism I wanted to convey in telling you my story. I wanted to take you back to the roots of a man and the story that created him. If this is an act of a madman, then I am proud to accept the name. I don't want to be said, like those white-shirted henchmen, to be unable to see beyond the universe that man himself has created. Leave me to be mad like the artists and the poets. Mad like Nature herself. Like those same people, those same gods who invented love. Having said that, and with great regret, I won't deny that I have seriously considered swallowing a clock. That's the truth. Other times I think about swallowing a fistful of nails, or maybe one of these days I'll simply hang myself. But not today. Today you have given me your time, lent me your ears and for that I am extremely grateful.

So for the moment, those bastards will have to kill me with electroshocks because I won't give them the satisfaction of killing myself. But before that happens, I want to thank you for having kept me company all this time. Thank you for listening to this story of a small corner of a sweeping plain with a few scattered shacks between the Sierra Maestra mountains of Santiago de Cuba and the copper mines of El Cobre, where the breeze blows and night enfolds us with its chill breath and the purple cloak that curls about the streets. Thank you for walking with me along the dirt roads of Pata de Puerco, this village of mud, fictional or real. This forgotten place where some day I will return for ever. My name is Oscar Mandinga. Don't forget it.

Acknowledgements

I would like to thank a number of people for their invaluable contributions to the creation of this book: José Adrian Vitier, Nick Caistor, Rupert Rohan, Olga Marta, Marina Asenjo, Elizabeth Woabank, Greg Heinimann, Laura Brooke and all the members of my family at Bloomsbury. I would particularly like to thank Felicity Bryan and Bill Swainson who, from the start, have had faith in me, and also Frank Wynne for his magnificent translation and for the crucial contribution he has made to the final version of the text.

A NOTE ON THE TYPE

The text of this book is set in Bembo. This type was first used in 1495 by the Venetian printer Aldus Manutius for Cardinal Bembo's *De Aetna*, and was cut for Manutius by Francesco Griffo. It was one of the types used by Claude Garamond (1480–1561) as a model for his Romain de L'Université, and so it was the forerunner of what became standard European type for the following two centuries. Its modern form follows the original types and was designed for Monotype in 1929.